GREEN FIRE

BOOKS BY JOY SMITH

THE PERFECT FIRST MATE

KITCHEN AFLOAT

OH, NO, THEY'RE ENGAGED!

GREEN FIRE

SEAGULLS DON'T EAT WORMS

THE SMART GUIDE TO CRUISING

GREEN FIRE

JOY SMITH

JSBooks Publications
www.jsbookspublications.weebly.com

GREEN FIRE

Copyright © 2015 by Joy Smith

Books may be ordered through Booksellers or contact:

JSBooks Publications

www.jsbookpublications.weebly.com

Cover Art by Raman Bhardwaj

Edited by Nancy Bell

Copyedited by Greta Gunselman

ISBN: 978-0-9862422-2-9

Second Edition January 2015 by JSBooks Publications

First Edition February 2013 by by MuseItUp Publishing

To the lovely people
who urged me to keep at my fiction writing.
You know who you are.

Acknowledgements

A special hug to all my writing friends at the Connecticut Chapter of the Romance Writers of America, who educated me, inspired me, and listened to me whine. A big smooch to my husband, Gil, and all my children and grandkids—the loves of my life.

Chapter One

How much longer could he go on with this charade? Victor Novak's client's gaze slid over his body, taking in every inch of skin, every mole, and every crease. Out of habit, he squeezed his buttocks to make them look firmer and tighter and sucked in his stomach. He'd slacked off on the workouts and it showed. Tugging on his black silk briefs, he hid his bare butt from the woman's assessing eyes. The woman; that was how he thought of Gloria Van Cleff, Eileen Goldwell, and the other lonely matrons who had used him since he had been a clueless teenager.

Victor caught his paramour's reflection in the mirror behind the door—cow-brown eyes fixed on his ass—and noted the plump white envelope on her bed table. He checked his watch. His cab should arrive soon. Brushing his hair straight back from his face, he secured it with an elastic band. The style was passé, but combined with his dark hair and olive skin, it gave him the continental look older women seemed to like. Leaning closer to the mirror, he frowned. Even though he exfoliated in the shower, the fine lines around his eyes and mouth hadn't budged.

Victor turned from his reflection. A glycolic facial would knock off a few years, but then what? He couldn't think about that now.

Surely, the woman would come through with a permanent position. The tightness in his shoulders eased. He would continue to live on this posh Coral Gables estate with all the benefits of being a kept man. And, because he no longer needed to troll for prospects, he could quit that pay-nothing job shuttling trays on *Ocean Pleasures* cruise line.

I'll dress casually for my visit to South America today. Pushing past the designer suits his client had supplied, he selected a floral shirt and tan silk slacks. He slipped into them and wiggled his feet into a pair of expensive Italian leather shoes. The woman continued to watch him from her canopied king-sized bed. His clients liked him best when he was naked, but he knew he wore clothes well.

For luck, he touched his mother's fiery emerald studs, stacked one over the other on his left earlobe, and pasted on a smile.

Show time.

When he turned toward the woman, she said nothing, nor did she smile. *Not a good sign.* He'd better pump up his charm or he'd be out on the street again. Raising his chin, he took his time walking back to her so she could appreciate his good looks and elegant poise. Then he eased beside her on the silken white sheet and propped his head with his elbow. He blew an imaginary circle over her surgically toned face, eliciting a moan, and caressed her thinning blonde hair—a combination move guaranteed to stir paramours' emotions.

Looking deep into her eyes, he dropped his smile. "*Ocean Pleasure* sets sail tonight. I'm supposed to go back to work."

His words hung in the air—every muscle in his body at a standstill—waiting for her to throw her arms around him and beg him to stay. He licked his lips. *Maybe a car this time—a Jaguar. Red.*

A smirk distorted his client's face. "Nice work, Victor." The words dripped from her thin lips like a death knell.

The muscles in his face froze. What the hell? *Nice?* He'd been fantastic. Why, the past night he escorted her to the governor's soiree, kissed up to all the politicians, and then screwed her brains out. What more could she have wanted from him?

Sucking in a breath, he rolled over and then sat on the edge of the bed with his back to her, squaring his shoulders. What did it matter? He was history as far as this client was concerned. Crap, what was he going to do now?

The woman slid her hand past him, picked up the white envelope, and knocked its edge against his arm.

He wanted to shove it away, shove *her* away. For a moment, he stared at the painted red fingertips that had scratched across his back during sex.

Take it. You need the money for your trip.

His spine stiffened. Schooling his face to hide the humiliation boiling inside, he grabbed the envelope and stood, towering over her. How had he allowed such a frail woman to have so much control over him?

"Thank you, Madame." He shoved his hand inside the envelope. Cash, of course. A thick slab of bills. Removing them, he glanced at the top one, a fifty, and then stuffed the wad into his pocket.

"It has been my pleasure to service you," he said with the usual courtly bow. The words rolled off his tongue by rote. He flipped the empty envelope onto the woman's bedcovers in the pathetic sort of rebellion that was normally beneath him, and turned on his heel.

Grabbing the handle of his roller bag, he strode from the bedroom.

Her loss. On his next stint on *Ocean Pleasures,* he would snag a wealthier woman, one lonely enough to want to keep him around for a good long time—if that was what he really wanted. His conscience niggled at him. With his mother dead, it was hard to justify selling himself. *If Mom only knew how I paid her medical bills...*

You're soft. Spoiled. Used to living a rich man's life without money and a home of your own. Victor drew in a breath. *Admit it. This is the fifth time in a row a client has curtailed your service. You're about done here anyway with nowhere to go but down.* A vision of him standing on a street corner, dressed in sleazy purple pants and a polyester shirt open to the waist, begging someone to fuck him sent shivers skating up his spine.

Squashing the horrid thought, he navigated the curved marble stairway and stepped onto the plush Oriental rug strewn across the foyer. If he were rich, he could be his own man, body and soul. He would buy a more luxurious home than this one and hire beautiful young women to wait on him and serve his every need. Once he was tired of them, he would throw them away and seek new ones—younger ones, prettier ones—as his clients had been doing to him.

The housekeeper stopped his progress. Her gray hair was caught in a loose bun, her uniform crisp and clean. "Breakfast, Señor Novak?"

His step slowed, and his manner softened. She earned her money through hard work, just as his mother had. It annoyed him how the client in the bed upstairs ran this poor woman in circles to please her every whim. He knew what that was like.

The dark-haired woman handed him a to-go cup of dark brewed coffee. "I fixed how you like it." Her smile smoothed the harsh lines of fatigue on her face. "A taxi is in the drive. When will you return?"

"I'm afraid I won't be coming back, Consuela."

Her face fell.

"It happens to us working people." He leaned down to kiss her cheek. "I will miss our talks in the kitchen." Reaching into his pocket, he pulled out one of the bills and pressed it into her calloused palm. "For your children back home."

"Oh, señor, too much." Consuela tried to hand it back, but he waved her away.

It was the least he could do. This kind woman had to have heard the orgasmic screams coming from the master bedroom—the old woman yelled loud enough to break the windowpanes— yet the housekeeper never showed she thought less of him for it.

"Stay safe," Consuela said in English. Victor's mouth went dry at the familiar words his mother had used whenever he left the Gallagher estate. She held open the front door for him, a heavy wooden thing with a brass knocker shaped like a pineapple.

"You, too, Consuela."

Victor hurried from the air-conditioned house to the waiting cab. A wisp of smoke wafted from the open window and disappeared into the steamy July air. Peon transportation. Had his client kept him on, her chauffeur would have driven him to the airport and picked him up when he returned.

The driver didn't move to assist him, so Victor tended to the luggage himself. When he opened the rear door, the cabbie gave him a dark-eyed look and then jammed his cancer stick into an ashtray spilling over with butts. Victor grimaced, by the time he reached the airport his clothes and hair would reek of smoke.

Shoving his bag along the dingy cloth upholstery, Victor slid in alongside it and pulled the door shut. He smoothed his hand along the luxurious silk of his slacks, *Fool. You left an entire wardrobe behind. Should've at least grabbed that cashmere sweater and classy suit. Now you're stuck with what little you've packed.*

The driver's head snapped around. "Where to, buddy?"

"Miami Airport, please."

With the ticking of the meter as background music, the cab swerved past the massive estates of Coral Gables and onto the expressway to Miami's business district. Victor tore off a small section from the rim of the to-go cup, and sipped on his coffee, the heat of it soothing the angst in his gut. The day had gotten off to a bad start, and he hoped to hell it got better. Maybe he should cancel this trip, tell the man who claimed to be his half-brother he changed his mind about a visit.

Yet he'd paid for the ticket out of his own money, and he wouldn't need to worry about a place to stay for a week, because he had an invite to this Carlos Rodriguez's country estate. It sounded impressive. Bogotá, Colombia was supposed to be beautiful, with lots of business opportunities, according to his research. Maybe he'd be lucky enough to come up with a plan for a new career—one less demeaning and more profitable than his companion shtick. Then he would hobnob with the wealthy and command respect.

And, if this stranger turned out to be family, so much the better.

* * * *

Six exhausting hours later, Victor stepped onto the tarmac and followed his fellow passengers to immigration, passing a pair of fierce-looking armed guards wearing camouflage. *Maybe this visit wasn't such a piece of cake.* A former client who traveled a lot once told him how she'd been held up for ten hours on some small technicality.

The tightness in Victor's gut eased when the customs official waved him through without questioning what might be in his luggage. For all the man cared, Victor could have smuggled in drugs or emeralds. Although he supposed most contraband goods must travel out of Colombia, rather than in.

The crowded terminal roared around him, and that annoying message to watch one's bag was on repeat. Pushing through the throng of charcoal-haired people, he headed for the exit through a modern terminal with tiled floors and well-marked concourses. *Man, with my height and American demeanor, I stand out above the crowd like the incredible hulk.*

In the men's room, Victor splashed water on his face, combed his hair, and retied it. He dropped some Bausch and Lomb in his ho-hum brown eyes to refresh the green contact lenses. Confident he looked as best he could after being squashed in coach for eons, he pushed open the double doors and stepped outside to weather cool enough to make him glad he had packed a light jacket.

New York-style skyscrapers towered around the terminal backdropped by a gray sky slashed with hazy, purple mountains. On the outside apron of the terminal, a collection of smells and sounds blasted: exhaust fumes from idling cars lining the curbs, and honking horns from drivers waiting for occupied spaces to empty. Car doors slammed and roller bags scraped along the pavement. Victor had barely set his bag beside him when a seedy-looking local snatched it.

"Taxi, señor?"

Victor pulled his bag from the man's steel grip. "No thank you. Someone is picking me up." He hoped. He should've called to reconfirm—although Carlos had his flight number.

Victor drew out his cell phone to check for a message from him. A voicemail. He dialed up the service. The racket around him made it near impossible to hear, but from what he could make out, the ship's maître d' wanted him to call ASAP. His boss thought every little thing was a fire needing to be doused. Most likely a change in schedule. He wasn't due back at the ship for another week, so what was the big deal? *Cedric, my man, I'll ring you back once I'm settled.*

With his fist wrapped around the handle of his roller bag, Victor paced in front of the Continental exit, scanning the triple row of parked cars. Carlos had told him to look for a Jeep. There had to be fifty such vehicles lined up here—and now many of them were pulling away from the curb, their pick-ups tucked inside.

Finally, an olive green Jeep wedged inside the stream of traffic, angling for the curb. A man hopped out and stuck his arm in the air.

"Victor." The voice was sharp, almost commanding.

Humph. About time. Victor raised his arm and waved. "Here." Taking loping strides, he approached a man with spiky black hair. Inside the car, he spotted a flash of color on the passenger side.

"Hey, my brother, got held up in traffic." Carlos pumped Victor's hand until he thought his arm would snap off. The man had the grip of an arm wrestler.

Victor wrenched his hand free and wiggled his fingers. *Not broken, at least.* "You are Carlos?"

He stepped back to get a better look. *Crap. This man couldn't look less like me.* He chewed at the inside of his mouth, a nasty habit. *Carlos's nose is lumpy, not straight and fine-boned like mine is.* If he had met this man cold, he would've never guessed they were related. Maybe they weren't, and this whole thing was some sort of scam. In fact, how had Carlos gotten Victor's cell phone number?

"*Si, si.*" Carlos rocked on his shoeless feet. He wore cargo shorts and a short-sleeved cotton shirt, open at the neck, revealing a heavy gold chain resting against a tuft of black chest hair. On his wrist, Victor spotted a Rolex watch. Not an upscale model like his own, but chunky and distinctive with an obvious scratch across its face. Both the chain and the watch could be knock offs bought on the street for a pittance. The man's jewelry tried to scream wealth, but didn't quite make it—given his bargain-basement-quality attire. But who knew? Folks with old money seldom flaunted it.

With a nod of his head, Carlos took in Victor's body.

He might have been offended if he wasn't used to being checked out, although for a different reason. Victor tipped up his chin. *Your turn. Find some way to convince me we're brothers.*

Carlos's face transformed as if he had put on a happy mask. He pointed to Victor's cheek. "You have a mole under your left eye, like our father did. Better money should run in the family instead, eh?"

A mole? That was the only resemblance between me and this Ernesto Rodriguez who is supposed to be our father? He wasn't buying it. Yet the man seemed sincere about being his brother. He'd play along, for now. Carlos didn't know it, but he was going to introduce Victor to the business side of Bogotá.

Without warning, Carlos enfolded him in a bear hug. The man was too close and breathing onto his neck. Not wanting to offend him, Victor endured the show of affection.

A tug on the hem of Victor's shirt sent him spinning around, ready to shove off the person who picked at his pocket.

"*Hola, Tio* Victor."

The dark eyes of a boy, perhaps in his early teens, looked up at him through a shock of thick black hair. He had been about this boy's age when he learned what women were all about. Victor managed a smile. "Your son?"

"Nah. Belongs to my sister-in-law. Kid sticks to me like glue. Joseph, speak English, please."

"Yes, *gracias*. My Spanish is a little rusty," Victor said.

Joseph eyed Victor. "You're taller than Uncle Carlos. What's America like? Mama says I should go to college there and get smart. Are you smart, Uncle Victor?"

"Whoa. I can't answer everything at once."

"Joseph. Get in the back seat, and leave the man alone."

Carlos slung a wiry arm around Victor's shoulder. "Shall we go, my brother? Mama Garcia has prepared a fine feast in your honor."

"How nice of her. You didn't have to go to so much trouble. I'd like to check into my hotel first." Victor paused, waiting for Carlos to reiterate his invite.

"Nonsense. My wife has prepared the guesthouse for you."

Victor exhaled. *So far, so good. Not a room, his own house.* Victor had seen such estates—huge mansions overlooking acres of farmland. There would be hundreds of workers and a full staff of maids, butlers, and valets to tend to his every need.

"That's very gracious of you. Give me a sec and I'll cancel my hotel."

Pulling out his iPhone, Victor punched in bogus numbers. After speaking gibberish to dial tone, he clicked off the call and tucked the phone into his pocket. "All set."

"Hop in the front with me," Carlos said.

American-made car, a low-end Jeep Cherokee. You'd think a guy owning a country estate would drive a flashier car. Judging from the fine layer of dust coating the dash and cloth upholstery, the car must not have AC. He brushed off his seat as best he could without attracting Carlos's attention and eased onto the passenger side.

Thirty seconds later, they roared out of the airport and onto the streets of Bogotá, a set of tacky dice dangling from the visor. Around them, horns honked as Carlos swerved into the passing lane, missing a car by inches. Traffic screeched to a halt, followed by shouts of what could only be obscenities, as a herd of white-horned animals paraded across the four-lane highway. While they waited, surrounding car radios blasted 60's songs via mega phones attached to their hoods.

Victor put his hand on his forehead. *What a God-awful racket.* "Is there always so much chaos here?" As he glanced over at his "brother," he zeroed in on a faded green tattoo. Without moving his head, he checked out Carlos's inner left wrist more closely. He could make out some sort of flame, a green one.

Carlos laughed. "Bah. This is nothing. You should see it in the morning."

Once they passed out of the airport traffic, the road dwindled to two lanes. *Better. Quieter.*

Resting his arm on the open frame, Victor took in the sights. Even though it was six, when most businesses thought about closing, vendors hawked wares at tables glittering with jewelry, and sold rich produce, fresh-caught fish, and delicate flowers. His nose caught a whiff of roasting chicken emanating from a kiosk on the side of a road. He had passed up the fast food in Houston, expecting a meal on the second leg. In coach, he had been lucky to get a bag of peanuts with his club soda.

He analyzed Carlos's face. Maybe around the mouth, but not the nose or cretin forehead.

"You keep staring at me, Victor."

"I'm sorry. You don't have my mole, so..."

"Hah. You think we need to have a mole to be brothers?"

"No, of course not. We have different mothers, so I expected we would be different."

"Are we different, Victor?"

"I don't know you well enough to answer that, Carlos."

Carlos laugh was hearty, which was good. For a minute, he seemed testy about Victor doubting their relationship. No matter what Carlos said, Victor wasn't buying into this brother thing until he had solid proof.

"Tell me about our father," Victor said as paved roads thinned to rocky, earthen paths. "Did he live on your plantation, also?"

"No, no. Our father never moved from our old apartment building. He served on the National Police Force. You have heard of it, eh?"

"*Tío* Carlos is a policeman, too." Joseph piped up from the back seat.

"True?" Victor looked over at Carlos, whose chest seemed to puff out at the mention.

"Off duty for a couple of weeks. I work security at a privately held emerald mine, La Esmeralda." Carlos winked. "Make sure no one is cheating."

Emeralds. Now there's a thought. He smoothed his finger over the flawless Colombian emeralds on his earlobe—his only inheritance. He used to catch his mother holding them to the light, turning them until they glittered, but he never saw her wear them.

Carlos's mouth dropped open and his head jerked in a double take. "Those earrings. Where did you find them?"

"My mother's...I..."

"Ah, but you are a visitor from the States. Everyone will think we have a wealthy relative, eh?"

The earrings. He thinks I'm rich. The studs warmed to his fingertips. He had tried to sell them—the jeweler offered him ten thousand dollars, which would've covered the cost of a proper funeral, and more. At the last minute, he reneged on the deal. He would never sell *these*, but what if he could get his hands on some of the emeralds mined here? Colombian emeralds, he had read, were the finest in the world. A handful of the gems must be worth *millions*.

Carlos's voice jolted him.

"You must run a profitable business back in America."

"Uh," —he flicked his hand in the air— "I dabble in finance."

Carlos's face took on an odd look. His eyes narrowed, as if in thought. "So," he said, as if choosing his words, "you are a money man, then."

Money man. The muscles in his chest squeezed. He would have graduated with a B.S. in Finance from Miami U if Mrs. Gallagher hadn't cut off his tuition and tossed them out when his mother contracted lung cancer.

"You might say that. I make investments here and there, and some pay off." *Like never.*

"I see." Carlos's head bobbed in a nod, and he was quiet for a while. Then his arm flew off the wheel and landed on Victor's upper arm with a healthy smack. "We will talk later of this, my brother, eh?"

You bet.

"Maybe you could help *Abuela* pay the bills, *Tío* Victor," Joseph said.

"Bills?" Victor turned his head. He'd almost forgotten the boy in the back seat, taking in every word.

"Speak English, Joseph," Carlos said, and then to Victor, "Since Papa Garcia kicked the bucket, the señora has been fretting." Carlos touched the side of his head with his forefinger. "The señora. She has no head for numbers."

Mama Garcia—must be Joseph's grandmother. Why does Carlos allow her near the bills if she can't add worth a damn?

"Could you help *Abuela*, I mean Nana, Uncle Victor? Could you?"

He would be foolish to pass up an opportunity to check out Carlos's finances. If, indeed, Carlos was next of kin, Victor could be in line for some big bucks.

Victor twisted in his seat to smile at Joseph. Had he once been

14

that uncomplicated? "If she asks me to assist, and I have the time."

"Are you *very* rich, Uncle Victor?"

The direct question caught him. "Not *yet.*"

Chapter Two

As Carlos swerved down the mountain and through the savanna, Victor inhaled air as crisp as freshly mown grass. During the drive, a few drops of rain spattered against the windshield. Now the sky was clear, leaving the lowering sun to cast golden sparkles over the greenery. Victor's vision blurred and the lush greens of the landscape became a field of emeralds waiting to be garnered. He had been in Bogotá a little over an hour and already the very idea of getting his hands on those precious emeralds consumed him. If he could make something work here, his dreams would become reality.

They approached a small village. The wooden sign mounted on a stake read "GARCIA." Pastel adobe buildings lined a rough paved road, as if kneeling in abeyance to the monstrous cathedral that headed the main street. Victor took in an extensive garden shop overwhelming the doll-sized grocery store and post office on his left. On his right was a bar and a café.

"Saint Andrew marks our village. Most everyone here is very religious—Catholic. The head priest thinks *he* owns the town." Carlos's mouth curled in a sneer.

Victor drew an inward breath. Until he was old enough to rebel, his mother dragged him to church each Sunday—he had refused to go to confession. Carlos didn't appear to be the church-going type, either, which was fine with him.

They drove out of Garcia and onto a narrow, rutty road. The sweet smell of flowers drifted through the open window, reminding him of his love for gardening. He hadn't plucked a weed or planted a flower since his teenage years at the Gallagher estate. Signs marked the various plantations. From the road, Victor saw workers in the fields, some of them small enough to be children. It was well after six.

"SOTO FLORES," the sign to his right read. It seemed they drove miles before they came upon another plantation. "Who owns all this?" he asked, turning to Carlos.

"Gomez Soto, the largest flower grower in the savanna."

Victor filed away that little bit of info. *Never know when it might become important.*

Finally, they veered into a narrow drive marked "Garcia Jardines."

"Yay. We're here, Uncle Victor," Joseph exclaimed.

A man-high, chain-linked fence separated the two plantations. Rows and rows were staked and cordoned off to delineate one variety of bloom from another. Green stalks bore cup-shaped dots of budding flowers—lilies, from what he could see; masses of them in all colors, shapes, and heights.

"So this is your plantation," Victor said, leaning out the window. In other plantations they'd passed, he'd seen figures, even though it was nearing dusk. "Have your workers quit early?"

"The Garcias are more concerned about overworking their pickers than they should be."

"But don't you have a say in it? I mean, flowers are a delicate commodity. Won't your competition get ahead of you?" *Already, things aren't looking so good here. The Garcias, it seems, are not keeping pace with the larger growers.*

Carlos shrugged. "Mama Garcia runs the plantation."

Is Carlos such a weakling that he lets a grandmother make business decisions? Victor scratched his head. *And what's with the side job policing the emerald mines?*

After a seemingly endless driveway, they approached a cluster of squatty adobe buildings. Carlos parked in front of the largest building, a white, red-clay-roofed conglomeration with an attached greenhouse. No valet came out to park the Cherokee or even to greet them.

"What are you waiting for, Victor? We are here," Carlos said. A hint of annoyance tinged his voice.

"Oh, yes. Of course." When Victor got out of the car and did a three-hundred and sixty degree turn, his chest muscles contracted even further. Where was the three-storied colonial mansion with the pillars and the wrap-around porch? What were those little sheds plopped here and there? Now he was conscious of a droning sound. He pressed a hand against his forehead. *Make it stop. Please make it stop.*

He glanced around once more to be sure he hadn't imagined this...this...hovel of a plantation. Sure, the grounds were pretty, but where was the money? Coming here was a mistake, not even worth the plane fare. And Carlos—he snuck a sidelong glance at him—an okay sort, but the man needed polish.

"Come on inside. Mama Garcia and Rosario will want to meet you," Carlos said.

Victor nodded, not trusting himself to speak.

"You have to meet *mi madre*, first, *Tio* Victor." Joseph's voice changed octaves.

Carlos's mouth turned down. "I will meet you inside, then."

"Come on." Joseph tugged at his shirt sleeve.

Show time, again. Victor blanked the emotion from his face, so as not to dampen Joseph's exuberance, and smiled. "Yes. I would love to meet your mother."

Leaving his bag by the car, Victor followed Joseph toward a skinny woman hovered over the plantings nearest the greenhouse.

"Mama," Joseph called.

The woman stood, took off her straw hat, and slapped it against her hip. Wavy chestnut hair tumbled over her shoulders and down her back. A broad, Julia Roberts smile lit up her rather gaunt face. High cheekbones, suntanned skin, and not a lick of makeup—except for the smear of dirt at the tip of her narrow nose.

When she saw him, her smile dropped away, not the usual effect he had on women.

The boy swung Victor's arm up into the air. "Say 'hi' to my new uncle. He's American."

A smile teased Victor lips. "I speak little of your language, señora." He extended his hand in greeting and gave her his killer smile.

"Marisol Garcia." She ignored his outstretched hand. "And, it is señor*ita*."

He let his arm swing at his side. "Sorry about that. I mean the mistake in your title." *An unmarried mother. Wonder what that's all about?* "Marisol, a pretty name for a pretty woman."

"*Gracias.*" Her cheeks flushed. Casting her gaze downward—*long, dark lashes*—she said, "If you will excuse me, I need to finish my planting."

Victor shoved his hands in his pockets and tilted his head; something about this woman grabbed at him. "Yes, you grow lilies here. Maybe you'll show me your gardens, later."

"Maybe." Dismissing Victor as if he were a bug on one of her flowers, she turned to her son. "Joseph. Change into your work clothes. We need to finish setting in these bulbs before the light goes away."

The boy's shoulders dropped. "But, Mama, Carlos told me to take Uncle Victor to meet *Abuela*. And then, I am supposed to show him where he is going to sleep."

"Yes. The guesthouse," Victor said, hoping to she would give him some hint as to where it might be hiding. But Marisol didn't bite. *Nada*. For all she seemed to care, he was a stick in the ground.

Marisol's mouth tightened. "Okay, then, get on with it." Twisting her mane of overly long hair in a coil on her head, she plopped on her hat and turned her back on him. Her bag of a dress stretched across a nicely rounded rear end as she stooped to return to her work. She moved with the grace of a swan. He could have stayed on, just to watch her, but Joseph was tugging at his shirt.

By the time Victor turned, Joseph had run ahead, waving for him to follow. He kept up as best he could, determined not to step into puddles left by the rain they must have had here earlier.

Crashing through the front door of the main house, the boy shouted as if some dignitary were arriving. "*Abuela*, he's here."

Victor straightened his shoulders, head up, not wanting to disappoint the boy. He wiped his shoes on the straw mat, and then followed Joseph inside.

They passed through a comfortable-looking sitting room outfitted with a plump sofa, chairs, and a few tables. A huge, gold-framed representation of Jesus loomed over the room. Its eyes seemed to follow him into a steaming hot kitchen. Victor sized up the two women hunched over a green linoleum counter preparing something or other. Dark-haired, curvy shapes.

Carlos sat in front of a mug at a roughly hewn wooden table that took up most of the cramped floor space. He looked up, his straight lips curling up at the corners. "Ah, here he is." With a scraping sound, he pushed back his chair and stood. "Mama Garcia, meet my brother." His arm flung out to the side.

"Victor Novak, here." Stepping forward, he picked up the señora's hand. She was a tidy woman, petite, and rather attractive still. If she were wealthy, he might even give her a go. Leaning forward, he pressed his lips against the back of her hand.

She fluttered, as he expected she would. At least he hadn't *totally* lost his touch with women.

"And this" —Carlos turned— "is my wife, Rosario." He shot Victor a warning look.

Marisol's sister. Same shiny hair and oval face. Dispensing with the hand kissing, Victor acknowledged Rosario with a short bow. Tiny black flakes of mascara settled on cheeks thick with foundation when she fluttered her eyelashes and smiled—*lips not nearly as plump as her sister's, but if this Rosario backed off on the heavy makeup, she'd be almost as beautiful.*

"Oh, señor, you are so...big."

He'd been called "big" by women, but not in the way he was sure Rosario meant.

Rosario's hand went to her hip and she thrust her breasts forward, as if daring him to shove his hands into her low-cut top to fondle them, which he would never do, of course.

Carlos put a possessive arm around his wife's shoulder, gripping hard enough to cause red marks.

Whatever went on between those two behind closed doors, he planned to stay out of it. "So they say," Victor replied evenly. He turned toward the luscious odor emanating from the oven, where the señora prodded at a piece of roasting meat.

"Another hour," she announced, straightening her back. "Joseph, take your new uncle to the guesthouse so he can freshen up and get settled."

The boy grinned at Victor. "It is up the drive a ways. Come on."

Up the drive? There had been nothing on the way in but work sheds. He shrugged and followed the boy, sorry to leave the warmth and coziness of the main house for the crispness of the outdoor air. His accommodations would be just as comfortable, he supposed. It was a *house*, after all. He stared up the drive, scanning for the place, when a black dot hurtled toward them.

"Yipes."

He and Joseph leapt to the side of the driveway, clothes blowing flat against their bodies, as a black sports car barreled past.

Victor brushed speckles of damp dirt from his silk slacks. "Who was *that?*"

* * * *

Another pompous male—and he was movie-star handsome, to boot. One night stand material, for sure. Mama would not see him that way. She would see Victor Novak's too perfect manners and apparent wealth and begin matchmaking again. Marisol dropped another bulb into its dirt hole. Her basket was almost empty. Enough for one day.

She stood to relieve the stiffness from her back as a growing puff of dust hurtled down their driveway, moving fast enough to make the ground beneath her feet tremble. The sight of Soto's car, sleek and black as a panther on the prowl, made her stomach churn. She was not scared. Not of the beast inside.

As the car whizzed past, she followed it with her eyes, willing it to go away. The vehicle screeched to a halt, leaving deep treads in the damp dirt drive.

Soto's bodyguard, Sanchez, threw open the door and got out, a cigar dripping from his lower lip. Giving her a nod, the thug undressed her with his eyes. She folded her arms over her chest, but she would not give him the satisfaction of turning away.

Sanchez opened the rear door to allow Gomez Soto to climb out. Soto. The name that haunted her life. The man would not stop until he owned everything and everyone. *But not us.* Not if she had any say in it, anyway.

Soto reached inside the car for a bouquet of his cheap daisies. If he thought to impress Mama with them, he was dead wrong. Buttoning the jacket that hugged his skinny frame as if it had been custom tailored, Soto straightened his tie and strode to Mama's front door.

Marisol's hands clenched into fists. If she were a man with a gun, she would shoot him in the back. Anything to make him stay away. Now Soto's fist punched at Mama's door as if he already owned Garcia Jardines.

Mama opened the door, her dark hair coiled into a shiny bun, and her red lips curved in a smile. She had changed to her church dress, which was not unusual when they had a visitor, but she doubted Mama donned high heels and hose just for that Victor person.

With a curt bow, Soto entered. Then the door slammed as if Mama shut it in Marisol's face. Sanchez, she saw, watched for her reaction. Shooting her third finger in the air toward him, she packed up her things and shut herself in the greenhouse. Her haven, the only place on the plantation she felt she could call her own.

And Soto wanted it.

Marisol set her basket on the worktable and then checked her babies. Papa would have been proud of her new varieties of lilies. She tried to focus on pruning her plantings, but her eyes kept flitting to the door connecting the greenhouse to Mama's kitchen—and the only plumbed bathroom on the plantation. An excuse to go inside.

With a twinge of guilt for wanting to spy, Marisol eased open the door. The kitchen table had been set for dinner using the good china and crystal Mama only took out on holidays, and pots simmered on the stove. How odd that Mama would be away from the kitchen so close to serving time.

Mama's high-pitched giggle arose from the living room. Marisol shut her eyes, wanting to pretend her mother laughed at the *telenova*.

She knew better, and peered around the doorway to confirm her suspicion. Marisol muffled a gasp. Mama and Soto sat side by side on the good sofa. Soto's hand was on Mama's thigh. Mama was flirting with danger. Now Soto's raspy male voice spoke in low tones, she flattened herself against the wall outside the living room to hear what he said.

* * * *

It was a decent hike up the drive to reach the small cottage Victor had been assigned. His shoes were caked with mud, and he didn't even want to look at the wheels on his roller bag. Finally they stopped before a small adobe house with a red wooden door and matching tiled roof, like those clustered around the main house.

After wiping off his shoes and luggage wheels on the grass surrounding the cottage, Victor followed Joseph inside. As usual, Joseph ran ahead, pointing out everything from a bed barely large enough to accommodate Victor's bulk to a sink with a drain, but no faucets. The boy was so proud of this one room shanty that Victor didn't have the heart to show his disappointment.

He set down his bag on the woven coverlet, taking care not to get it dirty, while Joseph ran outside to fill an ewer. He hadn't asked where the source of water was located, but he suspected there must be some sort of tap nearby. While the boy was gone, he poked about, hoping to locate a proper toilet facility. The only door inside the room turned out to be a closet. This was going to be a problem. He'd hoped to shower before dinner, and what if he had to...

Oh, crap. A sickening thought went through his mind as Joseph burst in, carrying a pitcher of water.

"Er... Joseph. Is there a rest facility here?"

The boy's eyebrows wrinkled.

"Bano, el bano," he said, remembering that bit of the language.

"Ah, *si."* Grabbing Victor's hand, Joseph took him outdoors to a man-sized structure.

This time, Victor couldn't control the frown that tugged down the corners of his mouth. *An outhouse.* Now he'd hit the lowest of lows.

Joseph looked at him quizzically, as if he were wondering what the big deal was about using an outhouse. Perhaps that was all the boy knew.

"You can use *el bano* at Nana's. She doesn't mind, and if it is too cool to shower outside" —he pointed to a shower head mounted at the side of the outhouse— "you can bathe at Nana's, too."

Victor coaxed his lips into a smile. "That will be fine, Joseph." He patted the boy's shoulder. "Thank you for showing me around. Now run along. I will see you at dinner."

Once Joseph skipped off—s*kipped, to be that carefree*—Victor jammed his hands into his pockets. His right hand struck his cell phone. He had forgotten about Cedric. Taking his phone out of lock position, he punched in his boss's number.

*Connecting...*then, the tiny screen went pale.

There were supposed to be cellular networks in Colombia. He'd checked before he left.

One dot, analog.

Can anything else go wrong today?

He shoved the phone back into his pocket. Surely Carlos would show him around the area, maybe take him into the city where there had to be a stronger cell phone signal. He'd keep a watch on his phone as they drove. Yes, that would work.

Before Victor went inside the cloyingly small house to freshen up, he squinted toward the west. Despite being within a mountain range, from this angle the land was flat to the horizon. Glorious view, he had to admit. The sun had dropped so that it appeared to be sitting atop the distant mountain and shed a rainbow of light over the dots of color that must be flowers in bloom.

Real flowers, alive and growing in their natural environment, not dying in metal tubs in vendor booths on the streets of Miami. One day, *his* estate would be flooded with all varieties of plants——flowers, vegetables—and he would nurture them and help them grow.

His thoughts flashed to old Jake, the gardener. The man had taught him how to tend to the sumptuous and extensive flowerbeds at the Gallagher estate. Jake, not this Ernesto Rodriguez, the father he never knew. He was gone now, too.

Enough of this sappy stuff. Better primp for dinner. A hot shower would be just the thing to wash away his doubts about coming here; but that meant schlepping to the main house, towel slung over his shoulder. Maybe tomorrow, when he was better acquainted with the Garcias. He settled on taking a whore's bath and donning a fresh shirt. He eyed the stains on his slacks. He couldn't go to dinner in soiled clothes. No maid to take care of that. He hadn't spotted a dry cleaner's shop on the way in, but there must be someplace in Bogotá.

Setting the pants aside, he shook the folding lines from his backup pair of dress slacks and put them on. A few minutes past seven, so as not to be the first to arrive, he set out for the main house. *Crap. Isn't that the black muscle car that nearly ran us down?* He drew up his shoulders and marched toward it.

He leaned into the window toward the man at the wheel of the Jaguar. The driver was puffing on a cigar. Victor waved away the smoke.

"Hey, buddy. You splattered mud on my good slacks. You're going to pay to have them cleaned."

"I do not think so." The driver sent a puff of his cigar smoke into Victor's face, flicked his cigar ashes near Victor's expensive loafers, and guffawed.

"Well!" Victor turned on his heels. "I never..." He would talk to Carlos. Find out who this asshole was.

He scaled the steps to the front door. No knocker, so he rapped with his fist.

"Ah, Victor." Rosario linked her arm in his, giving him a whiff of heavy perfume. "How did you find your room?"

"I...uh, why it's wonderful. Thank you for preparing it for me."

She smiled, a full, lovely smile. "It was nothing."

As before, the kitchen was welcoming. He scanned the room and spotted a slight man with salt and pepper hair seated to Carlos's right. The Jaguar. Had to be. The insolent jerk at the wheel must be a chauffeur.

"Here he is now. Gomez, this is my brother, Victor Novak, from America. Victor, meet Gomez Soto."

Soto. The big cheese who heads the flower market here. The man had a face like a ferret, and was dressed like a Fifth Avenue bank president. Certainly, he could spare some change to pay a cleaning bill.

Stepping forward, Victor shook the man's hand. *Limp as a dead fish.* "Nice to meet you."

"Come. Sit." Carlos indicated the head of the table, opposite Gomez—both guests given seats of honor.

As Victor pulled out a rustic looking wooden chair to join the men, Señora Garcia bustled in from somewhere else in the house. She had done up her hair and wore enough makeup to hide the age spots he noted earlier.

Her attention was not on him.

"Gomez," she gushed," patting the bun on top of her head. "I am sorry to take so long to freshen up. Is Carlos taking good care of you? Oh, and I see you have met Victor."

Rosario cleared her throat as Joseph raced in.

"Oh wow, Señor Soto. You are having dinner with us?" The boy seemed to have forgotten his new uncle and was now tuned into the rich dude.

"Obviously," Gomez replied.

"Guess what? I am playing on the soccer team you are sponsoring. Are you coming to see me play this week?" Joseph went on.

The man almost smiled. "I am very busy."

"Oh." Joseph dropped his head.

Victor saw the hurt in the boy's face. The man *could* have been nicer to the boy, but he supposed a hotshot like Gomez didn't have to be nice to anyone. "Joseph, hello, come sit beside me. I used to be good at soccer. What position will you play?"

The boy's face lit up making Victor glad he made the effort to seem interested.

Within moments, the table was filled with platters of food, compliments of the ladies. The hand-hewn wooden table was large enough to permit dishes to be laid out family-style. No servants passed around entrées, but the chipped pottery and stainless flatware brought him back to the cozy meals with the staff in the Gallagher kitchen.

Gomez picked up his napkin and tucked it into the collar of his dress shirt—*how gauche*. As he did so, Victor noticed a flash of green on the inside of the man's wrist, like the mark he saw earlier on Carlos. Why would the only two men he'd met, excluding Joseph who didn't quite qualify as a man yet, have the same tattoo in the same spot?

He tried not to stare, but he wanted to get a closer look to find out if the design matched Carlos's.

"*Abuela*, maybe *Tio* Victor can help you with the bills," Joseph said.

Victor snapped to attention as all eyes turned to him.

Señora Garcia's eyebrows went up. "Indeed. Now how would *you* know anything about our bills, Victor?" She gave Joseph the evil eye.

"Beg your pardon, señora. Your grandson speaks out of turn. I have no desire to get involved with your financial situation."

"But he is a money man. *Tio* Carlos said so in the car."

Gomez's eyebrows went up. He leaned in, as if to hear more.

"Señora, if I may explain." He gave the woman an apologetic smile. "We talked about my investments in the car, and Joseph here must've taken it to heart." Victor spread his hands, palm up. "I am good with numbers. If you need help..."

"She does not," Gomez interrupted. "All you have to do is ask, Consolata, and I will have my accountant take care of things for you."

What was going on? Gomez was speaking as if the señora owned the plantation, not Carlos. He glanced at Carlos, who sipped at his coffee, not seeming to care that a financial conversation was taking place.

Uh-oh. Now it clicked into place. This is not *Carlos's plantation. It belongs to the señora. Carlos just lives here with the daughter.*

The señora blushed at Gomez's implications.

What price would she have to pay for that service? Clearly, she and Soto had a thing going.

Victor eyed Gomez, who oozed wealth. Certainly the smart suit Gomez wore was an Armani. And that car—what he wouldn't give for one like it. He thought of the red Jaguar in the dealership showroom back home. If only his last client had renewed his contract, he might have been tooling about the country club in it, attracting the young babes when he returned, instead of working at *Ocean Pleasures.*

Carlos raised his hand. "Enough about money. By the way, Joseph, where is your mother?"

Mama Garcia lifted an eyebrow. "Yes, where *is* Marisol?" She directed a pointed glance at Rosario.

Chapter Three

Finally, when she could no longer stand hearing Soto's voice droning on about promises he would never keep, Marisol slipped back into the greenhouse. Tension overwhelmed her, the muscles in her body contracted and her mind froze with fury. Without stopping to think, she swooped up the first potted lily within reach and strong-armed it toward the rear wall.

With a satisfying thud, the pot hit its mark, and then split apart. Lumps of soil and shards of pottery shot across the red clay floor.

Marisol's shoulders dropped, anger spent. What had she done? She had destroyed an innocent plant, and it was all Soto's fault. She moved to the thick glass wall that encased the greenhouse and felt for a crack. It had held, as bullet-proof glass should.

Stooping, she picked out the delicate green seedling by its bulbous roots and crooned, "Poor thing. I am sorry." She brushed off the extra soil, checked its spindly shoots were not bent, and then laid the plant on a nearby table along with a handful of moist soil. "I will repot you as soon as I sweep up." She picked up the straw broom she kept on hand and began the task.

"Marisol, I thought I would find you in here. Mama wants you inside. Now." Rosario's hand went to her mouth. "What happened?"

Marisol swallowed hard. This was not the first time her temper had gotten the better of her. "Did you not see Soto's car parked in the drive?"

"*Si.*" Rosario shrugged. "Mama sent me outside to give Sanchez a cup of coffee. Soto is making that poor man wait in the car all through dinner."

"Dinner?" Marisol voice rose to a yell. She peered out the window. *The black car. Still there.*

"I know you do not like Gomez..."

"Oh, it is Gomez now."

"Stop it Marisol. Is it not time to let go of the past? He has money. We need money. And he has taken a shine to Mama."

"Bah. He does not care about Mama, or us. All he cares about is getting his hands on Garcia Jardines and my lilies." Hands on hips, Marisol leaned closer to Rosario. "Does it not seem odd that Soto only became interested in Mama and our plantation when we sold that big order to Elite Flowers?"

"You and those lilies. Maybe you should worry more about yourself. You are raising a son without a father."

Marisol's mouth tightened firmly enough to make her teeth scrape together. "Do not try to change the subject. This is not about me."

"Look, come on. Do not make a scene about Gomez being here."

"You will not say that when you and Carlos get tossed out of your home. Oh, I forgot, Carlos is in bed with Soto, so you will be safe. Only Joseph and I will be homeless."

Rosario sucked in a breath, and then renewed her stance. "Mama would never forgive you if you missed a company dinner. Besides, we have a handsome gentleman at the table. Have you met Carlos's brother yet?"

Marisol snorted.

"Do you always have to be so critical? Victor has money, and Carlos says he is single."

"What do I need with such a man?"

"You cannot mean you plan to live out your days without a husband."

Marisol hesitated. Rosario spoke the truth. For the past twelve years, she had lain in bed alone; her only solace the child sleeping in the room across the way. One day, Joseph would marry and live in his own cottage.

"Maybe not, but the pickings in Garcia are slim...and that Victor Novak? I can see right through him. He is a ladies' man from Miami. I would be nothing but a fling."

"You are always so worried that you might get hurt. Take a chance. Loosen up your morals long enough to please yourself."

Marisol walked over to the sink to wash up, signaling the conversation was over. If she did not show up at the dinner table, Mama would be livid.

"I am not staying long. I...do not think I can."

Rosario's hand touched her shoulder. "Are you not going to change? I mean, for God's sake, that is your gardening dress. It is filthy! What will our guests think?"

"Ask me if I care."

* * * *

The back door opened. Rosario returned with her arm around

Marisol's shoulders. Nice that the two sisters get along, Victor thought.

"It is about time," the señora said, giving Marisol the evil eye.

Marisol froze in place. Her chest heaved, pushing up breasts that, earlier, had appeared sunken under the shapeless dress she wore. With a searing glare at Gomez, she walked to the table. Leaning toward her mother, she whispered into her ear. All the while, her gaze darted toward Gomez.

Whatever words she communicated caused the older woman to hiss a retort under her breath.

Chin jutting forward, Marisol plopped down in the vacant seat at the table and crossed her arms over her chest. Her plate had been prepared when they first sat down.

"Your dinner is cold," Señora Garcia said with a pointed look.

"I am sorry. I see you have started without me." Her lips trembled as if she were trying to communicate some sort of apology.

Rosario put a hand on Marisol's well-tanned arm and whispered into her ear.

Marisol shook off her sister's hand. "Mama, I do not wish to eat. Excuse me. Joseph." She touched the boy's shoulder. "I want you home as soon as you have finished dinner. You have school tomorrow."

In a single motion, she shoved back her chair with a grating creak and stood. Giving Gomez a final glare, she headed out the door, wavy chestnut hair swaying past her hips.

The room went silent. There were problems here, and Victor wanted no part of them.

"*Mi madre* has been sensitive lately." Joseph began forking down food as if it were going to run away on him.

Victor cleared his throat. "Señora Garcia, the meal is delicious."

The woman perked up like a peacock flaunting its tail. "Just our normal dinner." With a girlish giggle she glanced at Gomez, who looked up from his plate long enough to praise the meal.

Clinking forks against plates filled the silence that ensued. Surreptitiously, Victor picked the beans out of the helping of rice Rosario plunked on his plate.

Finally, Gomez leaned back in his chair, patted his belly, and belched. His face went serious. "We need to talk, Carlos." He shoved a thumb over his shoulder, which Victor took to mean "elsewhere."

Carlos's mouth formed a straight line. Sliding back his chair, he rose. "Gomez, how about a cigar?"

Gomez dropped his napkin on the table, stood, and then followed Carlos out the door.

I don't believe it. I come all the way from Miami, and my so-called brother leaves me hanging out with the women—and a boy.

"*Tio* Carlos and Señor Soto are in business together," Joseph said, as if sensing Victor's discomfort.

Victor had guessed as much from their matching tattoos, but what kind of connection involved a green fire?

"Joseph," Rosario said. "Mind your own business. Finish your dinner. Your mama wants you home."

"You will still be here tomorrow, won't you, *Tio* Victor?"

Much to his dismay, he would be. He smiled at the boy. "Of course, now do as your aunt says."

The meal over, Victor thanked Señora Garcia and headed for the door. Outside, dusk dulled the gardens to a shady green and the air had turned crisp. He turned toward the bright glare coming from the greenhouse. Inside, a shadowy figure he recognized as Marisol moved about. The woman intrigued him. Gutsy, but with a chip on her shoulder that, for some reason, he wanted to knock off.

He would have liked to stop by the greenhouse to get to know her, but he suspected his time would be better spent cozying up to Gomez and Carlos. Besides, this Marisol had been in a foul mood, which likely explained why she had blown him off earlier. When the timing was right, he'd hone in on her and she'd fall into his arms like the others had.

Had.

He drew in a breath. He couldn't go back to a life of humiliation. In that world he would soon be passé, but here in Colombia, opportunity was rampant. He would be foolish if he didn't take advantage of his time here. Somehow, someway, he was going to become the wealthy, respected man he was destined to be and forget his life in Miami ever existed.

He sniffed the air. Smoke. Behind that huge palm. Yes. Gomez and Carlos talking business—no, *shouting.* In Spanish. Fingering the studs on his lobe, Victor moved forward, ears tuned into Gomez's reedy voice, and caught the words, *La Esmeralda.*

La Esmeralda, the mine where Carlos said he worked.

Like it or not, he was going to join their conversation. A twig crunched under his feet. The voices stopped. Both men turned, like children caught mischief-making, and pasted on smiles.

"Victor, I did not mean to leave you. Gomez and I..."

"No matter," Victor replied.

Carlos's arm went around his shoulder, and Victor smelled booze. They'd been served only coffee at dinner.

"I overheard you talking about the emerald mines. I want to visit one, while I'm here."

A slanted look passed between the two men. *I struck a nerve.*

In a practiced manner, Gomez flicked a half-inch ash from his cigar onto the grass. "*No one* visits La Esmeralda without a permit. Now I must make my excuses to Consolata, and then vamoose. Nice meeting you, Victor."

"My pleasure," Victor said.

Gomez bristled at his mention of the mines. *Interesting.* He watched Gomez stride to the main house. The man spoke with authority, as if he had total control—or wanted it—over the mine. Well, Victor would see about that.

* * * *

Marisol peered out of the greenhouse window at Sanchez pacing in front of the black sports car. Taking a last puff of his cigar, he tossed it into the grass. How could anyone be so thoughtless, even Sanchez? She did not like the man. Still, he knew dry grass could go up in flames and had taken a risk at their expense. What had she expected from a thug without a conscience? Soto moved past him and went into Mama's. Rosario had left for her cottage, so Mama would be alone with that vile man again.

Her fist came down stingingly hard on the glass. She had to do something. Mama was buying into Soto's horse manure. She was needy, had been since Papa died. Ripe for the plucking, so to speak.

No way was Soto going to pick Mama like one of his flowers, and then take command of their plantation. Not after ten generations of Garcias.

She stood watch as time ticked on. Her hands itched to throw something, anything, to release the anger building up inside her. Her face felt as if it was on fire and her jaw ached from clenching it. She breathed a sigh of relief when Soto finally emerged from the building and approached the waiting car.

Sanchez started up the engine with a beastly roar. The car's headlights flared on, revealing Soto's puny figure. His eyes glowed like a cat's and his face wore a gloating smile.

He thinks he has won. Well, we will see about that.

Sanchez emerged from the vehicle and held the door while his employer climbed in. Slipping back into his seat the chauffeur put the car in gear and roared off.

Rage held Marisol immobile until the loathsome car disappeared into the night. Marching down the main aisle through her plantings, she mounted the stairs to the kitchen entry and slammed open the door.

Mama flew at her. "How dare you embarrass me like that?"

Marisol stiffened. She should apologize, but that was not why she was here. Before speaking, she took a few relaxing breaths. "Mama, what is going on between you and Soto?"

Her mother's nose tipped upward, a clear indication of her indignation. "I am doing it for you."

"For me?" Her voice rose. Mama never had done anything for Marisol, except give her grief.

"For all of us."

"Can you not you see? Soto wants our plantation, and he has been courting you to get it."

Mama's shoulders dropped, and her haughtiness dissipated slightly. "It is the best I can do. I have tried to keep things going without Papa, and I cannot." A tear spilled from her eye and traveled down the side of her cheek. She brushed it away.

"You do not need to carry the burden alone." Marisol touched her mother's cheek, soft and losing its firmness.

Mama shook her head to the side. "We need money to buy fuel for the generator, fertilizer for the plants, and to pay our workers." She smacked her hand against the side of her head, as if berating herself. "We can barely afford to pay the shipping now that prices have gone up. Even with the new orders your lilies have brought in, Marisol, there is not enough to pay our bills."

Mama sat down at the kitchen table, and patted her upswept hair. "If I marry Señor Soto, our worries will be over."

"Marry him? Mama, you cannot love that awful man. Why, he was Papa's arch enemy." *And more.*

"What has love got to do with survival? He will take care of us."

"How? By poisoning our crops with pesticides? Our workers will get sick. Besides, he will bring violence back to our household. He is an evil man. Can you not see that, Mama?"

With her elbows on the table, Mama dropped her head in her hands. "I have no choice, Marisol."

"Yes. You do." Marisol pulled her mother's hand from her face and forced her to look up.

"I saw the fax from Elegant Flowers in DC. Ten thousand blooms, the largest order we have ever received. Why have you not told me about it so I can get started on culling new bulbs?"

Mama shook her head to the side. "We cannot handle such a large order."

"Yes, we can and will. A big company like that pays on time, and will pay well. And, you will see, word of our exotic lilies will spread. There will be repeat orders from all over the world. We can hire extra workers, and Rosario and Joseph know how to plant..."

Mama exhaled and a look of pity clouded her eyes. "You always were a dreamer, Marisol. You think all you have to do is wish for something and it happens."

Drawing in a breath, Marisol dug her fists into her hips. "I am a grown woman with a child. I know plenty about life. Accept the order. She jabbed her thumb at her chest. "*I* will take on the responsibility for it."

With a sigh, Mama pushed herself up from the table. "Very well." She hustled off to the living room and returned holding a sheet of paper. "Here." She handed the fax to Marisol, and then tapped her finger on the letterhead. "Elite Wholesalers Inc. Read the requirements and you will see why we should turn this order down."

Marisol glanced at the sheet of paper, verifying it was the same one she had seen earlier. "Looks fine to me."

"Really? And you think you can handle everything this order requires?"

Marisol tipped up her chin. "I just said so. Fax them an acceptance."

"You understand that if we fail to fill this order on time, our reputation with wholesalers will be ruined." Mama's voice rose and Marisol took a step back.

Mama was baiting her, trying to intimidate her, but she was not going to budge. "Trust me, Mama. I can do it."

"You had better be right."

* * * *

Carlos' eyes narrowed when Gomez left to return to the main house. He puffed at his cigar, blowing smoke in Victor's face, and then flicked the ashes to the side.

Victor struggled not to inhale—second-hand smoke was as sure a killer as the real thing—and stood his ground. If Carlos thought to shoo him off with his nasty habit the man was mistaken.

"So you want to visit a mine. Why? They are nothing but filthy pits."

Filthy pits? What was Carlos talking about? The mines were mountains of green stones, waiting to be chipped off and marketed. Weren't they?

"Besides," Carlos continued. "As Gomez said, *no* visitors." He took a few steps away.

Oh no, you're not going to dismiss me that easily. Victor grabbed Carlos by the shoulder, spinning the man toward him. "Get me a permit."

Carlos's mouth twisted to the side, obviously deciding on a course of action. Then his face lit up in a smile. He clapped Victor on the shoulder. "Let us not spoil your visit, eh? Emeralds are beautiful, but they are trouble." He fingered the collar of Victor's silk shirt. His cat eyes looked into Victor's with enough intensity to cause him to swallow hard. "Besides, your nice clothes would get soiled." In the dim light of dusk, the green tattoo inside Carlos's wrist seemed to glow.

The man had a lot of nerve trying to intimidate him. Victor shoved Carlos's hand away. "You think I'm a lightweight because I wear decent clothes. You know *nothing* about me."

Carlos regarded him, a calculating expression on his face.

Victor changed his tactics, there was no sense making an enemy of Carlos at this point. He relaxed his face into an apologetic smile. "Sorry, pal. I overreacted there."

Carlos nodded, waiting for him to say more.

"I want to see where you work, to understand you better." *Lame excuse, but if it works, so what?*

Carlos paused, his jaw working. Then he slung his arm around Victor's neck. "I am on my break now, but since you are determined, I will try to arrange for you to tour *La Esmeralda*. It so happens I have an errand up that way. Give me a day or two, eh?"

"Of course." Victor smiled inwardly.

"Good. We will enjoy our time. Get acquainted. No?" Carlos's mouth formed a tight smile. From a pocket in his cargo shorts, he pulled out a bottle, took a slug, and passed it to Victor.

Ew. Covered with saliva, and God knows what else. Suck it up. I can't afford to insult Carlos. I need him right now.

He took the bottle and held it up in salute. "To...brotherhood." With his thumb covering the mouth of the jug, he pretended to take a healthy swig. Alcohol dribbled down his chin. With the back of his hand, he swiped it away.

"Strong stuff," he said, handing the bottle back to Carlos.

"Homemade." Carlos face broke out in a grin. "You know, you are all right for a *gringo*." He took a last swallow before tucking the flask into the pocket of his pants, and then winked at him. "Now, my brother, we are going out on the town."

Good idea. Carlos would be relaxed, and it would be easier to pick his brain.

* * * *

Marisol pushed open the door to her greenhouse, clasping the order to her chest. Mama was giving her a chance to prove her worth. She would fill that big order and save the plantation from Soto's clutches. Her lilies would bring in enough money to send Joseph to a top American university, where he would learn the management skills needed to take over the plantation and learn to speak fluent English. Of course, he would also study botany. He would learn from books, not by trial and error, as she had done. Her Joseph, grown with a family, his children playing in fields flourishing with lilies—newer, more unique varieties than even Marisol was able to produce.

With a smile, she held the order in front of her. She had scanned it quickly as it spit out of the fax, and not examined it carefully when Mama shoved it in her face. Now she needed the details. *Hmmm, all crossbreeds—dragon lilies, trumpets, whites. The largest portion is for my newest Hope Lily.*

She skipped to the note at the bottom:

"For display at political events associated with the 2012 United States presidential elections. Delivery no later than November 1, 2012. Call Alma to confirm."

Mi Dios. Three months. What was I thinking? Not nearly enough time

to germinate bulblets for outdoor planting. She would need all her resources for heat and cold at the ready and perfect weather. Her special
lilies were harder to grow. They required more exact temperature control and constant tending, which meant monitoring their progress day
and night, as well as hiring more workers.

As it was, Garcia Jardines survived from day to day on what little
money they received from wholesalers. The smaller ones dragged their
feet in paying. During the time Marisol was propagating the required
lilies, she would need to keep up with the other orders that drifted in.
At one time they only received a few orders a week, but since word
spread among wholesalers of her Hope Lily, they shipped out several
orders a day. None of those orders, even combined, demanded the
quantity and detail of the Elite order.

First thing in the morning, she would call Alma at Elite Flowers
and demand a ten percent down payment to help fund extra resources.
Even so, making sure the flowers bloomed perfectly and were ready to
pick, all at the same time, would be her responsibilities.

She glanced at the large, battery-operated clock hanging over her
planting desk. *After nine.* Her hand went to her mouth. *Joseph.* Tossing
down her pad, she flew out of the greenhouse and headed for the cottage, where Papa had given permission for her to live with her son. She
did not own it, not really, but after living in it for twelve years, it was
their home.

Leaving her shoes inside the door, Marisol padded down the short
hall, spying a slit of light under Joseph's door. *He should get to sleep.*
Lately, her son had shut her out, as if he were doing something private
inside his room, although she suspected he was only fooling with his

electronic games.

Peering inside, her heart melted. Joseph's eyes were closed in slumber. He had kicked off his covers, allowing his long legs to sprawl across the bed. The game rested on his chest. Shutting down the power, she set the toy on his night table and blew out the oil lamp. In the darkness, with his features softened, he was her little boy again.

"Goodnight, my son." Pulling his covers up over him, Marisol kissed Joseph's cheek and then left the room with the door ajar.

Marisol started for her own room, as she usually would at this time of night, when the weight of the ceiling seemed to crash down on her. *I must take inventory and get going. Now. Tonight.* This Elite project could break them.

Why had she ever thought she could manage it?

* * * *

"Out on the town" turned out to be Barra de Luis in Garcia, a sleazy joint no larger than the efficiency apartment Victor kept in North Miami. A neon sign flashed "CLUB COLUMBO" over the antiquated cash register. The shelved, rear wall held an assortment of colored bottles and was flanked by a bored bartender, presumably Luis, wearing a Boston Red Sox hat and tee shirt.

Victor's nose wrinkled at the stale odors of beer and cigarette smoke. The gray Formica counter was littered with overflowing ashtrays and stained with the rings left by sweating glasses and bottles. The chrome-legged stools lining the bar were backless, with vinyl cushioning. On them, two surly-looking men in filthy denim pants hung over bottled beers. The big one, he recognized as Gomez's chauffer—the man who blew smoke in his face. As if on cue, all eyes zeroed in on Victor.

"Who is the fancy *gringo*, Carlos?" the chauffeur said, as if he had never before set eyes on Victor.

Victor sizzled inside. He wanted to bring up his soiled pants. But from the way everyone here sized him up, doing so would only fuel their ridicule. Tomorrow he'd forget to shave so he'd fit in better with Carlos's cronies, although there was little he could do about his height. Carlos and his friends must take short pills.

"Be careful how you talk about *mi hermano*," Carlos warned.

"Your brother?" The man laughed. "That is a good one."

Carlos stepped forward and bunched the front of the chauffeur's tee shirt in his fist, a gutsy move given the man was at least fifty pounds heavier and bulked up like a body-builder.

"Victor, do not pay attention to Sanchez. He does not know how to show respect to our family."

"Victor? Who names a kid Victor?" the second man at the bar said.

"Enough, Miguel."

The men seemed to calm and turned around in their seats. As Sanchez slugged back his beer, Victor caught a flash of green on his inner wrist. He peered over at Miguel, trying to check out the under-side of *his* wrist.

"What are you looking at, pretty boy?" Miguel stood, stuck his thumbs in the front pockets of his jeans and lifted his pointed chin in challenge.

Enough putdowns. Miguel was asking for a fight and, from his puny build, getting the best of him wouldn't be a big deal. Victor's fists came up in front of him. He didn't know much about street fighting, but he'd learned wrestling at Lawrence Academy—and Jake taught him a few karate moves.

"What did you call me?"

"Sit down, Victor," Carlos said, holding him back. "Miguel, lay off my brother."

With a surly glare at Victor, Miguel turned away.

"Do not mind him, Victor. He has parked his butt at Luis's too long."

With a nod at the pair, Victor slid onto a cracked vinyl stool that made his ass itch. He didn't need Carlos to protect him. Yet he was in a foreign country surrounded by strangers who appeared to be in some sort of street gang or secret organization.

"Carlos," he whispered, playing dumb. "What's with all the green tattoos?"

A muscle twitched under Carlos's eye. "You ask too many questions for a *gringo*."

Okay, so the topic was off limits. Not the right time. He would wait Carlos out for now.

Luis stood in front of him, dark-haired and swarthy with a neatly trimmed moustache. "What will you have?"

Victor glanced at the offerings behind the bar. First class liquor and beer on tap. Not bad for a dive. After the day he'd had, something strong was in order. "I'll have a Gentleman Jack on the rocks."

"Jack who?" Luis laughed. Carlos laughed. And Victor wondered what was so funny.

"Gentleman Jack," he repeated, not feeling the need to explain to a bartender that the whiskey was the high-end version of Jack Daniels.

"He will have a shot of Aguardiente," Carlos said, "and so will I."

In moments, two small glasses of potent, but clear liquor appeared in front of them. They toasted and drank.

Again.

Again.

Pleasantly numbed and in an alcohol haze, he found Carlos's friends were actually very friendly. Maybe Garcia wasn't such a bad place, after all—and the counter looked so cool and comfortable.

Chapter Four

Dawn came far too quickly for Marisol's liking. She lifted her head and realized she had fallen asleep at her desk. A rainbow of colors from the rising sun poured through the glass promising a glorious day, but she would not enjoy it. No, she had too much to do.

With a pang of guilt, she remembered Joseph. She left him alone all night. Although he was certainly old enough and safe, the guilt of not having slept in the room across the hall from him pressed against her heart. He was all she had.

Rising, she rinsed her face in the greenhouse sink. Water dribbled from the tap when it should have gushed, and it was not as warm as it should be. Something was wrong. She cocked an ear for the ever-present drone of the generator.

Dead silent.

They must need fuel again. Since Papa died, Mama had been lax about keeping ahead of problems and it was hurting their production. Why, last week, they had run out of manure to fertilize the plants. Money. It always came down to that. Yet Mama had worn a new dress last night when Soto had come calling.

Marisol squeezed down her resentment. It was not Christian to blame her mother for their problems. Mama never asked to be proprietor of a flower plantation; she married into it. Carlos should have been next in order after Papa's death, but he seemed to be tied to his security job at the emerald mine and showed no interest in the plantation. If only Mama would let her, she could certainly do a better job of managing. Yet Mama held on to the control, waiting for the right man to come along and take over.

Marisol rechecked the thermostat. Down to nineteen degrees Celsius. The heat pump was supposed to maintain an even twenty-four so as not to jar the plantings. The room would warm up as the day progressed, but lack of electricity meant no power to bring water into the greenhouse complex, which included her mother's house. The plantings should keep until nightfall, so perhaps Rosario could pick up fuel when she took their shipment to the Miami shuttle. Before seeing to Joseph, Marisol posted a note on the kitchen counter for Mama.

* * * *

Something evil and bright blasted through Victor's eyelids. The blood moving through the veins in his head thundered like a rockslide. He attempted to wet his lips with his tongue, his mouth seemed stuffed with cotton. Insistent pressure in his gut made him aware of the need to relieve his bursting bladder. When he felt for another body in the bed, his hand dropped off the edge. He pried open his eyes, squinting against the glare streaming through the bare window.

Where am I?

Then it came back to him. *The flower plantation. Guesthouse.* A flash of memory: stumbling out onto the sidewalk and being poured into the back seat of Carlos's Jeep. Victor felt for his clothes. He was naked— well, almost. He still wore his boxers, but someone had undressed him

51

and tucked him in.

Pulling himself to a sitting position, he waited until the spinning in his head abated before glancing down. His expensive slacks were puddled on the floor. *The wrinkles will set. Have to hang them up.*

With a stretch, he picked up the pants and shook them out. *Wait. Something is missing.* He patted the back pocket for the lump of his wallet.

Fuck. I've been rolled.

Victor checked the remaining pockets, turning them inside out to be sure. He tried to think, which was near impossible, given that little men beat their fists inside his head. *My passport, my cash.* Had the theft occurred here in this cottage while he slept? The door had no lock. Anyone could have come in—and murdered him, even. His body went rigid, and sweat broke out on his skin.

"No-o-o."

Leaping up, Victor raced to his suitcase and flung everything out of it until he gripped his traveling documents and the remaining money from his last job. *Whew.* All there except for his designer wallet—which was worth more than the cash inside it.

What had he expected? He came to Colombia knowing it was filled with crime. He had been foolish not to be wary of theft. To think he stupidly flaunted what little wealth he had.

He grabbed his airline ticket. He could change the flight and get out of Bogotá today, although the change fee would be horrendous. Flapping the ticket against his palm, he thought back to the previous night. His wallet must have been lifted at the bar—all total strangers, until yesterday, and all apparent members of the same gang. Victor was an intruder. Did they plan the theft to scare him off?

No way.

Thief or no thief, he needed Carlos to commit to take him to *La Esmeralda.* Trading emeralds wasn't going to be a clean job, his instincts told him, but it would be fast money. What harm could come of hanging around long enough to give it a shot? He shoved the ticket back into its envelope, and then stashed it, along with his passport and the bulk of his cash, inside the inner lining of the pillow he'd slept on. With no maid service, it was as good a place as any for safekeeping.

Grabbing a shirt and a pair of jeans, he threw them on, slammed out the door, and strode to Carlos's cottage, to the far left of the main house.

He banged on the red wooden door until his fists stung. "Wake up, you son of a bitch." Victor bit back the coarse words. Cursing was for lowlife. This morning he couldn't care what anyone here thought of him. He'd been burned, and Carlos was going to know it. "Come on. Open up."

Rosario cracked open the door and peered out at him, wide-eyed and wearing a fluffy pink bathrobe. "Victor. What is the matter?"

Grabbing the knob, he tugged the door fully open and pushed past her into a sitting room dwarfed by a plasma TV set. "Where's Carlos?"

Rosario stepped back, her hands in the air. "He is..."

Carlos appeared from another room. Considering the drinking they had done last night, he looked in better shape than Victor felt. "Eh, my brother. What is going on? You come busting in here...you okay, Rosario? You make my wife all upset."

"Don't you 'brother' me. You...you, thief. My wallet. Hand it over."

"Calm down, Victor."

"Calm down? Someone removed my pants and tucked me into bed last night." He glanced at Rosario, who remained cowering by the door. *Certainly not her.*

He stepped nose to nose with Carlos, his feet digging into the plush carpeting. "I expect you took care of me, and lifted my wallet as a reward."

"You mean this one?" Carlos tossed over Victor's billfold. "I found it on the sidewalk outside Luis's place."

Victor flipped through it. His charge cards and cash appeared intact. "I'll bet you did." Stuffing his wallet in his pocket, he turned to leave.

"Victor." Carlos's hand clutched at his shoulder. "I tell the truth."

Victor heaved in a breath of resignation. He had his wallet back, and had already decided to stick it out here, so he might as well play along. Carlos's sidewalk story was bullshit. Though somehow he couldn't believe Carlos was low enough to steal from him, when he could have simply walked into Victor's cottage and taken anything he wanted.

Maybe he needed to thank Carlos for retrieving his wallet from whoever lifted it. He might've missed a good fight. If only he could remember how it went down. Then he'd know for sure if Carlos was friend or foe.

"The señora is making breakfast. Why do you not shower in the main house?" Carlos gave him a friendly shove. "You will feel like a new man, eh?"

He had run from the cottage without washing up. Victor finger-combed the tangles from his hair and checked his breath against his hand. *Raunchy.* Perhaps some dry toast and tea would settle his stomach, and a hot shower would put him to rights.

"I will meet you at Mama's in an hour, Victor," Carlos called after him. We will go to Bogotá. I will take you to the emerald exchange."

Victor slowed his stride. "Sure," he said over his shoulder.

Plodding toward the main house, Victor drew in a few breaths and caught the scent of lilies. The pounding of his heart began to slow, easing the tightness in his chest. Instead of going directly into the main house, he followed his nose to the flowerbeds outside the greenhouse. He stood a moment, allowing the beauty of buds in bloom to seep through him.

What if all that brother stuff is crap? Despite the issue of the stolen wallet, the thought zinged an arrow to his heart. For the first time since his mother died, he had not felt alone.

As he turned away, he noticed a figure inside the greenhouse. Without thinking, he pushed open the door. Marisol's back was to him—*bare feet and slim legs leading to a curvy behind*—bent over a table of greenery. His nose twitched at the smell of damp earth. His fingers itched to sink into the soil and press it tight against a rootling. The room was filled with aisle upon aisle of tables laden with cardboard bins sprouting greenies. Not high tech, like the Gallagher's, but functional. An assortment of flowers in various stages of blooming covered the length of the building.

Marisol's body straightened. She turned, her eyes steady, mouth tight. Her streaming brunette hair was caught back from a fine-boned face with a yellow print bandana. Her eyebrows arched above amber eyes, which were checking out his disheveled appearance, no doubt. But she made no comment.

"I couldn't resist your greenhouse," he said, moving toward her. "I used to help our gardener at the estate where I grew up, and I find I miss the plantings."

Marisol's nostrils flared. "Do you not have anything else to do? Like take a shower?" She turned back to her worktable.

So she had *noticed.*

This scamp of a woman wasn't going to blow him off that easily. "Sorry. Didn't mean to offend you."

Marisol's head swiveled around, hair flying behind her. "I thought you had gone."

He spread his arms. "Why don't you take a minute and show me around?"

"I do not have a minute."

"Well, then, don't mind me. I'll take a walk-through, and then let myself out." Victor ran his finger on the underside of a new leaf.

"Do not touch..."

Low move, but it got her attention. "Sorry." Victor held his hands in the air. "I saw some unusual lilies in your field. What varieties do you grow here?"

He leaned over to smell an exotic black lily. Bouquets of this flower had been sprawled throughout the governor's mansion—at the man's retirement, he believed. Very rare, very expensive. Maybe Garcia Jardines was more than it appeared.

"I've seen this flower before. I didn't know it was grown in your nursery."

Marisol's lips curved in a half smile revealing white teeth that would have been perfect, had one front tooth not been slightly crossed over the tip of its neighbor. Her eyes softened.

"The flower is not only grown here, but was created within these walls." The harshness in her voice became a musical lilt, as her hand made a sweeping gesture to span the greenhouse. Her shoulders seemed to broaden and her chest swelled.

Marisol moved toward him, bringing with her the clean scent of soap. He knew he reeked, yet she didn't wrinkle her nose and back away, as most women might have. Now he wished he were at least presentable. She had softened when he praised her lily. Perhaps, if he was better groomed, she would welcome his advances.

Marisol came up next to him, her nearness igniting heat in his groin. It had been a while since a woman turned him on without a lot of pre-coaxing. With the old ones, he had to use imagery, and even resort to pills to become erect. He positioned his hand to hide his crotch so as not to frighten this butterfly of a woman away.

"This is quite a large lily." Using his free hand, he spread his fingers to measure its breadth. I've only seen white lilies come close to this size."

Marisol smiled, not a wide happy smile, but a simple curve of her lips. "You are thinking of the Easter lilies that are so common in the spring."

"Yes, I suppose so. But the shape. It's a calla lily, is it not?"

"This particular one is the latest of a new variety I have developed. You see," —she traced the outer edge with a finger— "the white rim is nearly an even line now and the color, while actually a deep purple, is closer to black than any other botanist has ever achieved. I call it the Hope Lily. Its black center signifies the depth of despair. The white rim gives hope of goodness beyond the dark."

He'd found the way to the woman's heart, not with his looks or charisma, but through genuine interest in her flowers. He stood back, watching Marisol's lips move. She was so pure and untouched, and he was dirty inside and out.

Chapter Five

Señora Garcia trapped Victor in the kitchen before he could sneak into the shower. Her hair hung about her shoulders in the same type of loose waves as Marisol's. He'd bet she primped a bit, knowing he would be stopping in. And here he was, looking like something the cow dragged in.

The señora's gaze went to the towel and toiletry bag he held. "You will have to use the outdoor shower, today. Our generator is out of service."

Crap. He would bet that shower head was connected to a simple hose, which meant no hot water, no nothing. Yet he smelled...coffee.

"Ah. I see," the señora said, nodding her head like a bobble doll. "You are not used to being without modern conveniences." She spread out her arms. "We are simple people. You can see how far into the mountains we live. Did you expect we would have access to all of the utilities of a big city?"

He took in a breath. The woman had read his mind. Yes. He had expected to have all the amenities he was accustomed to in Miami, but maybe for a few days he could make do. He was already hobnobbing with the *in crowd*, as far as the emerald business was concerned. He needed to find the right niche. Besides, it wasn't costing him a damn cent to stay here.

"I can handle it," he said, sniffing the air. "I wouldn't mind a cup of that coffee, though."

The señora clasped her hands in front of her. "Forgive me. Of course. Sit." She pulled out a chair. "How do you like your eggs fixed?"

The steaming mug of coffee she set before him lifted Victor's spirits and doused his original craving for dry toast and tea. Suddenly, his acid stomach cried for food, and eggs sounded damned good. "Scrambled, please. Dry." He hated runny eggs.

Victor scanned the table. Finding no sweetener packets, he reached for the sugar bowl. Real sugar. He stirred in three teaspoonfuls and added cream until the coffee turned milky, the way he used to drink it. Once he was rich, he wouldn't need to worry about keeping down his weight. He took a sip. *Heaven.*

"What kind of coffee is this?"

The señora turned from the mustard-colored stove—propane-fueled, he guessed from the odor. "Colombian, of course, fresh-ground from beans grown at the plantation on the other side of Bogotá."

"Of course."

With such rich soil and temperate climate, Colombia could grow any plant from coffee to the coca used in making cocaine. Cocaine dealing. Now that was another lucrative option. It had been a party drug at Lawrence Academy. Nasty stuff if you got hooked. Victor had been smart to stay clean, but several of his school buddies hadn't. One of them overdosed and didn't survive. He could never involve himself in a career that destroyed people. Emeralds, now, they were clean and beautiful.

The señora set a plate of eggs in front of him, along with a platter of delectable-looking pastry drizzled with honey.

"Victor, I feel I should apologize for getting so upset about Joseph asking you to help me with our bills." Her head dropped. "Truth is I've made a mess of things. My husband used to take care of everything, but me, it never adds up right. Do you think...?"

He had hoped to get his hands on the numbers here when Joseph first suggested it. After seeing Marisol's magnificent black lily in the greenhouse, perhaps this pauper of a business was really a prince in disguise.

"Math was always my forte. Perhaps tomorrow, though. I'm committed today."

The back door rattled open. Carlos stomped in. His hair was gelled and he smelled fresh, as if he'd come from the hot shower Victor wouldn't have. Today, he had shucked his sloppy clothes for a trim pair of chinos and a collared shirt.

"Generator out again, Mama?"

The señora shrugged.

Without greeting Victor, Carlos picked up a sweet bun and ripped off a hunk. "I see Mama is taking good care of you, Victor." Carlos stuffed the food into his mouth, his cheeks puffing out like a chipmunk's.

Maybe Carlos could pretend everything was all right between them, but Victor still felt cool toward the man. Until he knew how Carlos came to have his wallet, he would be on guard.

"Yes, well, I've yet to shower." Victor stood. "Outside, I suppose. Give me fifteen minutes."

Carlos's hand pressed into his shoulder. "Take your time, Victor. Something has...uh...come up. Business."

"*Business?* I thought we were going to spend time together."

"Tomorrow." He gave Victor a light punch on his bicep. "We go to the cockfight, eh?"

"Tomorrow?" Victor sputtered. "What am I supposed to do all day today? Sit on my hands and sing?"

Carlos laughed. "That would be entertaining, would it not, Mama?"

"I'm not joking." Anger crawled up from Victor's gut and brought heat to his face. Stranded on this flower farm. No car, no phone. His cell phone might as well be a hockey puck, for all the good it did him. At least he had his wallet back, not that he'd be out shopping.

"Do not worry about Victor, Carlos. We will keep him entertained for you." The señora smiled at Victor. "Marisol has to run some errands this afternoon. I'm sure she would love company."

"Good idea," Carlos said, the tension dropping from his shoulders. "You and Marisol will get along good, eh?" He winked. "She has no husband, you know. Well, got to get going. Hey, see you later, Victor."

Turning his back, Carlos sauntered out the door.

Victor clamped his jaw tight enough to grind his teeth against one another. *What is Carlos's game, anyway?*

* * * *

Marisol burst into the kitchen, colliding with Victor. He grabbed her arms to keep her from falling. Every nerve ending in her body soared to high alert. He was *touching* her. "I...um...excuse me."

She pulled away, and then peered around him at her mother, who hovered over the sink washing dishes with water from a pitcher.

"Mama, did you get my note?" Marisol picked up a dishtowel to help, feeling the heat of Victor's gaze. He kept staring at her with those chocolate eyes.

"Yes, the generator. We need to pick up more fuel. I am sending you into town to get it this afternoon. On your way, you can drop off the flowers for shipment."

"Why me? Rosario usually does the errands. The sun is burning through the glass. It is twenty-seven degrees inside the greenhouse already. If I do not move the plants to a cooler area, they will wilt and die." The words spat from of her mouth.

"Do you need some help?" Victor asked.

His perfectly shaped, dark eyebrows knitted, forming two vertical creases in between them.

"N... Well, yes. I suppose it would take less time..."

"Well, good. I'll get washed up and be right over." Slinging his towel over his shoulder, he headed for the door.

His walk was smooth, controlled, as if he knew Marisol's eyes were following him. What was wrong with her? She no more needed this man fussing around her plants than a fancy ball gown. He was fluff; décor.

But it was too late. The door slammed behind him.

"Now there is a nice catch for you." Mama set a clean dish into the wire drainer.

"I suppose you would be happy if I married a man like Victor, but I do not need a man to take care of me..." Marisol bit back the words, *"like you do."* She did not want to hurt Mama; she loved her. She just wished Mama would love her back.

"What of your son? Do you not care that he is growing up without a father?"

"There are plenty of men around for him." The lie stung like a wasp crawling through Marisol's insides. Carlos was as poor a father image as she might find, and Papa had not been much better.

"I need to get back to the greenhouse."

"Not so fast," Mama said. "What about Victor? I told him you would take him into Bogotá. Carlos needs us to keep him occupied while he takes care of important business."

"So you volunteered me to entertain Victor all day...to help *Carlos?*" Her words came out as a shout. It irked her how Carlos wormed his way into Mama's heart after Papa's death. "You had no right..."

"I have every right." Mama poked at her chest with her thumb. "*I* own Garcia Jardines, not you."

Mama's comment stung. If Marisol had not followed her father's path in creating new species, their business would have dried up once the cartel money stopped coming in.

"Yes, I know that." She grabbed a stack of dried dishes and jammed them into the cabinet before whirling to face Mama. "But it is not our job to entertain Carlos's so-called brother, the man we never heard of until two days ago. What has Carlos ever done for us? Never once has he helped in the gardens. He sees we are hurting for money, but he has never contributed a peso."

"That is not fair. Carlos does not make that much at the mines."

"Bah. Open your eyes, Mama, and step inside his and Rosario's cottage. Carlos has more man toys than Santa Claus. Rosario told me he just put in a plumbing system, and it is hooked up to our generator. The least he could do is help pay for fuel."

"What can I do, Marisol? He protects us. Some of the townspeople resent us for Papa's part in the cartel. What is to stop them from destroying our fields or setting our house on fire?"

"How can Carlos protect us when he is never around?" Marisol put her hand on her mother's shoulder and pressed down until Mama's eyes met hers. "The women in Garcia will understand our plight, if we go to them and explain we are no longer affiliated with the emerald cartel, that we are running an honest business. They will talk to their husbands on our behalf, and we will be safe."

"And admit we are vulnerable? Doing as you suggest could stir up more trouble than we have."

Now Marisol understood. Mama had never stopped relying on the cartel's support. With Carlos gone much of the time, she saw Soto as their new savior. If Mama knew the horrible thing Soto might've had done to them, Mama would loathe the man, too.

"I had better get going. Victor will be along to help move the bulbets and I will need to show him what to do. I was up most of the night working on a planting schedule for that Elite order. We cannot afford to lose any plants right now."

At Mama's blank stare, Marisol went cold. "The order for ten thousand lilies. You faxed an acceptance. Didn't you?" Her voice rose.

"Oh. That." Mama took her time hanging the dishtowel over the rack, straightening it so it was even at the hem.

"We talked about it. You promised."

Mama's chest heaved with a deep sigh. "The fax will not work without power. I will take care of it later."

"There is always the telephone." She held up the order. "Shall I call them, or will you?"

"Give me that." Snatching the order from her, Mama shuffled to the mustard-colored kitchen phone.

Marisol was right behind her. Arms folded, she watched Mama's finger travel arcs around the dial pad, clicking each digit, and then listened as she told the agent Garcia Jardines would handle the order. The handset dropped into its holder with a snap. She wanted to let out a whoop, and at the same time crumple in a heap and cry. The fate of Garcia Jardines rested on *her* shoulders, now.

* * * *

The morning mountain air couldn't be more than sixty-five degrees Fahrenheit, or whatever it equaled in Celsius. In his cottage, Victor stripped off his clothes and shivered into his black silk robe. Over the pretend sink, he found a bar of soap. Grabbing his salon shampoo and a towel, he ran barefoot over the dewy grass to the curtained area of the outdoor shower Joseph had pointed out.

After a quick lather and rinse with the warm part of the water that must've been exposed to the sun, he dried off with the roughened terry bath towel, wrapped it around his waist, and high-tailed it back to his cottage.

It hadn't been the shower at Fontaine Blue, but at least he felt clean. By tonight the generator should be working, and he'd be able to shave and moisturize after a hot shower in the bath at the main house.

After tossing on a fresh pair of jeans and a long sleeved Miami Dolphin tee shirt, he peered into the crackled mirror hung over the sink and put in colored contacts. Would Marisol even notice his eye color had changed from boring brown to green?

When she collided with him earlier, the muscles in her arms had gone stiff, and her eyes widened in shock when he tried to brace her from falling. Under such circumstances, most women would have swooned in his arms. Of course, he hadn't looked—or smelled—his best, but he sensed that had nothing to do with her odd reaction.

He stood back from the mirror. *Day-old beard and hair in wet tangles. Man, if one of those rich babes saw me now, she'd turn up her nose and walk away.* He wasn't even going to try to shave, and his hair—he picked up a wavy strand—*girlie.* No wonder those tough guys he'd met last night picked on him.

He rubbed through some gel, combed his hair back from his face, and secured it into the sleek ponytail he always wore. *Better from the front, but that tail hanging at the nape of my neck has to go.* Maybe then he'd fit with Carlos's tattooed friends long enough to for them to let down their guard and cut him into their "business."

He turned over his left wrist. He might have to submit to a tattoo. He wasn't sure if he wanted to have permanent ink marring his body. His clients weren't into body art. They liked his skin to be pristine, touchable—and hairless. The truth was most women preferred smooth, silky skin to tickly fur.

In the mirror, Victor watched his lips curve into a smile. He wouldn't have to keep his chest, groin, and legs shaved smooth anymore. If he could pull off a deal here, he'd never have to worry about his appearance or demeanor again. He could be himself. Victor. The person inside. And finally have control over his body, his life.

After checking that his valuables remained intact, he headed down the drive toward the greenhouse. In the short time he'd been inside, the gardens had become populated with pale yellow circles. As he neared, each circle became the head of a straw-hatted worker. He slowed his step to watch one of the women methodically snap a bloom at its base and set it in the wooden bucket with the others. Her movements were rhythmic—pluck and place, pluck and place—a repeated action that must leave her arm sore by the end of her day. Hard work, but gratifying in that it put food in the mouths of her family.

Men wheeled carts overflowing with beauty toward the greenhouse. He waved to Rosario, who stood outside directing them. She smiled at him, a sign that the scene he made in her cottage that morning was forgiven.

"*Hola*, Victor. Marisol is inside."

At the sound of Marisol's name, he quickened his step. He opened the greenhouse door to chaos. Marisol's soft but commanding voice directed two slim men in soiled jeans and tees.

'Yes, over there in the shade. Set the pots from that table underneath, on the floor."

"Marisol. How can I help?" he asked.

She turned toward him, eyebrows lifted. "Victor. Yes, I had forgotten you were coming." With a wave he almost took as dismissal, she said, "The foreman's name is Jose."

She called Jose over. "Victor is going to help you." She spoke louder than normal, taking care to enunciate every word.

"What about this batch?" Jose said. "They do not look so good."

Marisol hurried over and pinched one of the leaves. "Take them outdoors and water them from the hose. It's connected to the cistern."

"Where...?"

Without an acknowledgement, Marisol turned to speak with a man barreling through the door with a cart filled with flowers. "Over there." She pointed to an area containing ceiling-high stacks of oblong cardboard boxes and a worktable.

Jose gave Victor the once over. "You a new hire?"

"No. Just helping out today."

The man nodded. "Cistern is out back."

"Thanks," Victor said, scooping up as many pots as he could manage. He glanced over his shoulder to see if Marisol noticed, but her back was to him. She stood at the worktable with an open crate set on top, dipping flower stems into some sort of liquid.

He kneed open the door, and tended to the plants by swishing the hose to water them evenly. Instead of bringing the dripping plants indoors, he wedged them under the shady eave of the greenhouse.

After the bulk of the plants were watered and protected, Victor came up behind Marisol. Her hair, held back by its yellow bandana, cascaded like chocolate silk to the small of her back. She smelled of wet earth and flowers, a perfume that never failed to stir him. While he'd been fussing with the plants, she finished packing several crates and stacked them on the floor.

"Can I store those crates for you?"

Marisol's shoulders bunched at hearing his voice, yet her hands didn't stop working. She turned her head enough for him to see the fringe of her dark lashes. Her chest heaved with what he took to be annoyance.

Irritation flooded over him at her cold shoulder attitude. He'd broken his back—*well, not really*—helping her and he didn't even get a thank you. What was he doing here, anyway? He was supposed to be in Bogotá with Carlos meeting his business associates and wedging his way in tight with them. He only had a few days to learn how the emerald business worked. Carlos promised he'd try to get Victor into a mine. Obviously, that wasn't going to happen today.

"Come with me," she said with a flip of her head that sent sunny highlights running through her hair.

Marisol opened the door to a refrigerated room where similar boxes were stacked. Beads of water covered the bare parts of the wall. Her hand flew to her mouth. "Oh no. I forgot about the refrigerator." Rushing inside, she pressed her hand against the wall. "Still cool, but not for long." She held out a set of keys. "Out back, there is a white van. Start it running and then flip the switch for the van refrigeration."

"Yes ma'am." Victor clicked heels and raised two fingers in a salute.

The corners of Marisol's mouth wiggled as if she couldn't decide whether to smile or not.

As Victor took the keys from her, his hand brushed against hers, leaving a lingering spot of heat on his skin.

"It will take a while for the van to chill and I have to finish packing," she said, the edge to her voice softening. "In about an hour, I should be ready to load the van and head into Bogotá. Come back then if you want to come."

Okay, so she wasn't hot on the idea of him tagging along. Tough. He had nothing better to do.

Dismissed for the moment, he remembered about Cedric and felt for his phone. It flashed the low battery sign—with no electricity available for charging. *Crap*. Cedric might forgive yesterday's slight, but he didn't dare put off the call any longer. Perhaps the señora would allow him to use her landline. He rapped on the front door.

"Victor, why so formal, you should have used the side door." The señora let him inside.

"I'm done helping Marisol. I...uh...need to make an urgent call. Do you by any chance have a telephone?"

"*Si*. Where do you need to call?"

"Miami. My boss needs to talk to me."

Her mouth formed an "O".

Reaching in his pocket, Victor pulled out a twenty-dollar bill and pressed it into her hand. "This should cover the cost for an international call."

"*Gracias*, Victor." She stuffed the bill into the pocket of her housedress and pointed to an archaic wall phone. "I will check on Marisol."

After she left, he dialed up Cedric.

"Victor," Cedric answered, his voice jovial as usual. "You are not normally remiss in returning my calls."

"I'm out of the country and haven't been able to call you until now. What's going on?"

At the other end, Cedric sighed.

A bad sign.

"Sorry old chap, but I have to let you go."

"Let me go? Go where?" Victor sputtered.

"Business is in the crapper and I was ordered to cut our staff in half. You understand?"

Victor swallowed hard. "Yes, I mean, *no*. How could you do this to me?"

"Not me. The powers above. Look, I'll call you when we are hiring once more."

"Yes, yes. Do that." He squeezed the handset, wishing he could throttle it. Make believe the call had never happened. In a swift move, he slammed it into its cradle.

Bastard. How dare the man fire him? Why, he was Cedric's top waiter. If he couldn't work things out here in Colombia, he'd have to return to Miami and go on the hunt again. There were other cruise lines, but *Ocean Pleasures* was the newest and most popular—and attracted the wealthiest women. While he might remain independent for a few more years by landing a job on a class B cruise ship, it would mean fewer perks and lower pay. Before long, he'd be on the streets flaunting his wares, like a common whore.

He was better than that; he deserved more, and damn it, he was going to get it.

Chapter Six

"Marisol, stop getting so flustered. It is not as if this has not happened before. Once we refuel the generator, everything will be back to normal," Rosario said.

"I have to pack this morning's pickings, but the refrigerator with last night's flowers is warming up fast. We are going to lose everything."

"No we will not."

"Yes we will. These lilies" —Marisol pointed to the boxes she had finished— "go to Elite in Miami. They have given us a huge order. If they do not arrive in perfect condition, they are liable to cancel."

"Seems as if everything is under control," Mama said, coming up to Rosario and Marisol.

"Not really. I was telling Rosario..."

"Yes, I heard. Victor is inside making a phone call. You *are* taking him with you."

Mama's look was accusing, as if she expected Marisol to back out, as if she ever had. She was more reliable than earth and Mama knew it.

"As soon as the van is charged," she replied.

"Rosario, can you finish up here so Marisol can get cleaned up," Mama said with a wink. Then she cupped Marisol's chin and looked into her eyes. "You are a beautiful woman, but no one would know it, the way you hide yourself."

Mama never called her beautiful. Rosario was the pretty one, Mama's pet. She was the plain daughter Papa pampered, until Mama decided Marisol should fill Saint Andrew's request to give one child to God and sent her away.

"Everything is pretty well set," Rosario said. "Mama, ask Victor if he will help Jose load the flowers onto the van while I take Marisol to my cottage and see if we can find something nicer for her to wear."

"But..."

"Yes, Rosario. Do that. I will send Victor along."

Rosario linked her arm through Marisol's. "Come on, big sister. I have just the outfit to make Victor's eyes pop."

Before Marisol could object, Rosario was dragging her toward the cottage. Rosario stopped to fill a bucket from the cistern, brought it inside, and set it in the sink.

Unlike Marisol's cottage and the guesthouse, Rosario's place had pressurized hot and cold water—which, without a working generator, was temporarily out of service.

She handed Marisol a bar of soap and a nailbrush. "Scrub up, then come on into our room."

Marisol pulled at her sister's arm. "Rosario. Stop. Why am I doing this?"

"You would have to be blind not to notice. Victor is a handsome man. He has money and class. What more could you want?"

"I really cannot afford the time to fool around with such nonsense. Victor can ride along, but I am going to pick up the fuel, see that the flowers get onto the Miami shuttle, and then hurry back here."

"Stop putting everything before yourself. There is no need for you to rush back. Victor will only be here a few more days." She smiled slyly. "Remember what we talked about?"

"Of course. According to you and Mama, I am supposed to throw myself at Victor so he will take pity on me and, and then he will want to..."

"Screw you?"

Marisol shut her eyes, wanting to block out the horrid word. She did not want to be screwed. She wanted to be loved. Yet after twelve years of celibacy, maybe she deserved to be...screwed. "Yes, Rosario."

"You are worried about getting pregnant again, are you not?"

Marisol swallowed hard, remembering how it felt to be held in a man's arms. Missing it, but not daring to pay the price. "One scandal was enough to ruin me for life."

"You are not ruined. You are human. Victor is a man of the world. I would not be surprised if he keeps a condom in his wallet. Besides, you do not have to bed the man to have a good time. Once you finish your errands, show him the town and then find a nice restaurant and make him buy you dinner. Certainly, he has the money."

Rosario leaned closer. "If you do not make it back in time for Joseph's soccer game, Mama told me she would go to the game and cheer him on for you."

Marisol's hand went to her mouth. "Oh my God. I forgot about his game. I cannot do this. I need to be here for my son or he will think I do not care." She grabbed Rosario's shoulders. "You need to take the flowers. I do not care what Mama wants."

"Sorry, Sis. You are not winning this one. Stop worrying about Joseph. You can watch him play next week. The season has just begun. He will understand. He loves you and wants you to be happy."

Marisol took a deep breath of air to clear the guilt racing through her mind. She had been so busy with her plants that she had not paid proper attention when Joseph announced he had made the team. Now he would think she was ignoring him again by missing his first game. Then she remembered the red soccer shirt she had picked up from the floor in Joseph's room. When she smoothed it out on top of his bed the name *"Soto Flores"* was emblazoned across it. Surely Señor Soto would be there cheering on his team.

No wonder Mama was so anxious to get rid of her today. She would bet Mama planned to go to the game with Soto and did not want Marisol to know. The thought brought bile into her throat.

"Stop over thinking this situation, Marisol."

"I suppose missing one game isn't going to make much of a difference."

If Marisol were right about Mama's reason for wanting to attend, what could she do, save plop herself between Mama and Soto and try to cheer Joseph on to victory.

She thought of Victor, tall, handsome, and seemingly kindhearted. Maybe a change of pace would be good for her.

Marisol pulled out a long strand of hair. "I am not sure how to style it. It has been so long since I have cared."

"I will help you fix it." Rosario leaned back, assessing her. "You could do with a dab of makeup and some perfume. Hmmm. You need to wear something flirty."

Marisol spun around in a circle, all of a sudden feeling like a teen-ager again.

* * * *

The last of the crates were cooling in the van. Victor sagged down onto a chunk of rock, backed by the high, chain-linked fence marking the property line.

Jose handed him an icy bottle of Club Colombo beer from his cooler. "*Gracias* for helping. Now I can go home to my wife for lunch and a siesta." He nudged Victor. "Know what I mean?"

"You're finished for the day?" He spoke louder than usual, so he wouldn't need to repeat.

"For the morning's picking. I come back in the afternoon when the children come from school."

"Children?"

"Two. They return with me to pick until suppertime."

"Don't you send out an evening shipment?"

Jose waved a hand in front of his face. "We keep the late-picked flowers cold, and then send them out with the fresh, morning pick-ings."

"So, this" —Victor pointed at the van— "is all that will ship to-day?"

Jose shrugged. "It depends on the demand." He smiled, revealing yellowed teeth.

From their labels, Victor noticed the flowers from the refrigerator and those Marisol had packed that morning were being sent to three different wholesalers, which meant very few orders must have come due between yesterday afternoon and this morning. Given the number of workers he'd seen in the fields, Garcia Jardines had to have a high overhead. No wonder the señora had trouble paying the bills.

Victor and Jose turned their heads at the clicking of high-heeled shoes against the stone path circling the greenhouse.

Jose whistled.

Victor's mouth fell open. His Ivory soap woman had turned into a tart.

He knew he was gawking at Marisol, but what the hell had she done to herself? Her eyes were shadowed in blue, her cheeks were too rosy, and her lips were as bright red as the dress she wore—a two-piece number revealing a bare midriff and the swells of her breasts. Her hair was done up in a knot of some sort with a matching flower tucked in. From the little he had seen of her, this getup was out of character.

Marisol's lower lip trembled and, for a moment, Victor worried she would dash away crying. He should know better than to allow his feelings to show.

He schooled his face. "You look lovely," he said with an approving smile.

She touched that knot at the back of her head. Her lips curved with a smile that made her appear more girlish than womanly. "*Gracias*, Victor." Her voice had a velvety tone.

Whoa, is she actually flirting with me? What happed to that cool, standoffish woman?

"We are all set here, *bonita señorita*," Jose said. "I will see you this afternoon."

"Ready, Victor?" Marisol tilted her head in that way women do when they are trying to look cute.

Marisol wasn't cute, but if she'd wash off the goop and change her clothes, her natural beauty would shine through.

"Shall I drive?" he asked.

"You do not know the way." She brushed past him, giving him a whiff of Rosario's perfume, and took mincing steps to the driver's side. As her hips swayed under that red miniskirt, he couldn't help but wonder if Rosario had loaned her a thong, a lacy black one. A man can only hope. Yet he knew without checking, that Marisol was a white panty girl. And he wasn't sure he minded.

Marisol kept pulling at the hem, as if trying to the make the skirt longer. He had to admit the outfit, though garish, made him want to toss Marisol on the grass and make love to her.

She grabbed the door handle of the van and hesitated. Casting her gaze downward, she said, "Wait for me in the van, Victor. I...have to get something."

* * * *

Ten minutes, and already her toes pinched from pitching forward in the torturous shoes. What had she been thinking by allowing Rosario to dress her up like a trollop? Once out of sight, Marisol kicked off the red shoes with a sigh as her bare feet met cool grass. Picking up the evil things with two fingers, she hurried into the cottage, grabbed her shawl, and slipped into comfortable shoes. Lord, she wished she could scrub off the makeup that covered her face like a mask, and shuck the skimpy outfit without hurting Rosario's feelings. Besides, Victor would wonder why she had changed.

As she skidded past Joseph's room, the soccer shirt laid out on the bed called to her like red flag. What kind of mother was she to go off on a lark when her son needed her? Her chin went up. She was committed to doing the errands, but not to trying to have a jolly time with a man she barely knew. She started at a rap at the door.

Rosario cracked it open and peered inside.

Caught.

Rosario's smile faded. "Not backing out, are you, Sis?"

"Of course not."

"Wait." Rosario blocked her exit. Her calculating, coffee-colored eyes zeroed in on the grey shawl. "What are doing with that old thing?"

"I...might be cold." She folded the shawl over her arm.

"Awk. And you've changed into those horrible old-lady shoes. They don't go with that dress."

Marisol picked up Rosario's red shoes from the floor and held them out to her. "These are pretty, but I cannot walk in them. I was afraid I would have trouble working the pedals of the van. *Gracias.*" She handed them to Rosario.

"Victor is pacing outside the van. Did he at least see the ensemble before you ruined it?"

"Oh yes," Marisol tried to make her voice bright and joyful, "and Jose whistled. After my grand entrance, I doubt Victor will notice my shoes are different."

"I suppose." Rosario's shoulders fell in resignation. "He will be looking at your face, anyway, *cariño.*" She kissed Marisol's cheek. "Have fun. I am going to grab some lunch, and then I will check on the new plants for you."

"Gracias."

Once her sister was out of sight, Marisol slipped the shawl over her shoulders and crossed it over skin that had not seen sunlight in over a decade. *There. Not great, but better.*

"Sorry I took so long," she said to Victor, who leaned cross-armed against the side of the van. Dressed more casually today, he exuded a raw sexuality that made her knees go weak. But she could not let him get to her that way. She would get hurt and she would never let that happen again. "Let us head out."

Tightening the shawl around her, she climbed into the driver's seat, made certain the gear was in neutral, and turned on the ignition. The engine sputtered and then stalled out. The van was overdue for servicing, it needed an oil change and some gear work, but it would have to wait. Had Papa been alive, their flower transport would be in top-notch condition. In fact, she would be driving the newest model, instead of this 2005 lemon.

Victor opened the passenger door, and then brushed at the cloth upholstery as if his magic touch would erase the embedded stains. A look of resignation crossed his face when he eased his rear end onto the seat.

"I see our shuttle van is not up to your standards." She glared him. "We are plain people trying to make a living. If you are displeased with our vehicle, you can get out. I do not need your help."

"Sorry. I didn't mean to offend you. It will be my pleasure to accompany you."

Words said by rote. How many times has this man covered up his true feelings? Without responding, Marisol shifted into first and pulled out of the drive behind the greenhouse. "Better buckle up. It is a bumpy ride."

Calm down, you jumped down the man's throat. Give him a chance.

As they chugged away from Garcia Jardines, Marisol rolled down her window to catch the sweet floral scent carried by the wind. Strands of her hair escaped from its clasp and beat at her cheeks. Speeding past acres and acres of beauty filled her, body and soul. Ahead, the curve in the road seemed a smile.

"Do you get to Bogotá often?"

She blanked the emotion from her face. For a moment, she had forgotten she was not alone. "Rosario usually takes the flowers."

Small talk, she hated it. "So, Victor, what exactly do you do in finance?"

"Investments."

Marisol chewed at her lower lip, biting off some of Rosario's greasy lipstick. *Another evasive male.* "That is your source of income?"

"You might say. Tell me more about you."

He turned his knees toward her and rested his arm on the back of the seat. His fingers mere inches from the bare skin of her neck.

Marisol ceased to breathe for a second as every muscle in her body tensed. Victor coughed, and then eased his arm away. She was not ready for a man's touch. Why had she allowed Rosario and Mama to talk her into this craziness? She could not sleep with this man, or any man. Not after the incident in the convent.

"You know all there is to know. I work with plants and live with my family."

"And you have a son. What of his father?"

Nosy man. "Look." She pointed at the tall building on the horizon. "The airport is ahead."

* * * *

Wrong question. Yet Victor couldn't help wondering how such a nun of a woman came to bear a child out of wedlock. Marisol didn't seem the type for a reckless love affair. Certainly she was skittish around men; the way she stiffened when she thought he might touch her made him suspect she might've been abused, raped even. The dark thought of *anyone* forcing sex on this seemingly innocent woman, as had been done to him, sent shivers up his spine.

He held back a relieved sigh when Marisol pulled into the cargo area of the airport, a flat stretch with a paved runway and a few shed-like buildings. The tension in the van was thick enough to slice, and he didn't want to deal with the concerns running through his mind.

You have a mission and you can't get all sappy over a woman.

He refocused on the boxy grey building he assumed was the check-in point.

Marisol parked and turned to him. "I will be right back."

"I..."

The door slammed behind her before Victor could complete his sentence. He wouldn't have minded going with her, just to stretch his legs a bit. Besides, he was curious. He shifted in his seat and peered out of the open window, watching Marisol flounce through the glass door and head for the counter. That awful shawl covered her upper body, but allowed him to view the curvy hips that jiggled under the short skirt. Long legs led to...what was she wearing on her feet? Gardening clogs?

An apparent ruckus inside the office interrupted Victor's thoughts. *Oh Lord, something is the matter.* He couldn't hear a word, but arms flew.

The man behind the counter shrank back, as if ducking a blow, with his arms extended, palms up.

Marisol's fists waved, as if she were punching holes in the air.

To see if he might be of assistance, Victor popped open the van's door. *Uh-oh.* Marisol was headed his way, her face red enough to set the building on fire. She stomped out of the door like a soldier going to war. Ripping open the truck door, she plopped onto the seat beside him, and then slammed the door so hard the vehicle shimmied.

"What's the matter?" Victor ventured, half expecting her to swing her fists at him.

Marisol's amber eyes flashed dark with fury. "Soto."

"Soto? You mean the gentleman I met at dinner last night?"

"You met no gentleman." She spat out the words with such venom that Victor vowed to stay on the good side of this woman.

"He has booked every shuttle until dinnertime."

Victor followed Marisol's glance to her left. He counted six shiny white vans lined up in the area he assumed was the loading zone for the shuttle. *Soto Flores* was painted in large green letters on the side of every single vehicle.

Six vans full of flowers, for the next five hours, meant Soto's business was blooming big time. By comparison, Garcia Jardines was a fly on a flower.

"You had a reservation, didn't you?"

Marisol turned to him, eyes narrowed, as if she considered biting off his head for even asking. "Of course, but Soto shows up and the charter company forgets about the rest of us growers."

Victor thought back to the past night. Carlos and Soto had been arguing about the emerald mines until he had interrupted. "Business," Joseph had called it. He needed to know more about this man—and what better source of info than a pissed off woman.

"What does Soto do? Bribe the officials?"

"He does not have to. He knows where their families live."

"You mean..." Victor ran his forefinger across his throat in a slashing motion. A bit dramatic, but he wanted to find out how far Soto would go to get what he wanted.

Marisol stared straight ahead without responding.

Damn. Soto kills people—or has them killed. Involving himself in Soto's business could cost him his life. And what of Carlos? He and Soto had that same green tattoo, which had to mean they were in cahoots.

Victor's mind flashed back to the *tête á tête* under the tree. When Victor had asked to visit the mines, Soto made it clear they were off limits. Soto, the little man with the big balls, was aware of Victor's interest in emeralds. Had Carlos planned this excursion to prevent Victor from getting involved in Soto's affairs? Or to protect him?

This whole emerald thing could get out of control. What good would making a ton of money do him if he were dead? Marisol must be exaggerating. Women did that, sometimes, to make a point. Surely, Gomez Soto was no killer. He might, however, be a savvy business-man, one worth kissing up to. Besides, Victor knew how to handle people. He would be careful.

On the tarmac, a group of men unloaded Soto's flower crates into a commuter plane hooked up to a fuel truck. Victor checked the cheapo watch he had brought along. After having his wallet stolen, he wasn't taking any chances on losing his diamond-studded time piece. "It's nearly noon, perhaps we can kill some time getting a bite to eat. Will your lilies keep?"

"We will need to leave the refrigeration charging, which takes fuel." Marisol's bunched fist struck her forehead. "Now I will not make it home in time for Joseph's first soccer game."

Soccer game? Had he misjudged the purpose of this excursion? Victor knew he hadn't imagined the señora's sly smile, Rosario's sisterly prodding, and Marisol's out-of-character get-up was a matchmaking set-up.

Victor glanced at Marisol. Her lower lip trembled.

He molded his face into sympathetic lines. "What time does the game begin?"

"At four." Her words came out in a wail. "You do not understand. He needs me to be there. I am his *mother.*" She banged her hand on the steering wheel. A stray tear marked her cheek.

Marisol's emotions grabbed at him—and he wasn't having any of it. Most women in such a situation ended boo-hooing on his shoulder and staining his silk shirts. While he wouldn't mind having Marisol's body pressed against him, he could do without the waterfall.

He needed to do something though. Spending the next five hours coddling an upset woman wasn't what he'd bargained for. By now, she was supposed to be exchanging flirty smiles with him and, for God's sake, gotten rid of that awful shawl.

Now, soccer game or not, Marisol's don't-touch-me reaction

made his plan to bed her tonight a wet dream. Pity. He might've enjoyed the ride.

Before Victor could stop himself, the words were out of his mouth. "Look, the drive back to Garcia isn't that bad. I think I know the way. We'll pick up fuel and head back. If we hurry, you can see to the generator, tidy up your greenhouse, and still have time to make Joseph's game."

"But what about..."

Victor held up his hand. "Then, if you will permit me, I will drive your van back to the airport and see your flower shipment gets loaded on the shuttle."

You idiot. What did you just commit to? You didn't come to Columbia to coddle this woman or to babysit her flowers, especially if Carlos is at Garcia Jardines awaiting your return.

Marisol turned to him. The tremble in her lower lip became a smile that zinged straight to his groin.

"You're beautiful when you smile, you know." He expected her to throw her arms around him as any ordinary woman might have done. It was apparent that Marisol was no ordinary woman.

"Don't even think about it." Crossing her arms over her chest, she fixed her gaze on the windshield in an icy stare.

"Marisol, be reasonable. I'm trying to help. No obligation."

"Can you drive a shift?"

"Of course." Jake taught him to drive on the estate's pickup truck as a teen, but once Victor got his license, he went strictly automatic. Mrs. Gallagher even let him drive her BMW to school as long as he continued to please her. Certainly, the mechanics of shifting would come back to him, like riding a bike.

"Okay. *Gracias*." Marisol shoved open the truck door and hopped out. "Slide over. You can drive us."

Crap. What have I gotten myself into?

* * * *

Marisol clamped her lips tight to keep from smiling at Victor's efforts at figuring out the gears on the van. His offer surprised her. Perhaps he was not as self-centered a man as she thought.

"*Gracias*, Victor. You are kind to do this for me."

"No problem."

The van lurched forward and stalled. His face reddened, and she bit back a smile. "Do not forget to use the clutch when you shift."

"Of course. You're right. I'm a bit rusty."

"Would you prefer I drive?"

"No." He almost shouted the word. "I've got the hang of it now."

They moved forward and, indeed, he seemed to manage all right. Marisol leaned back in her seat. Rosario and Mama would be disappointed when she returned early. Too bad. This date had been *their* plan, not hers. Refueling the generator and watching Joseph's first game was more important to her than seducing a stranger.

She glanced over at Victor, his eyes were glued to the road. She could almost see his mind working, as if he were a little boy trying addition for the first time.

For a moment, his demeanor eclipsed his handsome face, affording her a glimpse of the insecure man beneath the façade. Pieces of their conversation flashed through her mind. He had befriended a gardener, lived on an estate with his mother that was owned by a rich woman. Yet he had grown up privileged. It did not make sense—unless said rich woman had taken him under her wing.

Still, his source of income remained an enigma. She eyed Victor. His clothing and jewelry screamed wealth, yet he claimed early poverty. Either he earned his money through smart investments or he was involved in something illegal. Deceit ran in the Rodriguez family.

Yet here she was, trusting this stranger to drive their only flower transport vehicle, and trusting he would do as he promised and get their flowers off to Miami.

She shook her head to the side. Either her standards had slackened, or she was beginning to heal.

Time would tell.

* * * *

The van coughed its way up the hill like an eighty-year-old man with the flu, and choked and hiccupped whenever Victor forgot to shift gears. He glanced at Marisol, so quiet beside him. The dreary shawl had finally slipped from her shoulders to reveal a hint of cleavage. A teaser, for sure. If women only knew how a tiny peek at creamy skin could tantalize a man, they would never stoop to baring themselves completely.

He took in the tight line of Marisol's jaw and the tension lines zigzagging across her forehead. Likely, she was worried about rescuing her precious seedlings from the fluctuating temperature of the greenhouse or wondering if they would arrive in time for Joseph's game. The past night, he had seen Joseph kicking around a beach ball in the drive. The kid had good moves.

"There. Pull in," Marisol said, pointing out the window at a gas station. Hopping out, she opened the back doors of the van and re-moved the empties. Like a pro, she pumped diesel fuel into the cans.

Once all tanks were filled, Victor heaved them up and into the bed of the van—but Marisol paid no attention to his manly prowess. She rifled through the tiny red purse—matched her outfit, he sup-posed—and handed a credit card to a grisly older man who seemed to be the only soul on the premise.

GGrrrrippppppp.

"What did you say, Victor?" Marisol turned at the sound.

He put a hand on his stomach, willing it to quiet down. "Is there someplace we can grab a quick bite?"

She pointed to a truck selling meat pies parked to the side of the station.

Given his nose for food, it was a wonder he hadn't spotted it ear-lier. He had heard foreigners were lax about refrigeration What if he picked up food poisoning? "I'll pass on that. Is there any place else around?"

"Not really, but if you can hold out, I can fix us something back at the plantation."

Marisol was going to make him lunch. He would sit at the table while she fussed about the kitchen, or maybe he would pitch in. Then when their meal was ready, he would hold out a chair for her and they would sit down like a couple. As they ate, he would look into her eyes and she would say, "I want you, Victor." Then she would rip off his clothes and take him right on the kitchen table.

"Are we not going to get moving?" Marisol said.

"Huh? Yes, of course."

After some minor fits and spurts, the old clunker finally got going and they were off, bumping over the mountain road onto the flat plain of the savanna. With the windows rolled down, the sweet scents of blooming flowers drifted through the van.

As Victor inhaled, he noticed Marisol wore a dreamy smile, as if she too enjoyed the scent of the outdoor air. In his mind's eye, he plucked a few blooms, cradled them in his arms, and then lifted them to his nose. When he handed them to Marisol, she would smile and kiss his cheek.

Oh man, you are really way out there with this woman.

* * * *

Marisol stole a glance at Victor's too-perfect profile, his gaze focused on the road. What would a man of the world see in a simple farm girl raising a son? She had no money to call her own, and if she could not get that Elite order out on time, she and Joseph might not even have a home. She looked away so Victor would not catch her staring at him. Had she imagined he cared? Yet he went out of his way to help her, first with the plants, and now with getting her back to the plantation so she could attend Joseph's soccer game.

Did he show the same consideration to all women? He was not wearing a wedding ring, but that did not mean a tall, blonde, and beautiful girlfriend was not waiting for him in Miami. Likely he was being extra nice to her because he had nothing better to do.

"Slow down, Garcia Jardines is just around the bend."

Gears screeched as Victor downshifted and spun the wheel into the drive. During the ride past the gardens, Marisol watched a black spot in front of Mama's place grow.

Oh no. Soto's car. Bile rose in her throat. *What is he doing here again?*

"Your mother has company."

"Yes. Pull around back. I...I can't go inside and get us some food without..."

"I understand. You and Señor Soto don't get along." Victor parked behind the greenhouse, hopped out, and pulled open the van's back door. "Lead me to the generator. I'll fuel it and make sure it's going, and then head back to the airport. I'm sure I can find something to eat along the way."

Reaching out, she went to shake his hand—although she had the strangest urge to kiss his bristly cheek. Did she dare risk starting something she doubted she could finish? "*Gracias*, Victor. I do not know how I can thank you."

Victor clasped her hand in his and held it a little longer than was necessary, but she did not mind. His grip was firm and the skin on his hand was smooth, with clean, perfectly trimmed fingernails. Her hand was calloused with ragged fingernails that never seemed to come clean.

"I'll think of something," he said with a wink.

* * * *

The generator, a boxy, metal device usurping a large space at the rear of the main house, slurped all the fuel in four big gulps, and then restarted with a belch and an ear-splitting roar. The electrical power was back in service. Marisol could stop worrying about her plants, and he would have a hot shower tonight. Big whoopee do.

Victor sniffed at his shirtsleeve. It reeked of fuel. He rinsed off his hands with the hose, and wiped them dry on the grass.

Before Victor got back into the van, he walked around the front of the main house. *Maybe Carlos is back*. No sign of the Cherokee, and Rosario didn't seem to be outdoors. He could knock on her door—or not. After busting into her home that morning, she probably wouldn't be welcoming to him. Humph. He shoved his hands in his pocket and stared at Carlos's house. *Asshole*. He sniffed the air. What was that?

Cigar smoke rose from Soto's driver, a brutish-looking man in a brown business suit and bowler hat who paced in front of the Jaguar. Maybe Gomez was getting a little nookie. No wonder Marisol was upset.

"Good afternoon," Victor said, using the local way of greeting, rather than the usual, "hi." The fireplug of a man lifted his head in acknowledgment. "You are Carlos's brother, Victor? Or is it, *Vickie?*" He laughed, or rather guffawed. "How are those dirty pants coming along?"

Victor's chest swelled with rage. His hands formed fists against his sides. One day, he would go head to head with this asshole, but this was not the day. "*Victor* will do nicely," he said through gritted teeth, "and my pants are no longer your concern."

His stomach had given up growling and had turned tortuously gassy, no thanks to inhaling stinky cigar smoke. He checked the time. Two hours to kill before the flowers were due back at the shuttle, and he knew just how he was going to spend them.

Chapter Seven

Entering Joseph's room always caught Marisol off guard, especially in the morning, when the sun made the reds and blues of his superhero posters strike an off-note against the green and yellow plaid curtains she had sewn. His room stood in stark contrast to the rest of the cottage. She preferred functionality and simplicity for herself.

It was nearly eight when she paused at his bed. His covers were in a tangle at the base of the bed, revealing not a little boy, but a young man with a lump in his underpants. She focused on the innocence in her son's face.

"Joseph. Wake up." She shook his shoulder.

He stretched and yawned, but did not open his eyes.

"Come on. You need to leave for school in thirty minutes."

His eyes flicked open. He stared into her face. "I am not going today."

"What do you mean, not going? Are you sick?" She held a hand to his forehead. Cool.

"I do not have a game today. I am going to stay home and visit with *Tio* Victor."

"Well, you cannot. He will still be here after school." Marisol tossed the navy pants and yellow shirt that made up his school uniform on the bed. "Get dressed. Cereal and milk from *Abuela's* are on the kitchen table."

She turned to leave, listening for the rustle of Joseph's covers.

Nothing.

"If you do not go to school," —she faced him— "you will not get a high enough score on the SAT to get into a college in America. Is that not what you wish to do? Go to America and study botanical science?" A chill ran through her. Joseph leaving.

"Carlos says I don't need to go to college. He did not go, and he has great job as a policeman. Everyone respects him."

She took a few breaths to tame her annoyance from spilling into a full rampage and chose her words. "Your uncle is a security officer, not a policeman. What about Garcia Jardines? It will be yours one day."

"Flowers are for sissies. I am not a sissy." Joseph rose, towering over her by a good six inches, fists bunched at his sides. "I do not want to go to college, and I am not going to school today."

Every muscle in her body went rock hard. If Marisol had spoken to her mother in that tone of voice, she would have earned a slap across the face. But she was not Mama. She could not bear to hit Joseph. Beneath his blatant rebellion was the child whose birth changed her life.

"No more arguing. Now get dressed."

She stomped out of the room, making it clear she was good and angry. The coffee pot had boiled over on the stove. Mopping up the mess, she brushed away the frustrated tears that welled in her eyes and dripped down her cheeks. *Why has my son become so defiant?*

With shaking hands, she dumped the burnt coffee into a mug, sat at the kitchen table, and waited.

Fifteen minutes later, Joseph emerged wearing his school uniform.

Marisol let out a breath of relief. "That is a good boy."

He met her smile with a cold stare, dropped his backpack on the floor, and sat down at the table. In seconds, his cereal bowl was empty. He dropped it into the sink for washing.

"Bye, Mama." He landed a perfunctory kiss lacking its usual warmth on her cheek.

"Have a good day, sweetheart."

Taking long strides, Joseph walked out of the door, body stiff, as if he were going to an execution chamber.

He will come around, she told herself. He has to.

* * * *

"*Gracias*, Señora." Victor blotted his lips with a napkin. "The eggs were wonderful."

"They are always wonderful when Mama makes them." Carlos entered with a slam of the kitchen door. "Hey, my brother. What happened to your ponytail?"

Victor lifted the steaming cup of coffee to his lips. He'd be damned if he would acknowledge Carlos. Yesterday wasn't horrible, just a waste of precious time. Carlos failed to show up at the plantation, even for dinner. And now the man has the audacity to stroll in here and speak to him as if he'd been a proper host.

Carlos's hand came down on Victor's shoulder.

The muscles in Victor's neck turned to stiff cords. Unspoken words clogged his throat.

"Thought we would go into Bogotá today," Carlos said, without so much as an, "I'm sorry."

Yeah, right. If you were really my brother, you wouldn't invite me to a foreign country and then forget about me. Victor pushed back his chair with a creaking sound that would have ordinarily sent goose bumps crawling up his neck. He rose to face Carlos.

Carlos's smile dropped. Creases of confusion furrowed his brow.

Doesn't the man understand what an asshole he is?

"I'm not going anywhere with you. You dump me here and then disappear like Houdini. Now you come in all chummy, as if nothing happened. The only place I'm going today is to the airport."

Victor's mind clicked dollar signs. He shot off his mouth without thinking this through. The cost to change his flight would be worth it to show this bogus brother he couldn't toy with him.

"Señora?" Her back was to him, her head tilted to the side, tuned into their conversation. "Can someone give me a lift to the airport?"

"Well, I suppose," she said, "but..."

"Now, now, Mama, he is not going anywhere." Carlos slung an arm around Victor's shoulder. "We are brothers, eh?"

Victor shrugged off Carlos's arm and stepped away. "Eh, yourself. I'm out of here." He headed for the door.

"But you cannot leave. I made special arrangements for us today."

Victor paused. "So," he said without bothering to turn around, "does that mean you'll dump me tomorrow?" His head was up, shoulders squared. *I dare you. Say something to make me want to stick around.*

"Victor, you are a tough one. I would never do that to you. After I show you around Bogotá, we will go to the cockfight—and then off to the casino."

Cockfight? He'd never been to a cockfight.

"And tomorrow..." Carlos flung his arms out wide, as if making a grand announcement. "I have arranged for you to tour *La Esmeralda*."

The mine. He could almost feel it. Things were ready to pop here. If he played Carlos's game right, in two days he could be set for the rest of his life.

"You *will* stay?" Carlos's eyebrows knit together. His pointed look pressed Victor to give in and stay.

He expelled built-up air from his lungs. He was close to changing his mind and staying at Carlos's mention of the cockfight, but the a trip to the emerald mine—that was the clincher. "Okay." He held up his hand. "Enough. I'll stay."

Carlos's shoulders sagged with what Victor assumed was relief.

"You will like Berto," the Señora said.

"Berto?"

"*Tío* Roberto. Our father's brother, your uncle. He is waiting to meet you."

First, a brother arises out of nowhere and now an uncle? Is Carlos really my half-brother after all?

"I think Berto is sweet on you, eh, Mama?" Carlos said.

Señora Garcia pinched Carlos's cheek. "Oh, you. You are teasing me."

"How about a cup of that wonderful coffee?" Carlos pulled out a chair from the table and sat down.

"More coffee, Victor?" the señora asked. The pot hovered over his half-empty mug on the table.

He waved his hand. "No, not for me. I should change my clothes."

Carlos eyed his jeans and tee. "Nah, we go casual today. Sit, Victor. Tell me about your day yesterday. How did you and the ice princess get along?"

Ice princess? He must mean Marisol. "I might have chipped away some of that ice." He relaxed into a smile.

"You devil you. Did you get her into..."

The señora seemed to stiffen. Her eyes narrowed and her lips pursed in apparent disapproval.

Victor waved his hand to the side. "No, nothing like that." He flashed back to Marisol sitting on the grass after dinner. She'd clapped her hands and smiled while he and Joseph played one-on-one soccer, almost as if the three of them were a family. He had always seen himself as a loner, but maybe...

Carlos bolted down the last of his coffee, set the mug on the table with a *thunk*, and scraped back his chair. "Let's get a move on."

"Uh...sure. Be right with you, as soon as I grab my windbreaker."

It was cooler than usual today, with the sun eclipsed by grey clouds threatening rain. *Marisol will be pleased. Her plants will get a good soaking without drawing on the cistern.*

Why, all of a sudden, was he worried about Marisol's problems when he had plenty of his own to deal with? His body was at stake. With a new career, he'd finally be free. An inlet, that's all he needed to get started on making serious money. Maybe an intro to the right person.

Ten minutes later, when Victor returned to the main house, Carlos waited out front.

"Let's go," Carlos said with a nod toward his cottage.

Following his supposed brother's self-assured stride, Victor made his way to the rear of the cottage to the Jeep, circumventing a small vegetable garden dripping with red tomatoes and long green peppers. His skin prickled with cool stickiness and his nose twitched from the heavy odor of moist soil as he slid into the passenger seat.

Two door slams later, with Carlos at the wheel, they rumbled along the dirt road out of Garcia Jardines. The radio blasted some ungodly rock tune, but all he cared about was that they were headed to the heart of the emerald trade.

As they passed Soto Flores, Victor pointed to the helicopter hovering over the gardens. "What's going on?"

"Gomez's private transport. His pilot sprays their flowers to keep the bugs away."

"This Gomez must make a lot of money with all those flowers he grows."

"Gomez has many interests."

"Like the emerald mines?" Victor licked his lips, expecting Carlos to spew forth some information he might latch onto.

Carlos lips clamped tight. He waved a hand in the air. The Jeep swerved to the right. "Emeralds are important to Colombia's economy. Everyone is interested in them." He laughed a hearty laugh—a fake one, Victor was certain.

So Carlos was going to hold back. Victor's spine stiffened against the curve of the bucket seat. The cold shoulder, again—but then, Carlos didn't know him very well. Victor needed to prove his worth.

Grabbing the handhold, he willed Carlos to slow down as they approached the rough spot in the road he and Marisol circumvented the previous day. But, of course, Carlos didn't. They hit the four by four pit at fifty miles an hour.

The top of Victor's head bounced off the padded ceiling and his seatbelt wanted to choke him.

"Yipe."

Carlos turned down the radio and slowed. "Did you hear something?"

"Yes. Back seat." Victor twisted around. "It's Joseph."

The boy's face was scrunched, as if he was trying not to cry.

"Are you hurt? Let me see," Victor said.

Joseph pulled his hand from his forehead.

"You've got a good sized lump brewing, fella."

"It is okay. I am okay. See?" Managing a smile, Joseph settled into his seat and clipped his seat belt into the buckle.

"Are you not supposed to be in school?" Carlos said.

The boy hung his head. "I wanted to come with you and Mama would not let me."

Carlos chuckled. "Playing hooky, eh? I used to skip school when I was your age, too."

"You *can't* be condoning the boy's behavior," Victor said to Carlos. "Joseph, you told me you wanted to go to America and get educated. I went to school every single day and to college, too. Carlos, how far are we from Joseph's school?"

"It's back that way, in the village."

"Good. We'll drop him off, won't we, my brother?" Victor

winked at Carlos. He must realize if Joseph came along it would crimp their activities in Bogotá.

"Are you going to rat on me to Mama?"

"Just between us men. We're buddies, right?" Victor held up his hand. "Give me five."

Carlos reversed gears with a screech, backed into the roadside bushes, and headed toward Garcia with the Jeep's wheels rimming that serious pothole.

Joseph was quiet until they pulled up to San Luis Middle School, a time-weathered, two-story building with a gated yard situated off Garcia's main thoroughfare. "I left my backpack and bike behind *Tío* Carlos's cottage. I do not have books, and I am not wearing my uniform."

"We are not going back for them. You will have to figure what to tell your teachers, and you can walk home after school." From the firm set of Carlos's jaw and the sharp clip of his words, it was clear the man was at the end of his patience. "Tell your teachers the truth, that you were planning to skip school but changed your mind," Victor told Joseph. "You've already lied to your mother. Adding more lies will only get you in worse trouble. Am I right Carlos?"

Carlos nostrils flared. "*Sí*, college boy."

Once a remorseful Joseph entered the school building, Victor and Carlos continued through Garcia. As they drove past Barra de Luis, Victor asked, "My wallet. Which one of your friends took it? Miguel?"

Carlos pursed his lips. Victor could almost see him locking them shut with an imaginary key.

"Okay, not talking about it." Victor folded his arms over his chest and stared straight ahead.

"You set yourself up," Carlos spit the words out. "You were bent over the bar passed out and your wallet bulged from your back pocket. I did not see it happen, but I shook down those two until one of them 'fessed up."

"You did that? For me?"

"You are my brother. You would have done the same if it happened to me."

Maybe...he didn't know. He never had a brother to worry about. "But you're not going to tell me who it was?"

"No. In Bogotá, it is important to know how to keep what happens private. If you know what I mean." His elbow shot out toward Victor in a friendly poke.

Victor shrank away, buffering its impact. The man was growing on him, but this jabbing shit was getting old, but knowing Carlos had protected him felt good. Fought for him. Still, now that Carlos seemed ready to talk...

"Brothers share, though, don't they, Carlos?"

"*Si, si.* I share my home with you, my car..."

"How about your business?"

The smile dropped from Carlos's lips. "You want me to share— my private affairs?"

"You've been skirting around my interest in the emerald business, Carlos. Fact is, I've seen all the green tattoos. Green fire. Emeralds. You must be involved in the emerald market." He leaned toward Carlos. "I want *in*."

Carlos's lifted an eyebrow, as if sizing up Victor. Then a slow smile spread across his face. "I will take you to my neighborhood."

What is that supposed to mean? Maybe Carlos's neighborhood was where the emerald hawkers roosted. Victor leaned back in his seat and crossed his arms over his chest.

By the time the Cherokee approached the fringe of Bogotá, the sporadic fits of rain seemed to have petered out, leaving bright cracks of sunlight peering through the wall of grey sky overhead.

Now the heat of the sun carved dry spots into the streets and walks.

They drove on past the vendor booths and into the outskirts of Bogotá, where poverty held court. Shabbily dressed vendors, mostly women and children, crowded the streets in colorful, mismatched clothing—candidates for the Glamour Don't Award. A very pregnant woman passed, one arm balancing a basket full of vegetables on her head and the other dragging a bare-assed toddler. Mostly, the women sat on the sidewalk, their backs against shop fronts with barred windows. Towels or blankets displaying fresh produce spread in front of them. One white haired, age-scarred woman held up a piece of fruit to a man passing by. The man ignored her and kept going.

Victor had seen this type of need in the back streets of Miami. It was sad how these people had to make their living; but at least they sold the fruit of their labor, not the fruits of their loins—although he was making an assumption. The need for survival was humbling.

They passed a black Jaguar parked against the curb. A curl of smoke lifted from the driver's side. Back in the bowels of Miami, a pricey car like that one would be stripped, the driver dragged out and beaten. The car spoke *power* by virtue of remaining undisturbed in what seemed to be a dangerous area of Bogotá.

A few yards past the Jaguar, two dark figures, one of them in a smart-looking business suit, were huddled under a storefront. The door of the establishment was barred, apparently closed for business. The men's heads were pitched toward one another.

The Jaguar. "Hey, isn't that Gomez Soto?" Victor said.

The man's head moved, as if he heard his name, but didn't turn to face them

"*Si*, he is...working."

Working? This Soto fellow appears to be dealing. Easing back in his seat, Victor wondered just how involved Carlos was in the Colombian underworld.

Chapter Eight

Raindrops spattered against the greenhouse in a barrage of tiny pings. A rain shower was a friend to the gardens, unless it turned stormy. Heavy winds could lay Marisol's blooms flat and rip their delicate flowers. Marisol bit her lower lip as she peered through the condensation on the greenhouse windows at the merging black clouds. She was in her glass house, protected and safe, while her lilies risked their very lives.

The door to the tool shed was ajar and there was movement within the shadows. It must be Jose watching for a break in the weather so they could call back the pickers for today's orders.

Rosario's blurry figure came into view as she hurried toward the greenhouse. The door burst open to admit her sister. She dropped the rain jacket she had draped over her head and shoulders onto the floor, along with a dripping wet bag of some sort, and kicked off her gardening clogs.

"Nasty out there." She fluffed her hair, which remained wavy and dry despite the downpour. "The wind is picking up. I think we are in for it."

Marisol made the sign of the cross. "Let us hope not." Her eyes dropped to the bag on the floor. "What...is that Joseph's backpack?"

Rosario pursed her lips. "I found it hidden in the bushes behind my cottage. His bike is there, too."

"How could he!" She strode over and picked the nylon backpack out of the puddle of water. "It is soaked." She shook it to knock off the worst of the water, and then rummaged through it. "His uniform. Look, it is all wrinkled, and his books..." She examined Joseph's history book. "The pages are wet around the edges. The school will charge me to replace this."

Marisol willed herself not to kick the bag and each one of the items across the room. She wanted to hear the thud of connection. Then she would feel better.

"He defied me," she told Rosario, trying to steady her voice. "He wanted to go to Bogotá with Carlos and Victor, and I would not let him. Oh, Rosario, what am I going to do? Joseph used to be so sweet and now I do not know who he is anymore."

"Give the kid a break. If he misses one day of school, it will not scar him for life."

"That is not the point. He *lied* to me." Marisol realized she was clenching her teeth. She tried to relax her jaw. "Just wait until he comes home." She paced in front of the backpack, which she had set on a dry spot on the floor. Every time she looked at the damage, she wanted to throw something. "His bike will get rusty in all this rain. He can walk to school from now on...it is only five miles. I will take away his electronic games...and tell him he has to give up soccer."

"Give up soccer? Come on, Marisol, you know he loves the game. Mama says he is the best. If Joseph does not play, the team will start losing games."

"What do I care? It is Soto's team, anyway."

"Ah, now I see. Some of this is about Gomez." Rosario put her hand on Marisol's shoulder. "Find some other way to punish Joseph for not being truthful."

"I suppose you are right about the soccer, but what am I going to do? I want him to grow up to be honest. He needs to go to school and learn so he can get into college. One day, God willing," —Marisol blessed herself— "he will take over Garcia Jardines."

Rosario's mouth lost its soft caring look and her jaw went tight. "How very presumptuous of you to assume your Joseph would inherit this plantation. Carlos and I are trying to have a son."

"Pah. Two years and nothing has happened. Tell your Carlos to stay home once in a while, and maybe you will get pregnant."

"That is not fair, Marisol. His job takes him to the mines for much of the time, but when he is on break he is home ten whole days."

"Really? Where was he last night? And where is he now? Do you expect him home for dinner?"

Rosario crumpled into the chair at Marisol's desk. "You are right, Marisol. I get only the piece of him he wants me to have." Her lower lip trembled. "I...think he is sinning with other women. A few days ago, I was gathering his clothes from the floor to wash them and found a big smear of red lipstick on his shorts and, yesterday, he came home late smelling of a woman's perfume."

"Have you talked to him about it?"

"I tried, but he denied everything and then got mad at me for asking." She pressed her hand on Marisol's arm. "Oh Marisol, I still love him, but I think he is tired of me."

"Carlos does not know how lucky he is to have you." She smoothed her sister's hair.

"I do not know what to do."

"You will do what I have had to do. Make the best of it. Think of the good things. You, Mama, and me are together, and we live among beautiful flowers. Like paradise, true?"

"Our so-called paradise will be hell if Mama decides to sell. Carlos thinks if we have a baby, Mama will accept him as family and turn the business over to him. You should have heard him rage when he learned Gomez Soto was courting Mama."

"Papa despised Soto."

"I know, but what can we do about him and Mama? She has some old fashioned idea that only men can operate a successful business."

"That is not true, Rosario. You and I could do it if she would let us. I have already spoken with her. We made a deal of sorts."

"Did you sell your soul? You know how Mama feels about you. I am sorry, Marisol. I see it in her eyes. If not for Papa, she would have disowned you. I am glad she did not. I am glad you are here. Who else could I talk to, if not my big sister?"

A lump rose in Marisol's throat, the type that came on when she tried not to embarrass herself by crying. Today, she had no time for tears.

"*Gracias*, Marisol."

"For what?"

"For listening to me. For understanding. I did not mean what I said about Joseph. One day he will make a great businessman. If I am fortunate enough to have children, they can grow up as we did, among beauty and love."

...And deceit, Marisol thought. Like Mama, Rosario chose to ignore the extra money Papa funneled through Garcia Jardines, as well as his leadership in the Green Fire Cartel.

A thunderous crash ripped through the greenhouse and the world around them flashed as if someone had turned on a light.

"Oh no!"

Across the field, lightning zigzagged down a threatening sky, followed seconds later by a rumble loud enough to make the greenhouse tremble.

Marisol and Rosario ducked, hands over their heads, even though they knew the glass would hold.

"My lilies," Marisol cried. "They will be destroyed."

Crashing through the door, she and Rosario raced outside.

Water poured over her, as if from a bucket. Her hair hung in wet strips and her clothes clung to her skin, but Marisol did not care. She would survive, but her babies might not.

"I have to protect my specials," Marisol cried. "Ask Jose to call in the pickers to gather whatever blooms they can. We have two orders that need to go out to Elite on the late shuttle. If we miss, they are liable to pull the November order. Hurry."

Rosario hesitated. "They will not want to work in this rain."

"Too bad. This is an emergency. Now, go, go." She shooed Rosario toward the shed. Jose was standing in the door, frowning. The man knew what had to be done.

Marisol's heart pounded with urgency. *Focus. Prioritize.* She grabbed several lengths of tarps and some poles and dumped them into one of the carts stacked outside the greenhouse. Her feet wanted to run, but the two-wheeled cart took its time. She gripped the slippery metal handle and pushed with strength she did not know she had, forcing the wheels out of muddy ruts that splattered her skin and clothes with filth.

Cold tremors ran through her body, raising prickly goose bumps to her arms and legs. What if she lost everything?

* * * *

They hadn't traveled a quarter mile into an area Victor might classify as slums, when Carlos turned down a side road and parked in front of a three-story, yellow building. Like the others they passed, the exterior thirsted for a fresh coat of paint. Chipped wrought iron bars caged the lower windows, making it appear as if each of the rooms behind them were jail cells.

"There is Berto, where he usually is," Carlos said, pushing open his door and stepping out onto the still-wet concrete sidewalk. He waited until Victor got out of the Jeep, and locked its door with a key.

Victor moved to join Carlos. Out of the corner of his eye, a big-haired, heavily made up woman wearing a fishnet top, too-short skirt, and spiked heels leaning against the side of one of the other buildings straightened out of her slump. Her eyes brightened. Taking a puff of her cigarette, she strutted toward them, hips swaying in an attempt at a seductive walk.

That could be me one day, Victor thought, working the streets and hoping to pick up some money for a blow job, or something worse. He would be old, so it would take a few tries to get anyone—

man or woman—to want to pay him for sex. He would work for a pimp—everyone in the business had a pimp—who would beat him if he didn't earn enough. If he went back to Miami without working a deal here, he could end up like this woman approaching them with a come-hither smile on her smeary red lips.

Then how much longer would it be before he was as broke as this poor woman and had to sell what was left of his soul?

"*Hola*, señor." The whore pinched her nipples so they poked out from the net and thrust her breasts forward.

"How much?" Carlos asked, reaching to touch her.

Victor pulled away Carlos's arm. "No, we're not doing this." He fished in his pocket and handed the woman the first bill he laid his fingers on.

She clasped it to her breast, and then opened her hand. Tears welled in her eyes. "Oh, señor. *Gracias.*" She glanced over her shoulder toward a beat-up, purple Chevy parked beyond the building, where she had first waited, and then hid the C-note deep into the waist of her skirt. "Are you sure? I give good..."

"I'm sure you do."

He couldn't afford to hand out hundred dollar bills as if they were candy, but if doing so kept this woman off the street even for one day, it was worth it. If he should ever be needy, maybe a kind person would do the same for him.

Victor steered away Carlos, who continued to leer at the woman. "You have better at home."

Carlos scraped a hand though his bristly crew cut. "I do, but that woman wanted me. I could tell."

"She wanted your money."

"How would you know?" he said, giving Victor an odd look.

Victor didn't reply. "So, where is this Uncle Berto?"

Carlos nodded toward two men seated at a folding type metal table set on the sidewalk outside a yellow adobe building playing Dominos. "The grey-haired guy on the left."

Victor smoothed his hair, and then remembered he chopped it short. Following Carlos's lead, he duck-walked with his thumbs shoved into his front pockets toward the game in progress.

The man Carlos pointed out as Uncle Berto raised a hand and gave Carlos a high five, muscles rippling under the skin of his arm. "Ram. It has been too long."

Ram? A light bulb clicked on inside Victor's head. The word painted on the back windshield. Was he supposed to call Carlos "Ram," now he was privy to the nickname?

When Berto rose, he stood at least a head taller than Carlos. Adjusting his steel-rimmed glasses on the bridge of his nose, he directed his gaze toward Victor. Berto's skin was a shade or two lighter than Carlos's, even with a tan. He touched his own cheek. More like his.

"Berto," Carlos said, once he pulled free. "This is my brother, Victor Novak."

"Ernesto's son from America?" Berto's mouth dropped open beneath a silver brush of a mustache and his bushy eyebrows shot up. He turned to his friend. "Look at him, Jocko. Does he not look like my brother?"

Jocko rocked back in his metal folding chair and gave Victor the once over. "The mole, and a little around the mouth."

The mole again. Victor scanned Berto's face. From what he saw, the man hadn't been blessed with the family mole. Yet Berto's nose was straight, like his own, and the smile was vaguely familiar.

Victor's heart thudded. If this man really was his uncle, then Carlos must be telling the truth about being his half-brother.

"Welcome, *mi sobrino.*" Grabbing Victor's hand, Berto pulled him to his chest. When Berto was satisfied his new-found nephew had been sufficiently hugged, he linked his arm in Victor's. "Come inside. We will have coffee and talk."

With Carlos following them, Berto pushed a buzzer to unlock the door leading into the musty-smelling foyer. With Berto's hand on Victor's shoulder, the three of them climbed two sets of creaking wooden stairs to a third-floor landing, and then headed down a railroad-style hallway with doors on each side.

Berto stopped to key open the door marked 3G. He waved Carlos and Victor inside what appeared to be an efficiency apartment, much like the one Victor rented in North Miami.

Carlos flopped on the brown sofa and clicked the remote to turn on the TV, while Berto lit a flame under a pot on the stove.

Without regard for manners, Victor headed for the table by the window covered with framed photos and stooped to examine them. He picked up a photo of a man resembling Berto. His arm wrapped around the shoulders of a squatty woman with a lumpy nose like Carlos's.

My father?

He was about to ask Berto, but the words caught in his throat. His breath came in short gasps and his fingers closed around the lacy edge of a gold-framed picture. Not trusting his knees to hold him upright, he eased down onto a stiff-backed chair and stared at the picture. His mother kept this exact same photo on her night table.

"Nesto received that photo in the mail from America," Berto said. He seated himself on a chair near Victor. "The envelope had no return address. He saw the mole, and knew at once he was seeing his son. I found it in his wallet after..." Berto bowed his head, his lips trembling with emotion. "I loved my brother."

Victor put a reassuring hand on Berto's shoulder. "I never knew."

"It took some time, but your father finally tracked your mother down. When he called her, she refused to let you meet him. My brother told me she did not wish to complicate your life by having you know a man who could never be a true father to you."

Victor's heart clenched with pent emotion. "He could have come for me, anyway, or at least sent Mom some money. She was a maid, and I was...no one."

"He wanted to. He loved you from the second he saw your photo. You look very much like him, you know."

The man in the photo.

"Your father was not a rich man," Berto continued. "By the time he found out about you, he had married and his wife, Carlos's mother, was fat with his child. Nesto carried the guilt of not supporting you to his grave."

As he should have.

Victor sucked in a deep breath and held it, swallowing the anger that threatened to lash out at Berto. He wanted to cry. He wanted to scream, *"It's not fair,"* and he wanted to punch something—hard. If only he could relive all those wasted years he spent mourning a bogus American father, who supposedly died in the Viet Nam war. He could have spent them with the father he never knew existed. But Ernesto Rodriguez was dead—and Victor hadn't even met him. Felt the love Berto spoke about.

Knowing his birth father existed might've changed his life. He would have found some way to come to Bogotá for a visit, even if he had to stowaway. When life got rough, he could've sought out his Co-lombian family instead of turning to prostitution.

"At least he could have called me, or even sent me a damn post-card." His words came out in a hoarse rasp.

Berto's arm went around Victor's shoulders. "It was for the best. Look at you. Educated, wealthy. Here, you would have had nothing but a clean bed."

"And family." He stopped himself from going on. Carlos sat a few yards away, ears cocked. All along, he'd doubted Carlos's word. While Carlos wasn't exactly a prince of a man, they were bound by blood, and that was enough.

Berto pressed a photo of two men in uniform into his hand. "Here, keep this. Your father and I were part of the National Police Force. He was a good man."

Victor glanced down, already aware that the tall, lean man linking arms with a younger version of Berto was indeed his true father. The man had Victor's same killer smile. No wonder his mother had fallen for him, but why had she kept the knowledge private? He fingered his earrings. Likely a gift from his father.

"Did he love my mother?"

"When they were dating, he asked her to marry him. She turned him down. She would not give up her life in America for Colombia, even for love. They went their separate ways. If Nesto had known your mother carried his child, I doubt he would have accepted your mother's rejection without more of a fight."

"You guys done hashing around old times yet?" Carlos's voice dripped with boredom.

"Forgive my bad manners." Berto left Victor's side and hustled to the stove to pour their coffee.

Coffee became lunch and more coffee, until Carlos announced, "We had better get moving."

Carlos rose, not making a move to help Berto clear off the dishes. Victor might have helped the old man—he apparently lived alone—but feared the goody-two-shoes image might not be in his best interests, especially after Carlos's "college boy" slam. Obviously, Carlos had rebelled against his family by hanging out with the wrong crowd; yet Victor knew he was no better. One day this uncle who seemed to care about him would find out he was a sham. A fake. A pretentious fool who had let one rich bitch after another determine how he lived his life. If he ever made it good, he would be true to himself, and answer to no one but Victor Novak. Depend on no one but Victor Novak.

"I promised Victor I would show him around before the cockfight tonight. I can get an extra ticket if you want to come along, Berto," Carlos said.

"Ach. You know I cannot stand watching two chickens murder one another. There is enough violence in the streets. Besides, Jocko will want to finish our game."

Berto scribbled something on a scrap of paper. He handed it to Victor. "Keep my telephone number handy in case you have any problems." His gaze went to Carlos. "I still have connections with the *policia.*"

"Carlos," Berto shook his finger at him. "Keep your brother out of trouble. You understand."

"*Si, Si, Si.*"

* * * *

The storm left as quickly as it had arrived. Despite its severity, Marisol said a thankful prayer the damage had been minimal. A passing squall, that was all. Yet she had panicked as if Garcia Jardines had been threatened by a tropical storm.

She inhaled the clean sent of ozone that followed such a storm. Blue patches poked through the brightening grey sky. The sun would come out soon and her plants would be better for the experience.

The tarp Marisol had erected over her Hope Lily beds sagged with water but it had protected the delicate flowers from being pounded to the ground. The blooms the workers gathered from the outer field now lay soggy but intact on the lawn outside the greenhouse.

"The workers need a break," Jose said, dropping off the final cart of blooms. "They want to go home for lunch and put on dry clothes. He pulled a soaking shirt away from his wiry body. "I could stand a change out, too."

"*Gracias* for your help," Marisol said, pushing wet strands of wet hair from her face. "I do not know how Rosario and I would have managed if you had not come to work, despite the rain. Please tell the crew to expect a little extra in their paychecks this week."

Rosario grabbed her arm and hissed into her ear. "You cannot..."

"Hush. We will figure out a way." She shrugged off Rosario's hand.

"They will be pleased." Jose smiled through a wiry black beard and then, after giving his crew a thumbs up, headed for his pickup truck.

"We had better get started organizing this mess," Marisol said.

"I will run inside and get some newspaper so we can lay these stems out to drain before we pack them for shipping."

"Good idea."

A few minutes later, Rosario returned with her arms full and began to spread newspapers on the floor. Mama was right behind her. Her eyes were wide and her face pale. As a child, she had been told thunder and lightning meant God was angry. Marisol would bet her mother had been hiding under her bed until she heard Rosario come inside.

"That was some storm," Mama said. "I see you girls handled the flowers all right."

To Mama, they would always be girls, even though Marisol had just turned twenty-seven and Rosario was twenty-five.

"Jose brought the pickers in," Rosario said. "Marisol told him we would pay them extra."

One of Mama's eyebrows went up. "And who gave you the authority to make that kind of promise?"

Marisol bit back a retort. "I have no authority." Her chin went up. "Our pickers risked their lives out there in the field with lightning going to ground all around them."

She heard Mama suck in a breath. "I did not realize..."

Of course, she would not. Mama never set foot out of the door if it even *looked* like it might rain. Marisol was not sure what her mother was afraid of. As far as she knew, God had little reason to be angry with Mama.

"It has been handled, Mama. Our orders will go out on time." Rosario let out a breath.

"And if the money is a problem, you can take it from my portion of the profits," Marisol said.

"What profits? We are running at a loss, although that nice Victor helped me to balance the checkbook last night. He is a wizard with numbers, you know. He found a deposit slip for two-thousand dollars that I forgot to enter." Mama made the sign of the cross. "Thank God we can meet our bills this month."

Mama pulled out the metal folding chair from Marisol's desk and plopped down in it. She pressed her palm into her forehead. "I am so tired of having to worry about everything here. I do not understand why you girls are so set on holding onto Garcia Jardines. Look at you two. Your clothes are soaked and you are covered with mud."

"This has always been our home, Mama," Rosario said.

Mama lifted her head and seemed to brighten. "If I marry Gomez, we would be able to live here as we are now. Garcia Jardines and Soto Flores would be one. We would not be selling our business to a stranger, after all."

"No, not a stranger. A *killer*."

"W-what?" Mama bolted out of her chair and stared at Marisol.

Rosario grabbed Marisol's arm. "No, do not say anything."

"Have you forgotten about Papa's accident?"

"Quiet," Rosario hissed.

"No. This pretense has gone on far too long." Drawing in a breath, Marisol spewed out the facts that had haunted her for the past year. "Mama. Papa was murdered. *Murdered.*"

Mama's face crumpled. All of a sudden she looked older and defeated.

"The Green Fire Cartel. I overheard Papa and Soto arguing. Soto wanted control and Papa would not give it up. Now that Papa is gone, Soto runs the cartel."

"No. That cannot be. A worker lost control of the tractor. That is what happened. You are wrong, Marisol." Mama stepped forward, her hand ready to slap Marisol for lying.

Marisol's hand went up. "No, Mama. Think about it. Did you know the worker? Was he one of ours? Have you seen him since?"

Mama's lips trembled. Rosario moved behind Mama and held her shoulders. It was how it had always had been; Mama and Rosario pitted against her.

"She has had enough for one day, Marisol. Back off." Rosario rested her head in the crook of Mama's neck.

Rosario was right. Mama appeared ready to collapse. If Mama had been displeased with Marisol before, she must hate her now she had opened her mother's eyes to the truth about Papa's death. She should stop now—except it was too late. She had to finish what she started. Then maybe it would end—the tortuous nights of not sleeping, the anguish over Soto's attentions to Mama, and the threat of losing their heritage.

Sniffing back a sob, Marisol smoothed a stray hair from Mama's forehead. "Did it never occur to you that Soto had Papa killed?"

Mama's eyes narrowed. She pulled away from Rosario. "How do you know all this Marisol? Tell me."

"The pieces fit. After they brought Papa back to the house, I was so upset I had to find out what happened. When I ran out to the back field, the rear of a tractor was heading up the road toward Soto Flores. The soil of the new beds we had been plowing were red with Papa's blood. It was awful." Marisol put her head in her hands.

"Tractors travel the road all the time, Marisol. Why would you think..."

"That is not all, Mama. I examined the tire treads and compared them to our own. They did not match. That tractor was leaving our land, not working it. What was it doing here? You tell me, Mama." She dug her thumb into her chest.

Marisol went over to her desk and pulled open the top drawer. She held up a sandwich-sized plastic bag. A marker indicated a date— the date of Papa's death. She dangled it from her fingers. "I found this at the scene."

"What is it?" Mama wrinkled her nose. "A cigar butt?"

"I did not know it was important, but I saved it anyway. This week, when Soto visited you, his bodyguard Sanchez was waiting out front smoking a cigar. He threw the remains into our grass."

Marisol drew out a second plastic bag from her desk and then held it next to the older one. "Look. The writing. The same brand. Cuban."

Mama grabbed the two bags and stared at them. Her eyes glistened. "I did not know. I did not think... The police said it was an accident."

"Did you even wonder how the police knew to come so quickly? *We* did not call them."

"And to think, I brought Sanchez coffee that night." Rosario shook her head to the side. "Now I believe you, Marisol." Tears brimmed in Rosario's eyes. With a gut wrenching sob, she reached for Marisol and engulfed Mama and her sister in a hug.

"It is over now, Mama," Rosario said. "There is nothing we can do."

Mama pulled away, tears spilling over onto her cheeks. She sniffed and then her face went hard. "Yes, there is. With such hard evidence, we can reopen the case. I want Sanchez behind bars."

"Everyone knows the police are corrupt," Rosario said. "It is not worth the trouble."

"Not all of them. Your husband's *Tio* Berto is a good man. He is retired, but he still has honest friends in the force," Mama said. "I will call him."

"But Soto is the real villain. He will still be free. If he had Papa killed so he could take over the cartel, how far will he go to get our land?" Rosario asked.

"Your husband must protect us," Marisol said. "Talk to him, Rosario. He works for Soto."

"I will try, but he is not around much."

"Then we will have to protect ourselves. We can beat him," Marisol said. "Soto is trying to use his money to control us. We need to be profitable enough to fight him off. If we work together to fill the ten-thousand-lily Elite order, we have a chance at climbing out of the financial rut we have fallen into."

Marisol lifted her hands, fingers splayed and nails caked with soil. "I will work day and night to keep our plantation out of the clutches of Soto's cartel."

Rosario raised her filthy hands. "And I will, too."

Mama's shoulders went back, and she seemed to grow taller than her petite five-feet. "Show me what to do."

Marisol could not help but smile. Mama's place had always been inside the house tending to meals, seeing to the needs of her family—and defending Papa's part in the cartel. Now her mother was working alongside her daughters. A sense of harmony sang through her. For the first time since she had been ousted from the convent, Mama was not bucking her every suggestion.

Marisol stood back watching Rosario show Mama how to pack the flowers for shipping. A crate lay open on the shipping table. A bag of cotton balls sat alongside it. Rosario held a cotton ball between her fingers. "Now, Mama," Marisol heard her say, "put one of these inside the cup of the calla. It will keep the bloom open and protect it from crushing during transit."

Finally, Mama and Rosario washed up and went into the kitchen to fix sandwiches, while Marisol continued to cull bulbets from the sodden stalks, not wanting to waste a moment.

She happened to glance outside. Joseph shuffled along looking at the ground, minus his school uniform. He knew she would be in the greenhouse, yet the boy turned in toward their cottage.

Bike left in the woods, wet backpack. Skipped school! Shoving open the door, she stomped outside and hurried to block his path.

He stopped, refusing to meet her eyes.

The urge to grab her son by the shoulders and shake sense into him made her clasp her hands in front of her. "Stop right there, young man."

Joseph lifted his head and met her eyes. The corners of his mouth turned down. "I am sorry, Mama."

"You *should* be. You lied to me. Where have you been? The truth. All of it."

"I disobeyed you. I hid in the backseat of *Tio* Carlos's car because I wanted to go to Bogotá and see the cockfight."

"And..." She tapped her foot, waiting.

"And *Tio* Victor made *Tio* Carlos turn around and take me to school."

"Victor did that?" Victor Novak was turning out to be a decent man although there was a phoniness about him she could not explain.

"He said I needed to listen to you and study so I can go to school in America."

"So they drove you to school. Why are you home so early?"

Joseph pulled at his shirt. "I...did not have my books and was not dressed properly so Mr. Martinez sent me to the principal's office. I have detention tomorrow afternoon."

Marisol pressed her lips together. "Well, good. Now that you are here you can finish packing this morning's flowers. They need to go out on the five o'clock shuttle."

A shadow passed over Joseph's face.

Chapter Nine

A warm feeling filled Victor, as if he'd downed a shot of whiskey. He was sorry to leave the comfort of Berto's flat. All his life he'd felt alone, even when his mother was alive. They kept secrets from each other under the guise of protection. Now his heart swelled. He held back the smile of pure joy that threatened to reveal his giddy emotions.

He belonged.

He had an uncle and a brother—and the Garcias seemed like family, too.

Ahead of him, Victor observed Carlos—truly his half-brother. What did it matter if they shared no resemblance? He and Carlos were flesh and blood. "Did father live in this neighborhood, too?"

"We lived downstairs." Carlos rapped on a door labeled 1B as they passed by.

When he and Carlos exited the building, Victor looked at the street with new eyes. He might've grown up here, been among kids like those playing kick ball in the street, instead of playing footsie with Mrs. Gallagher.

Victor watched the boys playing. They appeared to be about as old as he had been when he lost his virginity. Back then, Victor thought of himself as the cock of the walk. He'd had sex, when none of the boys at Lawrence had even kissed a girl. Unfortunately, the great education Mrs. Gallaher funded hadn't bought him freedom. These boys laughed freely, ran about joking with each other, being boys, not men. He would have rather been raised among such boys knowing his life—and his body—were his own.

"You okay, *amigo?*" Carlos punched his arm.

Victor grinned wide enough to make his cheeks hurt and slung an arm around Carlos's shoulder. Now it was confirmed that he and Carlos were related, Carlos must surely trust him. "Of course. Where to next?"

"The bar at Club Galilistico. A hot spot. You will like it. Meet my friends," Carlos said.

"I'm looking forward to it."

Thirty minutes later Carlos and Victor sauntered into the Club, which turned out to be the site of the cockfight they were to attend. The rather large room had a collection of tables and a mahogany bar. The rear ends of a few hefty men draped over stools in front of it. The place smelled of spilled beer, smoke, and chicken feathers. In one area, a crowd of men hooted and cheered.

With a nod for him to follow, Carlos headed over. They wedged themselves into the front of the group.

Victor gawked. Two roosters were being held down on one of the tables by their handlers. The birds strained to peck at each other, hissing. He always thought roosters said *"cock-a-doodle-do,"* but those must be happy roosters. These cluckers were in a foul mood. Some of the men were counting out pesos and handing them to a man who likely was a bookie.

"Is this the cockfight we're here to see?" Victor asked Carlos.

Carlos gave him an "are-you-kidding" look, and then laughed. "Oh no, those two men are teasing their cocks."

Only a filthy mind would assume the men were jacking off, but Victor understood what Carlos meant. Victor continued to watch the two roosters straining to get at each other until he could no longer stand it. He turned away.

"Does it always reek of bird shit in here?"

Carlos chuckled. "Ah, college boy, you are not used to squalor. I will bet back in Miami you sit in your plush house watching football on the television."

"You know nothing about me, Carlos."

"Then tell me. I want to hear all about Miami." Carlos nodded toward the far end of the room. "The back side of the bar will not offend your sensitive nose, my brother. Let us get a beer."

He and Carlos settled on stools beside two heavy-set men—one of them he recognized from Barra de Luis in Garcia. Out of habit, Victor zeroed in on the tattooed wrists of the pair.

"You remember Miguel," Carlos said to Victor. "He is a supervisor at *La Esmeralda*."

"Ah yes, Victor, or is it Vickie?" Miguel smiled showing his full set of teeth, minus one eyetooth on the left.

Miguel was goading him and he was not going to give the man the satisfaction of knowing he'd been offended.

"I answer to Victor, *Mickey*. By the way, steal any wallets lately?"

"Uh..."A flash of guilt passed over Miguel's sun-roughened face.

His shadowed eyes cut to Carlos.

"Back off," Carlos hissed into Victor's ear. "You are not supposed to know."

Victor smiled. He'd made his point.

"*Hola.*" The curly-headed man who sat near Miguel swiveled around on his stool and rose. His had a pushed-in face and a skewed nose that gave him a tough-guy look. With a curve of his lips, his bad-guy demeanor turned friendly. "I am Angel." Standing at eye level with Victor, the man extended his arm and gave Victor's hand a firm shake.

Now there's a gentleman, Victor thought.

"Angel is a professional. Eh?" Carlos nudged the man's hairy arm. "His magic hands separate our valuable stones from shale."

"Are you a jeweler, then?" Victor asked, leaning forward.

"My brother," Carlos said, patting Victor's back, "does not know much about our business."

Miguel swiveled around, beer bottle in one hand. "And why should he?" His chin lifted with an air of superiority. "Our business is closed to outsiders."

Carlos grabbed the front of Miguel's T-shirt and pulled him so they were nose to nose. He spoke through clenched teeth. "My brother is *not* an outsider." When he let go, Miguel fell back, rocking the legs of his stool and spilling beer down the front of his shirt.

"Okay, *amigo.*" Miguel held up one hand in surrender. "I get the point."

For the second time since he arrived, Carlos was defending him. Guilt stabbed at Victor's gut. Would Carlos feel as brotherly if he learned Victor had come to Bogotá doubting their relationship—and now intended to use him as a stepping-stone to the emerald market?

He glanced over at his brother. Carlos must truly care about him. Could he care for his brother in return? He wasn't certain he even liked the man. Carlos was rough-cut, as were his seedy-looking friends, and Victor was all about grooming and manners.

Behind them, the crowd rooted for their favorite cocks. Carlos and Victor moved away from Miguel and Angel and settled into the two lone seats at the far side of the bar.

"I'll have a Club Colombo," Victor told the bartender, a light-skinned, sandy-haired man who spoke perfect English. Knowing he was among a mixed group of Colombians made him feel less of an outcast.

When the beers came, Carlos tipped his bottle against Victor's. "A toast to brotherhood." He raised his drink.

"*Salute.*" Victor tapped bottles with him and took a slug of his beer.

"Keep them coming," Carlos told the bartender.

Crap. He knew this would happen, but he had come prepared. He felt inside his pocket for the two aspirin he had tucked away and popped them into his mouth, using the beer as a chaser.

Despite all the time he and Carlos spent together today, Carlos hadn't mentioned anything regarding Victor's request to join the Green Fire Cartel. The words had spilled out, meant to shock. To get Carlos's attention. He didn't *really* think Carlos would snap his fingers and Victor would become an instant member. No, there had to be some sort of ritual—*oh God, what would that be?* He glanced at the pink flesh on the inside of his wrist. Thin skin there. It would hurt like a mother. Carlos seemed relaxed, now he had a couple of brews in him, and no one sat within earshot—not that anything they said could be heard over the racket in the room. *Good time for the push.*

"To the emerald business," Victor said.

Carlos tapped his bottle against Victor's and slugged it. Then he leaned in close enough for Victor to smell his malty breath. "Gomez."

"Gomez?"

"Sh." Carlos held a finger to his lips. "He runs the emerald cartel here."

"Runs it, like a don in the Italian mafia?"

Carlos pointed to the fire tattoo on the inside of his wrist. "I got this tat when I was initiated into the cartel."

"Nice."

Carlos held his gaze, waiting for Victor to say more.

If he joined, he would be scarred for life as a criminal. Maybe he should back off. There had to be more legitimate ways to get into the emerald business than joining the cartel.

I want out, and I'm not even in. No, that sounded ridiculous. "How profitable is it, your cartel?" he said, deciding on polite conversation.

"Not enough for me." Carlos picked at the label on his bottle. He gave Victor a sidelong look. "Gomez controls the money. It takes months before I get my share."

"Is this a large group, your cartel?" He knew the answer—he had been surrounded by members ever since he arrived, but Carlos seemed to want to talk, so he would encourage him.

"Too large." Carlos stared into Victor's eyes, as if struggling with himself about talking further. Finally, Carlos turned from him to slug down another shot.

I get the point, Carlos. You're not thrilled with your cut. Don't tell me anything else. I don't want to hear it.

As if Carlos picked his mind, he broke out into a wide smile and whacked Victor on the back. "Tell me about South Beach." He wiggled his eyebrows. "The sexy babes. You are a handsome devil." He nudged Victor. "They must be crawling all over you."

Carlos licked his lips, and was close to drooling—the man's mouth was moister than usual. Given the way his brother reacted to the whore's advances earlier, there was no telling what Carlos expected him to say. Carlos wanted him to talk about babes—hardly an apt description of his clientele. He settled on giving Carlos a sly smile. "Wealthy ones."

There, that was the truth. For the right amount of money, he would call any of his has-been cougars "babe."

Carlos's lips curved in a lecherous smile. "Young ones, rich and beautiful, I'll bet." He leaned uncomfortably close to Victor.

"Not worth it. They want me for free." *No. I didn't really say that. I just thought it.*

Carlos's eyes narrowed. He peered into Victor's face, his breath reeking of stale beer. "Women pay you to fuck them?"

Oh, fuck. He drew back, summoning what little dignity he had left. "I beg your pardon. I am a professional escort, not a low-life whore."

Carlos laughed, and then threw an arm around Victor. "You are a sly one."

"Wh-what?" *Sly?* Carlos hadn't rejected him. He was—proud of him? The burden of hiding his past floated up and off his shoulders,

Victor leaned against the back of the stool and folded his arms across his chest. With a pitch of his head to the side, he rolled his tongue inside his cheek. "Big bucks."

"You got pictures?"

"Not on me."

"Later then. Come on, it is time to place our bets."

"Bets?"

"Over here." Carlos pointed to a rather attractive yellow and red cock. "A sure winner."

Victor dug into his pocket for what was left of his cash, ripped off a hundred dollar bill, and handed it to the bookie.

"That is all you are going to bet? Look at this cock. He is healthy and feisty. It is a triple play."

Not wanting to appear cheap, he added another hundred, praying the cock with a name he couldn't pronounce would come through. His cash was running low. Without a steady income, he didn't dare charge much more on his credit card—and it was clear this emerald thing had taken a wrong turn.

Victor's cock lost, of course.

After a bitching two hours sitting on a hard seat in the foul-smelling, circular arena, Victor's ears burned from all the yelling and hooting. He stared at pairs of cocks flying at each other with death on their agenda. Feathers erupted into the air, and blood sprayed onto the green bull's eye that marked the center of the ring.

Victor's cock went down in two minutes. Two-hundred dollars gone up in bloody feathers.

"Better luck next time." Carlos smacked him on the back again.

"Please don't do that, you're bruising my back."

"Oh, are we delicate?"

Victor froze for a moment. "What did you...?" Then he saw Carlos's grin. "No more delicate than you," he said, returning the favor with a hearty whack on Carlos's back.

They left the stench of the arena and headed for the bar, along with other losers. "I'm going to need something stronger than a Club Colombo," Victor said. "Your treat this time."

"I know just the thing," Carlos replied.

* * * *

Either Carlos was weaving on the stool or he was. Victor couldn't tell. It had to be that Aguardiente again. He should have shied away from the drink after having passed out cold the last time. He was tired of always having to be in control of what he did or said, lest one of his client's dump him prematurely. Now he was in a different place in his life—and it felt damn good.

"Victor, I have a confession to make." Carlos stared at Victor bleary-eyed.

The muscles in Victor's abdomen tightened and he struggled to fight off the fuzziness in his head. Earlier, his tongue loosened by the fiery liquor, he had spilled his guts to Carlos about his companionship business. Carlos apparently had decided to share his own secrets, which wasn't a good thing. Hearing details about the Green Fire Cartel could get him killed.

"I am no good. I cheat on Rosario." He shook his head to the side. "I do not deserve her."

Oh, that. Tell me something I don't already know. "Of course you deserve her. You're a good man." Victor slapped his brother's back. It felt good, like a release. Now he understood why Carlos had developed the backslapping habit.

Carlos coughed.

Fearing he was going to yak all over him, Victor leaned back on the stool. *Whoa.* He was falling backward—

A hand grasped at his arm and pulled him up. "*Gracias.*" Victor righted his body on the stool. "Maybe we should switch to water."

"*Dos aguas,*" Carlos called out to the bartender, his two fingers raised, "and two more of these." He pointed to their empty shot glasses.

Laying his hairy forearm on the drink-spotted bar top, Carlos turned to face him. "Why do you say I am a good man? I lie, I cheat on my wife. Our father tried to make me behave, but I never listened."

Christ. Why is he getting religion?

Carlos continued to stare at him, waiting for some pearl of wisdom Victor might offer to exonerate him.

"Look." Victor spread his hands palms up. "We are men. We *own* women."

It was a blatant lie, because the truth was women owned *him*—and right now, he could use a cash cow. No job, no way to meet the right cronies, and he was nearly broke from betting on those stupid cocks. He had to get moving on something here or in a couple of days he'd be on a plane to Miami hawking his wares. Emeralds. He couldn't get them out of his mind. *All* the jewelry stores carrying precious gems couldn't have come by them legally. If he went with Carlos to the mine and learned as much as he could it might be possible to develop a business of his own.

"I want to change my life," Carlos said.

Uh-oh. He's boozed up, getting morose on me. "How? You have a good life."

Carlos leaned in and belched in Victor's face.

My reactors must be numb, because I don't give a damn about the smell.

Carlos lifted his head and scanned the bar area, and then he hunkered down nose to nose with Victor and spoke in a low tone. "I have an idea for making money, but I need someone I trust to help me."

Money. The word struck like a shot of adrenaline. "You can trust me." A hiccup bubbled up in Victor's throat. He threw his arm around Carlos's shoulder. "We're family."

A sly smile crept onto Carlos's lips. "Here is my plan..."

Chapter Ten

The roar of an engine roused Victor to semi-consciousness, he cracked open one eye, and then the other. His nose twitched with the foul odor of morning mouth and his butt itched from the stinging little pellets beneath him. Something heavy and smelly lay against him. He moved, and stopped abruptly when the object groaned.

"Carlos. Wake up. We're on the sidewalk."

With a snort, Carlos lifted his head from Victor's shoulder and struggled to his feet. Unzipping his pants, he pulled out his penis and took a leak against the side of the building, not three feet away.

Victor's nose wrinkled, and then his bladder squawked for release. Rising, he stumbled over his sneakers. Shoving his feet into them as far as they would go, he shuffled over to follow Carlos's expeditious example.

A down-in-the-mouth woman dragging three toddlers gave him and Carlos a dirty look. "Disgusting," she said, never pausing as she passed.

As if Victor wasn't already aware of that fact. Admiring his graffiti, Victor smiled at Carlos. "I've always wanted to write my name on a wall like that."

He glanced down at Carlos's crotch. "Better zip the chicken in the coop, if you know what I mean."

"*Sí.* Heh, heh."

This morning, he was Victor, but not Victor. If his clients could see him now. He ran his fingers through his hair, still not quite used to it taking less time, and came away with a wispy, blood-speckled feather. He glanced sideways at Carlos, who brushed similar feathers from his shirt and jeans.

The cockfight.

The bar.

The true confession.

Shit, Carlos knows I screw women for a living. He vaguely remembered talk of emeralds and some plan Carlos had cooked up.

"We have a good time last night, eh, partner?"

Partner? What exactly had he committed to? Victor's insides turned to ice. He focused on the bare skin on inside of his left wrist and sighed in relief. "I need coffee and maybe some dry toast," he said, ignoring the partner comment.

With Carlos's arm slung over Victor's shoulder, they wobbled down a narrow street littered with used coffee cups, crinkled newspapers, and discarded candy wrappers. Automobiles and pickup trucks zoomed by. Decently dressed men and women ignored them as they hurried past. It might be just another workday for most, but not Victor. Today his brother was going to lead him to the wealth he deserved.

Carlos pulled open the door to a coffee shop. The odors of coffee and cinnamon drifted out. Inside, the place was retro with red vinyl seating and a chrome-edged linoleum counter.

"Two black coffees and a couple of those." Carlos pointed to a tray of sugary pastries.

The gum-chewing woman behind the counter wrinkled her nose and then turned away to pour their coffee.

Victor and Carlos slid onto stools, joining the jeweler Victor met at the cockfight.

"How did you do last night, Angel?" Carlos said.

Angel lifted his cup to sip his coffee, revealing the cartel tattoo inside his wrist. A shiver ran through Victor. The only friends of Carlos he had met seemed to be part of the Green Fire Cartel. By joining forces with these men, he would be operating beneath the law. The image of Gomez Soto in his pricey power suit flashed in his mind. Money could buy anything, even immunity.

"Pretty good, Ram." The man smiled, revealing a gold front tooth. "And your brother? Uh, sorry your name is..." His forehead wrinkled.

"Victor Novak here."

"Ah, yes. *Victor.*"

Carlos laughed. "My brother needs a street name, eh?"

"Just call me...Money Man," Victor said without thinking.

Carlos lifted his eyebrows. "Good choice."

Money Man. The obligation that came with his choice of street name preyed on Victor's mind. Bits and pieces of the past night's discussion came back to him. Had he *really* promised to use his contacts in Miami to launder emeralds? Did he even have any such contacts?

When their coffee arrived, Victor swallowed his down neat, its bitterness clawing at his insides. His head weighed ten tons and the coffee was doing a jig in his stomach. Tums and aspirin lay tucked inside his roller bag at the plantation, along with his toothbrush—he ran his tongue along his teeth, slippery with gunk.

"Are we heading back to Garcia?" he asked Carlos once Angel left the coffeehouse.

"No, unless you changed your mind about visiting *La Esmeralda*."

"We're going? Now? But... look at me. Look at you. We've slept in these clothes and we stink. I need a shower."

"Bah. What for? The mines are dirty. We will fit in with everyone else there, eh?"

Yes, fit in. That's exactly what he wanted to do. But now he saw having his hair chopped and not shaving wouldn't be enough. From the looks of things, being clean and neat was undesirable.

"I went to a lot of trouble to get you into the mine on such short notice, Victor. You are not happy?"

"Uh, yes. I'm happy. Thank you. See, I'm smiling." He flashed his teeth in a grin.

"Good. We should get a move on. It is a long ride."

"Sure." Victor reached into his pocket to pay the tab and came out with a twenty-dollar bill. *Not too many of the bigger bills left.*

"Are you going to pay me or are you flapping that twenty in your hand to tease me?" the waitress said.

"Of course. Here you go. Keep the change."

Departing the café, Victor followed Carlos toward the back lot, where they had left the Cherokee. As they passed a sporting goods store, Victor caught his reflection in the window. *Who is that old man?* He slowed his pace to take a closer look. The skin on his face sagged and the sun turned his black hair a dull brown.

"See something in the window you like?" Carlos asked.

"No...why, yes. I want to run inside for a minute. I'll meet you at the Cherokee."

"No problem, Money Man."

Accept it. You got what you wanted. Squashing the urge to wimp out on Carlos, he pushed open the heavy glass door, his tender senses stunned by the brightness of the florescent lights overhead and the gymnasium odors of sweat and rubber.

A chunky bald man leaned over the counter by the cash register. "Help you, señor?"

"I need a professional soccer ball."

The man's eyes gleamed. "Aisle two. Your son play?"

"Uh...yes."

Ten minutes later, Victor emerged cradling a colorful cardboard box holding a two hundred dollar soccer ball, charged to his credit card. The kid couldn't practice his game properly with a beach ball, after all. It was a win-win situation. Joseph would be thrilled and Victor would make serious points with Marisol.

He located the Jeep without much trouble. Carlos was lounging in the driver seat, the engine revving. When Victor opened the rear door to stow his purchase, coffee acid coagulated in his gut and rose to his throat.

What the hell? He swallowed the foul taste and croaked, "Why...the rifle?"

"For protection."

Protection? From what? Angry emeralds? One gun, two people. He didn't like how the odds stacked against him. He'd never handled a gun, much less learned to shoot one. His very life was in his brother's hands.

He closed the rear door, and slid into the front seat. He met his brother's gaze. "You expect trouble, then?"

* * * *

Today was a much nicer day. The sky was nearly cloudless and the mountains tops sparkled a grayish purple in the sunlight. The cisterns were full from the previous day's rainsquall, and the composted soil in the fields retained enough moisture to last until the second shift came in to water the plants.

"Everyone is here and working." Rosario approached her. "Do you need help?"

"Only if you have a magic touch that will grow bulbs."

"Sorry, Sis," Rosario held up her hand. "You have the green thumb. Do your thing. Coax those little babies and they will grow soon enough."

She followed Marisol into the greenhouse, where Mama waited. The sun blazing through the overhead glass cloaked her with a golden aura. Then she stepped forward, leaving a shadow. "I am here. Do you need me to stuff lilies for shipping?"

The dark circles under her mother's eyes told Marisol her mother had not slept well. She understood. Yesterday had been a rough road for all of them, except Joseph. Telling her son of Soto's deceit would change things; he would react with the rage of a hurt teenager. Certainly he would want to quit Soto's soccer team, and Lord knows what else. He'd find out about the murder as soon as the police made an actual arrest.

"Not yet, Mama," Marisol settled in at her desk to check over her planting schedule. "We must wait until the pickers bring them inside." Her head buzzed. She was accustomed to being alone in her greenhouse. Now she needed to find jobs for helpers.

The squeal of brakes outside the greenhouse startled Marisol. Her head turned swiftly toward the door.

"That must be Carlos now." Rosario clapped the soil from her hands. "Why is he parking out front?"

A car door slammed.

Rosario rushed to the greenhouse door and flung it open. "Oh no, Mama. Señor Soto is knocking on your door. And that awful Sanchez is pacing in front of their car smoking one of his smelly cigars. I will run over and tell him you are not home."

Mama pushed Rosario aside. "You will do no such thing. *I* will handle this."

"Be careful, Mama." Marisol pulled at her mother's arm willing her to stay put. "If he knows you have turned against him..."

Mama shook off Marisol's hand. Straightening her shoulders, she shoved open the connecting kitchen door and strode toward the living room.

Rosario and Marisol followed her.

Soto must have given up on polite knocking. Such loud pounding could only be produced by two-fisted blows.

Rosario bit at her cuticles. She turned to Marisol wide-eyed. "Did Soto beat his wife?"

"If you remember, his wife was a big woman. She could have

squashed Soto by sitting on him. Besides, Soto would not tarnish his good-guy image by doing his own dirty work. Did she not die in a car crash?"

"I... Yes. But I am sure it was an accident."

"An accident like Papa's?"

Rosario's face went white. She grabbed Marisol's arm. "I am scared."

She patted her sister's hand. "He is just a man, and a small one at that." They moved behind Mama, standing close enough to feel the rage radiating from her petite body.

Mama cracked open the door, straining the chain bolt she secured after yesterday's revelation.

"Consolata," Señor Soto shouted through the opening. "What took you so long? Let me in." He pushed at the door. "I have something for you."

"No, Mama," Rosario whispered. "Do not open the door."

Despite the warning, Mama undid the chain and stepped aside to admit Gomez Soto.

Stiff-backed, Soto lifted his pointed chin, stretched his turkey neck, and walked inside. "Consolata, what have you been doing? Why, there is dirt smeared on your face?" He grabbed her hands.

Mama's shoulders stiffened.

"Your hands. They are soiled also. You do not need to work the lands like a peasant."

Mama snatched away her hands and backed up. "Yes I do, Gomez. They are *my* lands. The deal is off. I do not plan to sell."

"What do you mean?" The pleasant smile fell from Soto's face.

His lips formed a straight line. He reached into the inside pocket of his jacket and brought out an envelope. "I have the deposit right here."

Mama held her ground, stiff and unmoving.

He undid the flap on the envelope and reached inside for what looked like a bank check. Marisol could not make out the amount, but the slight movement of Mama's hand toward it made it clear the deposit was substantial enough to tempt her.

But she was wrong.

Mama's hand rose to the side. With a hard swing, she clouted Soto across the face.

The envelope and check floated to the floor.

Soto's hand went to his cheek, which had turned solid red from the blow.

"Get out of my house." Mama shoved at the man's chest.

Not a big man, the force of her hand sent him stumbling backward toward door she had left ajar. His mouth opened, but no words came out.

"And take this with you." Mama dug her toe underneath the check and launched it over the threshold of the door. Soto's gaze followed the flight of the check as it fluttered onto the doormat. With a stabbing glare at Mama, he stepped on the check and ground it to bits before turning to leave.

Giving the door a whack, Mama shut it against the man's backside.

There was a rumbling noise followed by a high-pitched yelp and then silence.

"I think he fell down the steps," Rosario said.

"An accident. What a shame." Mama's pursed her lips. "I hope he broke something."

Rosario raced to the window. "Sanchez is helping him to the car. He is limping a little."

"Good riddance. Now I will make us a fresh pot of coffee and we will get Berto on the phone." Without waiting for a reply, Mama headed for the kitchen.

"What do you think will happen, Marisol?" Rosario wrung her hands. "Soto will want revenge for this insult."

"Whatever it is, it will not be good."

Chapter Eleven

Victor shifted in his seat. "What kind of trouble could we possibly meet en route to *La Esmeralda?*"

"Banditos hide in bushes and caves to attack cars, like ours, headed to and from the mines. They hope we are carrying *mucho pesos* to buy emeralds from a strike—or leaving to take a load to market."

"Nasty business. I didn't realize..."

"I warned you, my brother, but you insisted on a tour. Not to worry, though." He tapped on the windshield. "Bullet proof glass."

Bullet proof? Shit. Victor focused on the white line dividing the four-lane highway out of Bogotá. He had come to Colombia with high hopes of a new career, and now that it was in reach, he was sinking into a mucky pit of violence and deceit.

"Carlos, about your plan..."

"How about some music, eh?" Carlos switched the radio from Spanish news to American Rock, raised the volume, and drummed his fingers on the steering wheel. "You like Hot Chili Peppers?"

"A little spicy for me, but that's..."

"The band. Hot stuff." Carlos began to hum along with the music.

Okay, be that way. He let out a long breath. They would talk later, on the way out of the mine—barring no problems. Carlos had to be exaggerating about the danger, anyway. He was a security guard, after all. Why wouldn't they be safe? Maybe his brother was just trying to impress him. Besides, with luck, he wouldn't need to come back this way once he had the makings for a business plan of his own.

Carlos tapped the brake as they drove off the highway ramp onto an unpaved road rutted with stones and roots. They drove downhill for close to an hour before reaching the foothills of the mountain. The road thinned, becoming so narrow that roadside bushes scratched at the sides of the Jeep.

"How much farther do we have to drive to reach *La Esmeralda?*" Victor said. The loud music coupled with a lingering hangover from the previous night's festivities had his head throbbing.

"Relax, my brother. Travel is slow on the mountains. It will take us another few hours to reach the mine."

"You've got to be kidding. How often do you have to make this drive?"

"Twice a month. I am off for ten days now, but next Friday I begin my twenty-day shift. Like the miners, I must remain at the facility until my shift is over."

"Nice they put you up in a hotel."

"Not exactly, but making fewer trips means I do not have to worry about bandito attacks as often—even though guards posted along the road to the mines are always watching."

"And you are such a guard?"

"*Sí.* I head the security force at *La Esmeralda.*"

"But I don't understand. I read miners could keep what they find because they work for free."

Carlos smiled, showing all his teeth. "Not everything. Arrangements differ among various mines. In *La Esmeralda*, once the head honchos have culled the finest chunks of the lot, they allow the miners first pick of the rejects in exchange for providing them room and board. Other more generous owners will disperse a small percentage of the mine's profits amongst its miners, and some even offer them a small wage."

"So the miners get a raw deal, unless they hit it right."

"It happens. Even so, it does not keep them from returning— once the search for emeralds gets into their blood. Green Fire, we call it."

Money, people will do anything for it. Even consider becoming a criminal, like me.

For the next couple of hours, they navigated lumpy roads covered with loose stones that made musical clinks against the Jeep's undercarriage. Carlos had to shift into first gear to manage the steep, forested hills that dropped into valleys dense with plantations. Moisture hung in the air, turning the mountains hazy lavender and hiding their peaks in the clouds. Despite the bone-jangling ride, Victor couldn't help but gape in wonder at his surroundings. How could such beauty harbor violence?

Finally. They drove into a populated area. After that bouncy ride up and around the mountain, driving on the level, two-lane road running down the center of the small village was a treat.

"This is...?"

"Boyacá, where the miners live when they are off duty," Carlos said.

"Ah, so we are almost there."

"Almost. The hardest part of the drive is ahead." Carlos pulled the Jeep over to side of the road in front of a tin-roofed adobe building housing a few shops, including a café. "Come on, Victor. We will have a drink and a bite to eat before we tackle the last leg."

With a groan, Victor struggled out of the Jeep. All that jouncing couldn't have been good for his man parts and his head still pounded. Thin air, Carlos had said.

"You don't happen to have some aspirin around, do you?"

"In the glove compartment. I get those altitude headaches up here, too."

"*Gracias.*" Victor reached inside the Jeep, found the yellow tin, and swallowed two aspirin dry.

Ten minutes later, their thirst quenched and stomachs content, Victor and Carlos returned to the Jeep and got inside.

"Time to close up." Carlos rolled up his window. "Check the doors on your side. Make sure they are locked."

"Yes, of course." *So we will be safe from attack.* He'd almost forgotten about Carlos's earlier warning. The sausage sandwich he'd just downed roiled in his stomach. After shutting his window, he depressed the button to lock his door. Although they were somewhat protected inside this cocoon of a car, it was hot as hell. Already his clothing stuck to his skin from perspiration. How much worse would the heat be higher up the mountain at *La Esmeralda?*

They chugged out of Boyacá, leaving behind the smooth street and returning to the rock-riddled road. In the valley, a two-foot wide stream of blackened water gushed down the mountain road and pooled at its base. There, a motley throng of shabbily dressed people stood in the resulting muck, bending and scooping up the stuff as if panning for gold.

Victor watched a white-haired woman scoop up a handful of dismal grey sludge to examine it. Her gaze drifted to her surroundings before she stuck her fingers into the slop and ate some.

"Ew That woman just ate mud," he said to Carlos.

"You have much to learn, my brother. Those are *quaqueros*, treasure hunters prospecting for bits of precious stones that wash down from the mines, called tailings. She is biting on a stone to be sure it is worth keeping. See? She just spit it out—or pretended to."

"Can we stop? I'd like to check out that slop for emeralds, too."

"Not unless you want to risk your life. Others who come here every day hoping to find even a single gem would have killed that woman for her find."

There was that word again. Kill. "Thought you had police, guards to protect..."

"The gems. That's what they protect. Not people who are foolish enough to fight over them. We do not need our jails full of squatters. It is easier to let them kill each other than to house them."

Circumventing the area, they drove up the mountain road, tires sloshing through the slippery sludge spattering the underside of the Jeep. By the time they reached *La Esmeralda*, they would be as grimy as the *quaqueros*.

"My workplace is in the Chivor area, along with other privately held mines," Carlos said.

"Private? So people *own* mines?" *People who must have more money than God.*

"Not all. The Muzo mine is publicly held. It is regulated by the government and patrolled by the National Police Force of Colombia."

Hmm. Muzo must be on the up and up.

"You can tell we are approaching Chivor by the guards. Two, one on each side of the road. We space them a quarter mile apart."

Victor stuck his head out of the window. The men wore camouflage, which seemed to be the official police uniform of Colombia, and stood at the ready. "They're armed."

"Of course. How else can they get people to stop?"

Carlos held his up badge face out as they drove slowly past each set of guards. Finally, they approached a steel gate manned by two grim-faced men holding their rifles at the ready. Carlos put the Cherokee in park, stuck his head out the window, and waved. Still, the business ends of two guns remained pointed at them.

One of the guards, a stocky man with a military haircut and short, dark moustache, strode toward them. He motioned to Carlos with his rifle.

"Get out of the vehicle." The man's voice was gruff, but its youthful undertone undermined his authority. "Both of you."

"It is me, Carlos Rodríguez. I run security at *La Esmeralda.*"

"I do not care if you are Jesus Christ. Get out...and bring all your papers."

Victor's heart raced. He wiped his brow free of the cold sweat oozing from his pores. This was supposed to have been a simple visit, not an inquisition.

Carlos reached across him to retrieve a manila envelope from the glove compartment. "Just do as they say, Victor," he murmured.

Do as they say? Not, 'don't worry, I've got this under control?' Doesn't Carlos work here?

The guard stepped back to allow them room to get out of the Jeep. Meanwhile, his buddy came up behind Victor.

The muscles in his back stiffened. A loaded gun's business end urged him toward the gate station, as if he were a criminal headed into a jail cell. Behind them, the Cherokee's engine hummed the "lets-get-out-of-here" tune.

"Carlos, why didn't you tell me this mine thing was such a big deal? We can turn around and go back to Garcia. I've seen enough."

"Do not get your feathers ruffled. This is just a formality."

At the guard station, Carlos handed the first guard the manila envelope. "Everything is in order." Carlos tossed his badge on top of the table. "Victor. Give them an ID."

Digging into his pocket, he pulled out his driver's license and handed it over.

"Americano." Wrinkles formed on the guard's forehead.

"My brother. He wants to see where I work." Carlos shrugged. "Look, call Edwardo at *La Esmeralda*. He will vouch for me."

One of the guards moved to the side to speak into a two-way radio, while the other emptied the envelope and scanned Carlos's papers.

"Edwardo says he's good." The guard holstered his radio. "But your guest..."

Victor grabbed Carlos's arm and leaned in. "This is not working. Let's book out of here."

"I have permission from the office." Carlos pointed to one of the papers.

Horn-rimmed half-glasses perched on his nose, the guard rifled through the stack. "Ah. Yes. Here it is. You are both clear. Welcome to Chivor." The man had the audacity to grin at them.

Releasing a breath, Victor followed Carlos back to the Cherokee and slid in. "I thought you came here all the time. How come those guards gave us shit?"

"New guards," Carlos said. "My office did not notify them we would arrive today."

"But you showed them your badge."

"A badge must be verified. It is easy to duplicate."

"I see." So communication here wasn't good, which wasn't any wonder. High in the mountains getting a cellular signal would require lots of praying.

The rusted pair of gates opened, clearing entrance into the roads of the Chivor mines.

Victor ducked at a loud blast overhead, and then lifted his head in time to see a low-flying helicopter heading toward the mines.

"Looks like Gomez's." Carlos said with a shrug. "He does not like the drive."

"He's involved in the mines, then?"

"Owns *La Esmeralda.*"

"So, you work for him?"

"No, no." Carlos waved a hand in the air. "I work for the security company hired to guard his mine."

What about the cartel? Man, Gomez owns you.

They drove on until they reached a second chain-link fence, which was also flanked by armed guards. The sign bolted to the gate read, *"*LA ESMERALDA.*"*

Carlos rolled down his window and stuck out his head. "Hey, Wardo, it is me, Carlos."

A skinny man with a Mohawk haircut strolled over. *"Sí.* Got a call from some new guard at the gate. Are you not off duty?"

"Got an errand. I will only be here a couple of hours."

"Good enough."

The wrought iron gate creaked open, allowing them through.

"Well, that part was easy." The tenseness in Victor's chest eased. *Guards, guns, gates. What the hell is this place? Fort Knox?*

They drove into a clearing the size of a small airport. To one side, Victor spotted a helicopter; its blades spun in slow motion.

Carlos swerved to a remote section of the parking lot and jammed the front fender of the Cherokee into a row of man-high bushes.

When they exited the Jeep, intense heat and humidity descended on them like a wet cloud. Victor pulled his shirt away from his body to try to cool off, but it was a lost cause. "I thought summer in Miami was bad..."

"Tough up, big boy. Here. Put these on."

A pair of mud-splattered, slip-on boots landed in front of him, one toppling the other.

Plopping to the ground, Carlos kicked off his sneakers and pulled on his own set of boots. Unlike the rubber variety he tossed to Victor, Carlos's were leather with heavy-duty soles and a thick heel. The boots appeared brand new.

It took a few serious pushes, but Victor managed to get most of his feet into the boots. He ground the soles into the dirt to squeeze his heels down flat.

Scanning the clearing, he noticed Gomez Soto exit from the helicopter. Clad in his usual business suit and wearing boots, he inched down its pull-down steps. With a scowling expression, he shook off his chauffeur's helping hand and limped toward the cut in the brush. The black handle of a pistol stuck out from the back of the chauffeur's tan slacks. Gun toting seemed to be the norm here.

Neither man seemed to have noticed them. Carlos hadn't so much as waved.

"Gomez doesn't seem very happy," Victor said.

"He does not like it when things do not go his way. Let us get a move on." Carlos stamped his feet solidly into his boots. Grabbing the rifle from the back seat, he stuck it into the holder he'd buckled diagonally across his chest, locked the Jeep, and started toward the jungle at the edge of the clearing.

For protection. Knowing Carlos had a rifle at the ready, eased an iota of the tightness in Victor's jaw—but he hoped to hell they'd have no need to use it. Victor tramped after his baby brother along a trail cut through tangles of weeds and trees. Any minute he expected Tarzan might swing out at them, clinging to a vine. He looked up through the leaves at tiny triangles of blue sky.

Something wet plopped on his face, missing his eye. Victor wiped it away. "Ew. Bird shit." Well, didn't that put the icing on the cake? What he wouldn't give right now for a bar of soap, French-milled, and a steaming hot shower. He wiped his fingers as clean as he could with a large, shiny leaf he hoped wasn't poison ivy.

"Guano from birds means good luck," Carlos said.

"You've got to be kidding."

Carlos nudged him. "I am."

A clearing with groupings of shed-like wooden buildings lay ahead.

"Ah, civilization," Carlos said, as they marched into it. "The mine camp."

Camp? With a length of eight-foot high barbed wire separating the housing area from the woods beyond, it seemed more a prison. Crudely built one-room shacks with tin roofs formed a Congo line along the fence. A few of them had kettle-style grills out front, and some of the structures were open at one side.

As they trod through, crushed grey rocks and broken slats of wood cracked under their boots. A woman in a colorful dress hanging clothes on a line strung between sites, stood out in sharp relief against the pitiful grays and tans of the area. So far this was Slum Land Plus.

A couple of hundred feet ahead of them, two familiar figures headed into a building constructed of cinder blocks, in lieu of scrap wood.

"Isn't that Gomez and his driver?"

"Sanchez," Carlos finished. "A body guard." He put out his hand. "Stay back until they are inside."

After the men disappeared into the shack, Carlos kept his eyes on the door until they were well past. He pointed to a two-story rectangular building at the foot of the village. "That is the guard shack where I live when I am on duty."

"Live? As in sleep there, eat there? For twenty days?" Victor rubbed his palm against the grain of his jeans. *Itchy.*

"*Si.* It is hard to be away from my Rosario that long, but it is my job—and the pay is decent."

In minutes, they had passed the guard shack and resumed traveling into the heart of the jungle. The path narrowed further, forcing them to walk single file. Their boots splashed in ruts filled with water draining down the mountain.

"Carlos, what's the deal with all this water. It's not raining today."

"There is enough water on this mountain from its many streams to supply the city people in town. Gravity creates enough pressure to fill the reservoirs and direct it into canals, dug by miners, leading to the work area of the mine."

They moved on, coming across a group picking through sludge oozing from an opening near the mountain. A guard stood watch. "The work entrance," Carlos said, "for bringing heavy equipment in an out, plus it allows air to circulate between the two openings." He nodded toward the small congregation. "Those two men have just finished their shift. It is their turn to pick through the tailings fresh from the mine. In an hour or so, two more miners will have their turn."

"Those men can keep any stones they find, right?"

"Not really. The big bosses decide which ones the men can keep."

"Well that stinks. Hey, that man in the red shirt put something in his mouth. Is he hiding a stone?"

"Probably testing it against his teeth. It is common practice."

"You will begin your tour over here," Carlos said as they approached a large pit in the earth set against a sheer tower of stone. To the side, a group of men covered in muck sat on the rock-studded ground, smoking cigarettes and sharing sips from a filthy canteen.

A short, wiry guard with dark curly hair turned at their footfalls. "Thought you were off duty?"

Crap. Miguel from the bar.

"*Si*, Miguel. Victor wants a tour of our mine," Carlos said. He drew a slip of paper from his pocket. "I have guest permit."

Miguel's eyes narrowed, and Victor was certain the man was remembering their set-to at Barre de Luis. He snatched the paper from Carlos, and then moved to the side to speak into his two-way.

"I guess it is all right." He handed back the permit to Carlos, and then pointed the serious end of his rifle at the hole in the ground. "Go ahead."

Carlos waved his hands. "No, not me. I have seen the mine. I have an errand at the guard house. Would you take Victor down?"

"As you wish, *Jefe*." Miguel raised his hand in a military salute.

Carlos heads security. Miguel reports to him. Even so, the concept of "alone time" with Miguel in that hole didn't sit right.

Victor nudged Carlos and hissed into his ear. "How could you leave me with *him*?"

"You *will* take good care of my brother, Miguel."

"Of course." Miguel's small mouth formed a closed-lip smile. "The best."

Giving Miguel a meaningful look, Carlos headed back the way they had come.

Victor drew in a ragged breath. *Carlos and his fucking "business" trips.* He leaned over the rim of the hole and saw a vertical shaft fitted with a skinny ladder. Searing heat blasted him backward as hot air rushed to the surface. He scrambled for purchase.

"Whew. People actually go in there?"

"Not face first, *amigo*."

Amigo? Damn if the man wasn't smiling at him.

"How far down are the emeralds?" Victor brushed loose dirt from the seat of his jeans and ventured back to the rim of the shaft.

"About four hundred meters."

Four hundred? That's over one thousand feet!

Miguel set down his rifle and slipped a meta-banded light over his head. He tossed a similar headlamp to Victor. "Here, put this on."

With a metallic rattle, Miguel swung onto the first rung of the ladder and disappeared down the shaft.

"Well then." Working to swallow the bile in his throat, Victor grabbed hold of the top of the ladder, which protruded from the shaft, and stepped backward onto its rickety rungs. His feet grabbed hold a few yards above Miguel's head. The ladder was bolted to the side of the shaft, its treads wider than they first appeared. Gripping the sides, he continued stepping backward and down, feeling the muscles in his thighs pull taut. Sweat coated his body as the hot air whipped by him on the way to the surface. Acrid air closed around him, making every breath a chore.

A thump below him prompted Victor to flash his headlamp downward. *Thank God. Solid earth.*

Miguel tapped his foot, waiting while Victor navigated the remaining steps.

Relief washed over him as his foot struck ground. The area was furnace-hot with overhead spotlights breaking the blackness with their eerie yellow glow. He took a breath, feeling the caustic air burn the insides of his nostrils and travel down his throat.

"You will get used to the air in here, *gringo.*"

I doubt it. Walls of stone. Nothing here. No emeralds. No miners. What the hell am I doing in this God-forsaken place?

"This way," Miguel said, his voice amplified by the small chamber. He turned toward a tunnel cut into the mountain, expecting Victor to trail after him.

Victor nearly choked on the dust clogging his throat when he saw the man wore a holstered handgun, even though he had left his rifle up top. What was to stop Miguel from swiveling around and shooting him? Lord knows he couldn't trust the man.

"I...uh..." *Changed my mind. I don't want to go any further. I've seen all I need to see.* His hand went to the ladder. *I'm out of here.*

Miguel spun around to face him. "Aw. Can't handle a little dirt, Vickie?"

Victor ripped his hand from the ladder. His fists went to his hips. "Lead the fucking way, asshole."

With a satisfied grin, Miguel turned and continued forward into a tubular metal opening supported by cross beams. Ducking in after him, Victor's head knocked against one of two pipes traveling the length of the tunnel.

"Watch you do not damage that duct. It is how we get fresh air in and stale air out.

"Yes, a lifeline. I'll remember that. Whoa. This water's cold," Victor said as a fast-moving stream of water moved over his rubber-booted feet. "Refreshing though. I wish I could say the same for this sweating ceiling. Look at me. I'm soaked to the skin."

"Do you always talk so much?" Miguel turned to give him a disgusted look. Even though Miguel was in a similar state, the man showed no sign that he cared.

Only when I'm nervous. While the tunnel was narrow, a glow ahead told Victor they would soon enter the work area of the mine.

They stepped onto the dirt floor of a well-lit cavern. Victor's nose itched and all he could smell was tar. Sounds echoed off its stone walls, among them the drone of a generator pumping out electrical power and the whoosh of pumped in water. Clusters of miners covered in filth and wearing headlamps, like his, worked with intent at their stations.

One group chipped at a section of the walls with pickaxes and crowbars; pieces of coal-black rock fell from the wall in large chunks. Four miners set to the task of breaking up the fallen shale with their shovels, spreading it over a growing mound, and then dumping a few shovelfuls of water over the pile.

Like the tailings, only virgin pickings. Victor's fingers itched to dig out a handful of the wet shale, as he'd seen others do. He would uncover an emerald, maybe several of them. But he wouldn't put them in his mouth. That could wait until he was outside in the sunlight and the stones were rinsed clean.

He stepped forward, anxious to get going.

Miguel grabbed the back of his shirt and jerked him to the side just as a skinny man with a full, black beard whirled around and aimed the sharp edge of his shovel at Victor.

"Back!" Miguel's shout echoed through the chamber.

Victor stumbled to the ground, vaguely aware that Miguel had drawn his pistol. The other miners stopped working to glare at him, as did the man who tried to attack him.

"Foolish man. He might have killed you." Miguel extended his hand to help him stand. "Your brother should not have brought you here. Our miners do not take to strangers."

"No lie." Victor did his best to clear gummy muck from his bruised arm. By some miracle he hadn't cut himself on a jagged stone.

"They are more protective than usual. Last week, we had a thirty-thousand carat strike. Within hours, it was auctioned off and sold."

"But the emeralds, who buys them?" *Now this was getting interesting.*

"When our miners find a vein, hunks of the calcite the men chip off are sold in a lot as raw emeralds. They then go to a cutter who separates out the stones and prepares them for market."

Like Carlos's friend, the jeweler. Victor's mind spun. He would only want to deal in finished stones, not those buried in this muck.

"Miguel, *Gracias.* I'm ready to go up top."

With a nod, Miguel turned.

Victor followed him out of the cavern. Despite his earlier hesitancy, he was glad he had come. Hard labor went into extracting emeralds, the beauty to this beast of a mine.

At the base of the ladder, Miguel opened his hand. "After you, *amigo.*"

Grabbing the sides, Victor swung himself onto the ladder and scrambled toward the top. He poked his head from the shaft and inhaled. *Ah, fresh air.*

Miguel's footfalls sounded behind him.

No time to luxuriate. Gripping the rim of the shaft, he heaved his body onto the ground and landed on his knees. Pushing himself erect, he scanned the area for Carlos.

The point of something cold and metallic dug into the small of Victor's back.

"Do not move, *amigo*."

Chapter Twelve

Marisol threw down her soupspoon and leapt up, knocking over the kitchen chair. "Someone is trying to break down your door, Mama." She ran to the living room. *Maybe it was Soto, maybe...*

"Help. Open up. Help." A woman's voice cried out.

Rosario and Mama left their stew cooling on the table and stood behind her.

"One of the pickers is in trouble." Her fingers shook as she worked to undo the chain bolt on the front door.

The woman rambled now. "Please, my Jose..."

"Jose. Oh no." He was one of their best workers, conscientious and honest, a family man. Marisol ripped open the door.

Pilar fell into her arms. "Oh, señorita, my husband. He is hurt."

"Calm down, Pilar." Marisol patted the harried worker's back. "Where is he?"

Pilar drew back. Her dark hair had come loose from its bun and hung in strings on one side of her tawny face. She pointed to the field with an ugly snarl. "I think some bastard ran him down."

Marisol's knees went weak. *Just like Papa.* "Is he..." Behind her, Marisol heard Mama's breath catch. She shut her eyes. She did not want to ask. She did not want to know—

"He needs a doctor. There is a big gash in his head and he is bleeding... I am not sure what else...but he is in terrible pain. I did not want to leave him, but there was no one around." Her breath came in gasps. "I ran and got Pedro, and he sent me here."

"I will phone Doctor Ramirez right away." Rosario hurried to the desk and picked up the phone.

"I will take the van out there. The back field you said, Pilar?" Mama asked.

"Wait." Marisol shaded her eyes from the sun. "I see them. Pedro is bringing him here in one of our carts."

"Jose," Pilar screamed. She raced out the door and thumped down the steps, arms out.

"Thank God he is alive," Mama's voice was watery. "I will get our first aid kit."

Some bastard ran him down. Pilar's words replayed in Marisol's head. As Pedro neared, Marisol saw José splayed across the cart; his legs dangled over the side. He gripped his right arm. His face was bloody and his mouth clenched in agony.

She squeezed shut her eyes against the vision of her father being wheeled down the drive in the same way. From the field in a flower cart. He had been covered in blood, his chest smashed flat, eyes staring open with surprise. The horrendous grimace on his face reflected the pain he must have suffered before passing on to the next world. She had closed his lids over his eyes, kissed his cold cheek, and prayed God would have mercy on him.

"*El medico* is on his way," Rosario said. "Poor Jose."

"Bring him inside and lay him on the sofa," Mama directed.

Pedro set his arms underneath his brother's body to lift him. Jose let out a yelp.

"Sorry, my brother," Pedro said loudly enough for Jose to hear. "You cannot stay in the flower cart all day."

"*El medico* is coming, *querida*." Pilar walked beside Pedro holding her husband's hand.

Leaving a trail of bright red blood, Pedro muscled Jose up the stairs and set him gently on the upholstered sofa. Like his brother, Pedro was slim-built, but strong.

Pedro bent to Jose. "You are going to be okay, now. The señora, she see you get help." Righting himself, Pedro brushed a blood-spattered hand through his crop of black hair.

"Are you hurt? Anyone else?" Mama asked him.

"We are all okay, except for him." He indicated Jose.

"Did you see what happened, Pedro?" Marisol said. She knew she should not push, but she had to know.

Jose moaned and raised a hand as if he wanted to speak, but could not get out the words.

Pedro dropped his head, hiding his face. "I..." He looked up at Marisol, eyes glazed.

To save him embarrassment, Marisol said, "Why don't you use *el bano* and wash your hands and face, Pedro. You will feel better."

His face brightened. "Inside. Here?"

"Yes. Then we can talk."

"Here, Pilar." Mama rushed to Jose's side with a wet towel. "Hold this tight against that gash on his forehead to stop the bleeding."

"Your rug, your nice furniture..." Pilar's shoulders sagged." I am sorry. I will clean for you. Cold water and soap." She started to get up from her perch beside Jose.

Mama pushed her down. "Your husband needs you now. We will clean later."

"Can you talk, Jose? Who did this to you?" Marisol asked.

Jose moaned. His head dropped to the side, eyes closed.

Tears flowed from Pilar's eyes, dripping onto Jose's bloody forehead turning it a mottled pink. She shook her husband's good shoulder. "Do not *dare* to die on me."

Marisol rested a hand on the woman's back. "He is breathing. He must have passed out from the pain."

Taking a shaky breath, Pilar wiped her eyes, and sniffed back a sob.

Mama handed her a handful of tissues.

"Pilar, did you see the accident? Did he hit his head?"

Pilar shrugged. "I... No. I just heard a scream. I know it is my Jose. I run. And there he is, on the ground. Like this." She indicated Jose.

"You did not see anyone drive off? You do not know who might have done this?"

"Marisol, stop harassing the woman," Mama said. "Pilar, we can talk about this once Jose's injuries are under control."

Rosario ran to the window. "Doctor Ramirez just drove up...and here comes the *policia*."

Mama touched Pilar's shoulder. "Your husband will be in good hands, now."

"Yes, I know." Pilar put her hand on her stomach. "He deliver all our children."

Doctor Ramirez, a short, unassuming man with steel-rimmed glasses and a heart of gold entered carrying his worn, black medical bag. "May I have some privacy to examine my patient?" He adjusted his glasses on the bridge of his nose. "You can stay, Pilar. Jose would want you to."

The door was ajar. A uniformed officer strutted in as if he lived at Garcia Jardines. He flashed his badge. "Someone report a hit and run?"

"Yes, we did. The doctor is examining Jose. Can we talk outside, Officer? Come girls. You too," Mama said to Pedro, who had returned appearing to be in better control of his emotions.

Once outside, the officer took out a pad, licked the tip of a pencil, and prepared to take notes.

"Uh, Officer. Should we not go to the scene of the crime?" Marisol asked.

"That will be police business. First, I need a few details. Anyone witness the accident?"

Pedro stepped forward. "I was picking the left field and did not see anything, but I hear a loud noise...*Rrrrrrr.* Like that. Many of our people said a car was driving crazy-like through the back fields. They had to jump out of the way. Pilar came to get me when she found my brother."

"Let me get this straight." The officer held up his pencil as if ready to direct a show. "Everyone heard the vehicle and got out of the way, except your brother?"

Pedro pointed to his ear. "Jose does not hear well."

"Ah, I see. No one actually saw the incident, then. "The officer scribbled a note on his pad.

Doctor Ramirez came out with Pilar. "Jose's shoulder is bruised from the impact, and he sprained his wrist when he fell."

"His head?"

"Looks as if he smacked it on something jagged. Stitched that up. Pilar will keep an eye on him. He may have had a concussion. I will drop Pilar and Jose home on my way back to the office."

"*Mucho gracias*," Mama said. "Please send me your bill. Pedro will help you get Jose into the car."

The officer jotted down a few more notes. "Well, I guess that does it. No harm done. Your man is going to be okay." He closed his pad, stashed it in his back pocket, and turned to leave.

"Are you not going to *look* at the damage to our crops?" Marisol said, trying to keep her voice level. Local police were worthless. Mama should have called Berto instead. She wanted to take this man by the shoulders and shake him until his teeth feel out. He was one of *those* on Soto's payroll.

"Sure, I will check the area on my way out."

Mama pushed forward. "We had an accident in that field a year ago. My husband was killed."

Like this officer really cares, Marisol thought.

"Yes, Señor Garcia."

Everyone had known and respected Papa then, as they now respected Soto. The difference was, while Papa had been as corrupt as Soto, he had a kind heart. Soto's heart was black.

"Have you received permission to reopen the case?" Mama continued. "I think they may be related."

The officer shrugged. "I will check with headquarters." He tipped his hat. "Have a nice day, señora."

"Do you believe that?" Rosario said. "That man does not care about Jose...or Papa, for that matter. Why did he bother coming out here if he was not going to do anything?"

"Do you not know?" Marisol said "Soto tipped off one of his police cronies that the Garcias would call to report a hit and run. He made sure the *right* officer was sent to investigate."

Mama frowned. "It is my fault. If I had not angered Gomez, no one would have been hurt." She turned to Rosario. "Take the motor cart to the back field and send the pickers home for the rest of the day...with pay. Then come back for me."

Marisol heart filled with dread. "Wait, Rosario. I am coming with you."

Chapter Thirteen

"*Movimiento!*" Miguel dug the nose of his rifle into the small of Victor's back.

His ears roared with the *tick tick* of his heartbeat. One wrong move and Miguel's gun could go off, and he'd be dead—or worse, spend the rest of his life in a wheelchair selling flowers. Without moving his head, Victor looked to the right, and then to the left.

Where is Carlos? He hadn't returned to the pit. It crossed his mind that Carlos could have set him up. But what would his brother have to gain by doing so? Not when he had invited Victor to partner in his smuggling scheme. Carlos's evasive action toward Gomez Soto flashed through his mind. No, something was wrong. That his brother had not returned could mean he had met trouble as well.

A bearded, elderly man squatting nearby met Victor's gaze, and then turned away. *No help there.*

Easy now. He marched forward, prompted by the gun barrel, one foot in front of the other, until he stood before Gomez Soto.

Gomez crossed his arms over his skinny chest, creating a spray of folds in his pinstriped jacket. "So, Victor Novak, you finally got a chance to see my mine." His smile showed too many teeth to be legitimate. Read, "*what the hell are you doing here?*"

Victor focused on a trickle of sweat running down Gomez's neck into the collar of his dress shirt. Miguel stood to the left of Soto, now, his gun aimed at Victor's chest. Victor's mouth was cotton ball dry. *Think. Use your charisma. Talk yourself out of this.* He swallowed a few times to bring saliva into his mouth.

"*Sí*, Carlos arranged it for me. Quite a place." Victor worked to stop his lips from trembling. Taking a deep breath, he managed a smile and glanced around for a sign of his brother—anything: two boot tips sticking out from under a bush, a familiar cough.

"What is your game?" Soto squared his shoulders, making him appear taller, more formidable.

"Wh-what do you mean? I'm only visiting *mi hermano.*"

"Do not lie to me, Victor. You asked too many questions about my mine to play innocent. You and your brother are up to something. Take him, Miguel. Beat the hell out of him until he talks, and then call me on the two-way. I have other business to tend to."

In a flash, Miguel had Victor in an arm lock.

Victor struggled to twist away, but Miguel shoved his arm up higher, increasing the pain.

"Do not try it, *amigo.*" Miguel pushed upward on Victor's wrist to propel him forward.

He didn't know where Miguel was taking him, but he was damn sure he wasn't going to enjoy it.

"I'll do as you say. Just let go of my arm, Miguel. You're killing me."

"Always knew you were a pansy, Vickie." He dropped his grip. "Maybe you like this better."

Miguel's gun dug into Victor's back. His shoulders ached from the rough treatment but at least his hands were free. He scanned the wooded area they tromped through for some way to get free of Miguel without being shot. He lifted his arm, testing.

"Behave yourself. It will be more fun to beat you than to shoot you. Get over by that tree."

Miguel shoved Victor with vengeance.

He stumbled into the trunk of a nasty-looking tree, shoulder first. Pain shot through his arm. *No time to baby it.* Stretching his sore arm, he grabbed for the nearest branch. With a tug, he pulled it to him, and then ducked before letting it go.

Miguel let out a yelp. "You bastard. You got me in the face with that. I will..."

Twisting to the left, Victor slammed his good shoulder into Miguel. The thud of a solid connection sent an "oh shit" to his brain. *The fucking gun.* He dodged to the right.

A bullet whizzed under his extended arm and slammed into the bark. A hand grabbed at his leg. *Going down.* He rolled on his back, ready to—

Miguel hovered over him, reeking of the sweat that formed dark circles under his armpits and dripped from his dark curly hair onto Victor's face. A pair of handcuffs clipped to his belt gleamed silver. He pressed the hot nose of the pistol against Victor's chest. He didn't speak. Didn't have to.

"You can't shoot me. I have information your boss wants. Let me up. I'll talk."

Miguel's lips split in a smile wide enough to show his missing eyetooth. He motioned with his pistol.

Victor made a show of struggling to stand up. He raised his hands and let out a groan. "Smacked my arm. Hurts like a son of a bitch. Man, that branch did a number on your face."

Miguel's eyes narrowed, as if he just remembered the incident. His hand went to his cheek. "You..." He stared at the blood on his hand in surprise. His gun hand relaxed, finger off the trigger.

"Hey, sorry. Just defending myself. In my pants pocket I have a handkerchief you can use to clean up." He eased down his hand. With a low, quick twist of his shoulder, he threw his weight against Miguel's upper arm.

Miguel's feet scrambled for purchase.

Victor grabbed for the gun. Pointing its nose harmlessly away, he wrenched it from Miguel's grip and, at the same time, shot his knee into Miguel's groin.

Miguel fell backward and hit the ground solid. In an instant, the thug was on his knees.

Just like in the movies, Victor's man was down. He stepped back, gun held on Miguel. "My turn." The gun weighed heavy in his hand, cold and lethal. His finger grappled for the trigger. He'd never held a gun, much less shot one. It shouldn't be hard to figure out.

Miguel's eyes went wide, and then his mouth relaxed into a cocky smile. "You will not shoot. You are afraid of that gun."

"Try me."

"Okay, *amigo*." Miguel raised his hands. "Do not get crazy on me..."

"Make you a deal. Toss me those handcuffs dangling from your belt and I will let you live."

He was Dirty Harry and took no bull. He could do this tough guy act even better than Miguel if he had to. "One hand...and do it slow. No heroics." Then he added, "Make my day."

He heard Miguel's breath catch, and then a clinking sound. Whipping the cuffs free, he flung them.

Metal hit bone on Victor's cheek, just missing his eye. His head jerked back from the hot pain, but he kept his aim steady. He glanced down. Cuffs in the brush alongside him. Keeping his eyes on Miguel, he leaned to the left and scooped them up.

"I need a doctor." Miguel held his upper arm. "You could have killed me. His gaze zeroed in on a spot of blood on his shirt. Look. I am bleeding."

"Stop whining. Now put your arms around that tree trunk."

Miguel sniveled, but wrapped his arms around the sturdy tree in a lover's hug. He laid his cheek against the side and clasped his hands as if praying. "Do not shoot me." His face was oily with sweat and his breath came in short gasps. The red spot on his shirt widened.

Victor almost felt sorry for him. He hefted the cuffs, in his left hand. Pretty simple. Snaps on. The key was probably in Miguel's pocket, but he would leave it be. Moving to the backside of the trunk and keeping the nose of the gun aimed at Miguel's forehead, he performed a one-handed clip on each wrist. The short chain linking the cuffs gave Miguel a little wiggle room, but he wouldn't be going anywhere for a while.

Stepping back, he surveyed his work and then shoved the pistol into his belt.

"My arm. Look it is still bleeding. I am in pain. I am going to die making love to a tree."

Victor let out an exasperated sigh. Miguel was over reacting, yet he didn't want the man's death on his conscience. Reaching into his back pocket, he pulled out the handkerchief he kept on him to mop female tears and shook out its folds. He took two distant ends, spun them in a straight line, eased the make-shift tourniquet end under Miguel's arm, and tied a tight knot.

"There. You'll be fine until your boss comes to find you."

"You will regret this," Miguel spat out as Victor turned to leave.

Without responding, Victor followed the path Miguel had used, stopping beyond the mine area. Soto would be by the pit waiting for whatever information Miguel was supposed to beat out of him. When his man didn't show, Soto would send someone looking and learn Victor had escaped. The guards and supervisors at *La Esmeralda* were all on Soto's payroll.

Victor's blood ran cold. Even if he found Carlos and they made it to the Jeep, what were their chances of passing through any of the gates without being recaptured? This time, Soto wouldn't bother questioning Victor. He pushed down the fear that clutched at his gut. Now was not the time to think about that. He patted the gun. He had protection. His body vibrated with a sense of urgency, Carlos is in trouble.

As he crept along, he scanned the brush. His brother could be anywhere. He didn't dare call out. Staying hidden, he kept a sharp eye for a flash of movement, a scrap of Carlos's grey T-shirt. Victor angled through thorny brush toward the muddy path leading to the parking lot.

Carlos had gone off to conduct business. It must be something to do with the smuggling plan. His best guess: Carlos got accosted by Sanchez, as Victor had by Miguel. They would beat Carlos until he talked. Sanchez was larger and more powerful than Miguel. He doubted Carlos was strong enough to overcome him.

Of the two of them, Carlos was the primary connection to the cartel—the one he'd spoken of splitting from. Who else knew of his brother's scheme?

Duh. The jeweler. Angel could have leaked Carlos's plan to defect in exchange for a larger slice of cartel profits. The emerald business was trouble—more than just the stones. The kind of people who surrounded them were defensive, protective of their wealth—and deadly. He was lucky to be alive, and he hoped the hell Carlos was, too.

Through the brush, he spotted the miner camp. He ducked at the sound of voices coming from the nearby road. Parting the brush, he glimpsed two familiar figures, one hulking, the other puny and limping. He wished he were close enough to see if Sanchez knuckles were bloody, or his neat chinos mussed with grass stains. Surely Carlos would have not have gone down without a fight.

He stayed hidden until Soto and Sanchez disappeared into the town. They must not have found Miguel yet. If Soto was displeased with the man they might have left him bleeding and handcuffed to the tree.

A faint sound came from the snarls of brush to his right. His heartbeat thudded. *It's him. Got to be.* Thick woods separated him from the source of the noise. He searched for a path. Nothing but matted bushes. Victor plowed through a clump of taller foliage. Branches dragged across his bare arms. He scanned the area for a sign of life—a rustle, a fleshy something. One spot caught his eye. A hand wearing a large gold ring stuck out from a thick hedge.

"Carlos! I see you." Victor tore through to reach him.

The sight of his brother gave the phrase "babe in the woods" new meaning. With his butt wedged deep into a thicket, the man was stark naked. Bloody scratches covered what Victor could see of Carlos's body—the man was hairy. His jeans and T-shirt lay in a heap on the bushy thicket.

"Help me out of here." Carlos words came out in a slur. His jaw was swollen and tomorrow he would have one hell of a shiner.

Grabbing Carlos's hand, Victor yanked him out of the bush.

"Yeow. *Dios Mio!* You killed me." Carlos's feet landed on the ground, and then he fell back and doubled over. Pain creased his face.

"Sorry. Soto and Sanchez just went by, headed to the camp I think."

"Good. They should be going to his copter." He sat up and pressed an arm into his ribs. "Sanchez kicked me good. Hurts when I breathe."

"You're bruising up already."

"You do not look so good either," Carlos said. "What is the matter with your arm?"

"Soto was waiting when I came up from the mine. I had a go-round with Miguel."

Carlos eyebrows went up.

"Left him cuffed to a tree. Got his gun right here." He patted the hilt sticking from his belt.

"Good, because they took my rifle. We will need gun power to get out of here."

"You're going to need a doctor. Your ribs are probably cracked. Sanchez may have busted a spleen or something."

"No doctor." Carlos pointed to his clothes.

Victor tossed his brother the jeans and shirt, releasing flakes of mud.

Carlos peered around, a look of panic on his face. "My boots. I must have them. That way. See if they left them."

Following Carlos's pointed finger, Victor pushed through the bushes to a small, grassy clearing. The boots were sprawled like small brown animals, about ten feet apart.

He returned to find Carlos struggling into his pants, groaning. "Guess they didn't expect you'd be walking anywhere soon." Victor held up the boots, realizing the pain in his shoulder had dulled.

A wave of relief crossed Carlos's face.

He set the pair of boots next to Carlos. "Can you get into these okay?"

"I will manage."

Carlos stood a minute, getting his bearings.

"You're dizzy? Take a minute."

"We go."

With Victor's arm around his brother's waist, they carved a path through the tangles of brush that ran parallel to the main road. A few sooty miners passed, but Victor saw no sign of Miguel. He was damn glad he'd found Carlos alive.

Half an hour later, they reached the parking lot. Soto's helicopter was gone, but the Cherokee was still embedded in the hedge, but sitting low to the ground. Holding his sore ribs, Carlos limped over to check. His movements were slow, and he walked half bent over.

"*Los cerdos* slashed our tires."

"Now what?" His heart thumped in fast-time. Crap. Carlos held up a hand. "I will handle this." He reached inside his glove compartment to retrieve his two-way radio and flipped it on. "Wardo. Need your help."

Victor waved a hand in his face. "No. He'll tell Soto, and then..."

"Not to worry. Wardo is a trusted friend."

"Humph. I've heard that before. One of your so-called *amigos* must've leaked your plan to Soto. Why else would he have set Sanchez and Miguel on us?"

Carlos's shoulders dropped. "What would you have me do? We have to get out of here by dark and we are in no condition to make it home on foot."

Victor blew out a breath. "So..."

"We wait."

Ten minutes later, Carlos's guard-buddy, Edwardo, stooped by the Cherokee and shook his head. "I do not know how you are going get this car out of here without tires. These are *ruina*."

"I have to get home," Carlos said, holding his side. His words came in short, garbled breaths and his chin had swelled like an apple.

"Who got you? A band of *quaqueros*?" Edwardo took off his cap and rubbed his hand over his bristly crew cut hair. "Where is your rifle?"

"*Los hombres* who attacked me took it."

Victor understood why Carlos didn't mention Soto. Edwardo might not be so helpful if he learned the owner had all but kicked him and Carlos out of *La Esmeralda*.

"Did you report the men?"

"Not yet, Wardo. Know anybody who can tow us out of here now?"

"Let me think." He snapped his fingers. "I will call my friend in Boyacá. He runs an auto repair shop. He fix you up good."

"*Gracias, mio amigo,*" Carlos mumbled through a poorly working jaw.

Victor watched Edwardo walk toward the gate, hunched over his two-way radio. "Are you sure we can trust that guy, Carlos?"

Edwardo's call to his friend, assuming it was the only call he made, turned out to be legit. By three o'clock, Tomos's Auto had replaced the Cherokee's all-terrain tires with a set of bald, but functional ones. Carlos, who had downed a few aspirin, lay across the back seat. Oddly, the repairman never asked what happened—but, Victor supposed, Edwardo might've told him something.

"Carlos." Victor poked at his shoulder. "Tomos is finished changing out the tires."

Carlos struggled to a sitting position and touched his jaw.

"Feeling any better?" Carlos's face didn't look any better, but he hadn't moaned as loudly.

"It helps when I do not have to move."

Tomos poked his head into the car window. "I can repair these for you in a day or so." He indicated the damaged tires he stowed in the back of his van, and then swiped at his forehead with a grease-streaked arm.

"*Si, Gracias*, Tomos," Carlos said. "Not sure how soon I will be up this way. I am on leave. You will mail me the bill?"

"No." Tomos motioned away Carlos's offer. "It will hold until you come back through Boyacá. I trust you are good for the money."

Trust, that word again. Did it actually mean anything here in Colombia?

Once Tomos hopped in his van and was permitted through the hallowed gates of *La Esmeralda*, Carlos shoved open the rear door and stood on shaky legs. With keen eyes, he scanned the lot.

"Just us," Victor said.

Carlos nodded, and spoke into his radio. "Edwardo, fix it so the guards at the Chivor entrance let us pass without a pat down."

Victor eyed Carlos. "What if Soto got to them first? Are they going to listen to your friend?"

"Soto controls only *La Esmeralda*. Once we are clear of the gates, we will be fine."

"I hope you're right. I've had enough drama for one day. Want me to drive?"

Carlos's back straightened, and Victor saw his brother summoning his strength, his authority. "If I have a problem, you takeover, eh?"

"Of course." Shift car, no problem—anymore.

Carlos eased behind the wheel and stuck the key in the ignition.

"Wait, "Victor shouted, pressing on Carlos's hand. "What if they planted a bomb or something?"

"You watch too many police shows, *mi hermano*. Soto does not know anything. He only suspects. If he knew, we would be dead already."

Carlos fired up the engine, backed out of the space, and honked for Edwardo to open the gate. *"Gracias, amigo,"* Carlos said. "I owe you."

Edwardo winked.

Once they were clear of *La Esmeralda*, Victor exhaled. *Close one.* "I gather our emerald scheme is kaput now."

Carlos shot him a look. "Are you backing out on me?"

"Oh no, of course not. I would never do that." *Oh my God, he's going through with it—and by helping him, I could be dead.*

Victor grabbed for the hand strap as Carlos's foot stomped on the gas pedal. They shot forward, careening over the bumps, pits, and loose stones. The tires weren't good and skidded in the muddy streams.

"Hey, slow down, we're jumping around on these seats like jelly beans. Don't tell me you aren't in pain."

"I need to get away from the mines. I need to get home." Carlos focused on the road ahead, his lips pressed in a straight line.

"Yes, you need to see a doctor, or at least get some ice on that jaw."

"Si, but, more important, we need to get moving on our plan. The longer we wait, the more likely Soto will hear something...and then we are in real trouble."

We. Meaning him and Victor.

"Now that I have the gems, we need to get them out of Colombia as soon as possible. Tomorrow."

The emeralds were in hand. A tremor of excitement vibrated through Victor's body. His fingers touched his earrings—cold, hard, and beautiful. *Like these, only larger, more valuable.* His dreams were about to come true. He was going to be rich. He could tell those picky clients who dissed him to go to hell. He would show them he was better than they were. He would own more real estate, buy ten jaguars, and maybe even a yacht. *Coral Gables, here I come.*

"Where are the emeralds now?"

Carlos smiled. "Once we get to the plantation, I will show them to you. You will need to be in Miami when they arrive."

Sooner than he expected. He had hoped to spend another day or so with Marisol and Joseph. He'd been away from the plantation carousing with Carlos for two days and, already, he missed them. *Stop being foolish. You can always come back for a visit—if she will have you. She.* Marisol. So proper—and honest. Would she even want to see him once she learned of the scheme with Carlos—or found out about his past?

"Of course," he replied. A frisson of dread grabbed at Victor's gut. He had confirmed his commitment to Carlos. Carlos might be running the show here in Colombia, but the control would be in Victor's hands once he arrived in Miami and got hold of those valuable emeralds. *He*, not Carlos, would take them to market.

"I trust you, *mi hermano*, to be honest about the transaction amounts," Carlos said. "To be safe, the gems will be assessed and prepared for market here in Colombia to insure the profit you gain is in sync with their true value."

He's thought this out. Perhaps he's even hired a snoop to check on me. I should have known the trust Carlos professes is superficial. But wasn't I just thinking about cheating Carlos? Victor stared at the seams in his jeans. What kind of brother was he to think about pulling a fast one on the only family he had? He was slime, a scumbag. A pretentious fool.

"You okay with that, Victor?"

Victor looked up. "Oh, sorry. I was thinking. So far, I count three people involved: you, me and this other person, the assessor."

"He is also a stone cutter."

"Angel?"

"Yes. To keep his mouth shut about preparing the stones on the sly for us, I had to cut him in on our deal."

"Are you certain he didn't tip off Soto about your plan?"

"Only threat of death would make Angel do such a thing. He is solid."

"I read you, but there's got to be one more person, unless *you're* handling the shipping."

"Victor, stop worrying. I know how these things work. It is unfortunate you met Angel. The less you know about who is involved the better, especially if we are caught."

If we are caught. Victor gagged on the lump that formed in his throat. United States customs officers were less apt to look the other way that those in Colombia. Once the gems were in Miami, customs could arrest him at the airport or tail him as he left.

"If you want out, Victor, just say so. I can find someone else to handle the Miami end."

Someone with more guts, Victor thought. If he quit now, he'd be back in Miami hustling wealthy chicks while that "someone else" raked in profits that should have been his.

Victor gave Carlos his killer smile. "I'm *in*, buddy. All the way to the bank."

Chapter Fourteen

"Almost there," Carlos said. "Rosario will be angry I have been gone so long without calling."

"And she will worry that you are hurt." Victor's mind flashed to his mother. With her gone, there was no one to care if *he* was hurt, emotionally or physically. Carlos was a lucky man.

As they approached the savanna, the scent of the flowers he had come to love wafted in through the window. He was going to miss being here, except for dealing with the nastiness of the cartel.

As they passed Soto Flores, Victor wished he could slink lower in his seat without having Carlos notice. At the far end of Soto's gated drive, he noticed the top of a large white building—a house, maybe. "Does Soto live on his plantation?"

"Soto would not stoop so low. No, he has a huge estate in northern Bogotá...a little too fancy for me. Lives with his daughter and two spoiled dogs."

Of course, he would. Soto had money and power. Victor would bet Soto could live any damn place he wanted to.

Elation hammered at his heart. Once he got his emerald business going, he would be as rich as Gomez Soto and command the same kind of respect. He could buy a red jaguar—the latest model, of course, and splurge on clothes—whatever took his fancy. The image of the whore who had approached Carlos and him flashed through his mind. Why, he could be a humanitarian and help such people. Give them a fresh start, a new life. Open up a safe house, even. Victor's dreams of wealth flew from his mind the moment they turned into Garcia Jardines. *Something is wrong.* He could feel it. No, smell it. Freshly turned soil mingled with the flowery aroma.

"Carlos." He pointed out the window. "The chain linked fence is down over there and..." He craned his neck to see. "The lilies look mowed down."

Carlos glanced over. "*Si.* You are correct. The señora put up that fence after her husband died to keep the gardens safe from intruders."

"We've got to check this out. Stop the car."

With a bored sigh, Carlos pulled over. He tapped his fingers on the steering wheel. "I will wait here."

"Sorry. Forgot you were hurting. Go on down and see to your wounds. Meet you later."

Victor threw open the Jeep's door and stepped out. Shading his eyes against the lowering sun, he inspected the fence. Something wide and powerful had plowed through it and continued on through the beds. He climbed over the bent wire and started down the path of destruction. Stakes supporting strings that separated one variety of lily from another tipped every which way. Lovely lilies that should be standing straight and tall to seek the sun lay like corpses on the ground. The vehicle's pattern was erratic, catching some groupings and sparing others.

Victor knelt to run his hand over the smashed ridge made by the fallen stalks. Tire treads. Not a plow. A tractor would have a double set. Curvy S-shaped tracks—maybe a car. He did a three-sixty turn and squinted at the moving figures. It was past six. From what he knew, the Garcia's workers should have gone home for the day.

None of my business. I'm leaving. Why do I care? The smart move would've been to ignore the damage and continue down to the main house with Carlos. They had business to discuss about tomorrow.

Damn if that doesn't look like Marisol—the long hair, the yellow bandana—and Rosario, the señora, and Joseph?

Victor picked his way through the aisles of plantings, heading toward the distant figures. How long had they been out doing damage control? He wasn't sure what had to be done to rescue plants from such devastation, but he was going to find out. He broke into a run, following the tire treads.

Once he had a clear view of the Garcia family, he stopped for a break. Bending over, he took some deep breaths. Next week. Back to the gym. He bit at his lower lip. Next week he would be in Miami hawking emeralds. Even if he had a gym to go to, he doubted he'd have the time. Besides, what did it matter if he were buff and appealing? After tomorrow, the only beautiful things he needed to impress were hard and green. He doubted the emeralds would care if he painted himself purple.

Marisol's hand shot up. "Over here."

He sucked in a breath at the sound of her voice. Musical, sweet. Her long dark hair glowed chestnut in the dipping sun. After tomorrow, she wouldn't ever want to see him again. Joseph was standing next to her, smiling. He'd miss the kid, too.

* * * *

"A man is running towards us, Marisol," Rosario said. "It looks like..."

"It is...*Tio* Victor." Joseph took off like a streak down the stalk-beaten path.

"Be careful, the flowers," Marisol shouted after him, shaking her head. Joseph was far too attached to Victor, which was not good. He would be disappointed when Victor left—and so would she. If not for Victor, Joseph would still be trailing after Carlos and rebelling against her.

"But where is my husband? I do not see him with Victor." Rosario shot Marisol a look.

Carlos. How could she worry about him when their finest lilies had been mowed down? "Carlos is Carlos. He will show up when he is good and ready. Right now, we need to gather as many stalks as we can. Soon, it will be too dark to see. It is supposed to rain again tomorrow."

Rosario turned on her, eyes flashing fire. "You and your flowers. That is all you think about."

"Stop it, girls. Marisol is right. We do not have time to bicker. Rosario, Carlos will be along. You will see."

"I am sorry," Marisol said. "It is so frustrating. Every time we make progress on that order, we get slammed."

"What's going on here?" Victor came to a stop and leaned over, catching his breath. His face was smudged with dirt, shadows underlined his dark eyes and his clothing appeared to have been dragged through mud.

"What happened to you?" Marisol asked. Joseph's arm was around Victor's waist.

"We...met with some trouble at the mines."

Mama frowned. "You are holding that shoulder funny."

"I had a date with a tree."

Rosario's hands went to her face, smudging dirt on her cheeks. All of them were tired and grimy. "Oh no. My Carlos."

"He took a few jabs to the ribs and his jaw's puffy." Victor nodded toward the driveway. "I sent him to the house."

"Take the golf cart, Rosario," Mama commanded. "Joseph, go with her, unload it, and bring it back here. Wait. Victor needs to go, too, his shoulder..."

"I'm fine. See?" Victor lifted his arm part way. Nothing's broken. Just a little stiff."

Joseph, who loved the chance to drive, even if it was only a golf cart, jumped in. "Come on, *Tia* Rosario."

Marisol looked after Joseph, and then turned at the feel of Victor's warm hand on her aching shoulder. She wanted to lay her cheek against his knuckles, feel the roughness of his skin against hers.

"You never answered me," he said. "Your fields are trampled. Who did this?"

Allowing Victor's hand to drop away, she stepped up to face him. She longed to lean against him and let him shoulder all her troubles. She did not need to ask who attacked him and Carlos—she already knew. Soto ruled the mines, as he ruled everything else in their small area of the country. She was not sure what Carlos and Victor had done, it did not take much to incur Soto's wrath. Marisol gazed at Victor, any trace of the cocky arrogant man he had seemed were gone, he looked beaten, tired. It was a wonder he cared enough to ask what had happened.

"It was him." Her words came out in a whisper.

Victor's head tilted to the side; his shoulders went up in a small shrug. "Why?"

"He wants our business and we told him we were not selling." The injustice of the deed angered Marisol all over again. Her shoulders straightened. "We will replant. He is not going to win."

"But..." Victor's arm spanned the damage surrounding them. "How?"

"We are collecting the fallen stalks to cull for new bulbs." Mama's chin was raised, determination plain in every line of her body. Her expression dared anyone or anything to stop her.

Marisol swallowed hard. Mama expected new flowers would bloom in days, when it would take weeks of tedious work to sort through all the stalks they gathered for surviving bits of life that might be coaxed to spawn new plants. The beds would need to be raked to loosen the matted soil and coax the existing bulbs into rejuvenating. Recouping today's loses would take time—time they did not have—and work. Then, once the damaged half-acre was restored and the fence rebuilt, what would stop Soto from crashing through whenever he was in the mood?

"I can't undo what's been done," Victor said, "but I have two hands and two feet. Let me help."

Mama lifted her eyebrows at Marisol, as if to say, "see, he is a good man, a good catch."

Marisol looked away, enough of Mama's meddling. The less Mama knew about her growing feelings for Victor, the better. She could not deny she had a soft spot in her heart. But she must remember he was leaving Garcia Jardines. If he came back, he would visit his brother, not her, not Joseph. But now, the fact that he chose to be with her, willing to work, when he might have gone to nurse his sore shoulder warmed her heart.

The three of them worked side by side, bending over to snap off the wilted blooms low on their stalks and tossing them into the garden carts they had brought up to the fields.

As she knelt, Marisol felt her father guiding her hand and heard him speaking in the soft voice he used for her. "Feel the length of the stem for small nodes and pinch them to be sure they are vital. Like this." Marisol's back ached and her thumb and forefinger blistered from the repetitive motion, yet she realized she and Mama had never been in such harmony. Papa taught her to love the soil, and Mama had resented him for it. Had Papa been alive, Soto would not have dared come near their plantation.

With a clatter and clunk, Joseph returned towing a flatbed on which he had loaded four wheelbarrows. "Thought we would need these." After parking the cart, he let down the ramp on the flatbed.

"I'll give you a hand with that," Victor said, walking over to help Joseph unload the wheelbarrows.

"How is Carlos?" Mama rose and pressed her hand in the small of her back.

"He seems okay," Joseph said. "Aunt Rosario is clucking over him."

"He is...very fortunate." Mama's cheeks were sunburned, even though Rosario had made her wear a sun hat, and her perfectly coifed hair was in tangles. Her eyes clouded over.

The sun was down and the blue of the sky had faded to dusky grey. Using the flatbed, Victor and Joseph shuttled flower-laden carts to the greenhouse, returning with empty ones to fill. On the last trip, Mama and Joseph went along to clean up. Mama needed to start dinner, and Joseph had homework. Marisol sized up their accomplishment. They had not cleared the entire acreage, but it would suffice until the workers arrived in the morning.

Now Victor returned alone. His cropped hair hung in damp strings around a face streaked with dirt. Yet his strong legs and arms had done the hauling three women and a boy had not been fit enough to handle.

"Last load." He wiped his brow with the back of his arm. "Ready to go, princess?"

Princess? Hardly. Her heart swelled. This man, this wonderful man, after being attacked by *gaguerros*, tramped through the mountain and helped his beat-up brother get home. He had put aside his own pain to help them deal with theirs.

Emotion overflowed her heart. She moved to stand by Victor, her lips curved in a smile. "If you had not stopped to help us, we would have never accomplished so much. *Gracias.*"

Cupping his face in her hands, her fingers aware his days old beard was gritty with road dirt. The shine of the emerald studs he always wore had dulled. She bent toward him, touching her lips to his. Warm, tender. She had forgotten the feel of a man's lips.

His mouth moved under hers...

Dios. What was she doing? She jerked away. "I am sorry, Victor. I did not mean..."

His hand went to his mouth, which spread into a slow smile. He dipped his head toward her—

She took a few steps back, hand out front. "I...uh... have to check on Joseph. See you at dinner." Turning, she raced out of the field and started down the drive.

What was I thinking? She had pushed herself on Victor and, now he thought she was an easy woman. *Fool. Have I not learned the hard way I cannot do everything my body demands of me? There are consequences.*

Behind her, the chug of the golf cart with the flat bed rattling with its last load of stalks bore down on her.

Victor shouted, "Wait, Marisol. Don't do this. I liked that you kissed me."

She slowed and turned her head enough to call back. "Do not get any big ideas. It was only a thank-you."

"Marisol, for God's sake. Will you stop running away?"

She should ignore him and keep going, but her strength was waning and she was not sure she could make the quarter-mile down the driveway without falling flat on her face. Marisol stopped, arms crossed over her chest, and waited for Victor to drive up to her.

Victor braked and stepped out of the cart. "Thank you." In seconds, he was in front of her. "Now, where was I?" He tipped up her chin.

She stood perfectly still, her heart banging inside her chest. He was going to kiss her. And she was going to let him.

Victor's lips met hers, not with aggression, but gentleness—as if she were as fragile as a one of Mama's teacups.

Her arm went around his neck, pulling him closer, wanting more. His kiss sent frissons of energy to every nerve ending in her body.

His lips were hungry. Now he deepened the kiss. Parting her lips, his tongue sought entry.

Enough. Her eyes flashed open. She stepped away, lips parted.

"Sorry. I got carried away." Hands resting on her shoulders, his eyes softened. "I've wanted to do that from the moment we met." His voice was a hoarse whisper.

His finger stroked the curve of her cheek. He was going to kiss her again. This time, she was not sure she could stop the urges that swelled within her.

"You are leaving soon. Why would you care about us?"

He shook his head. "Beats me. Look, we've both been working our asses off for hours. How about we clean up and I buy you a quiet supper in Garcia. Just the two of us."

Marisol wanted to say yes. To be with a man she cared about, even for one evening. "But Joseph..."

Victor put a finger to her lips. "You have been using Joseph as an excuse for too long. Joseph will be fine. Come on, Marisol. We've both had a rough day. An hour or two of R and R will do us both good."

She narrowed her eyes at him. He was too good to be true. "Why are you being so nice? What do you want?"

"I don't know. I feel differently than I did when I first arrived. More complete. As if I *belong*. I know I have no business even thinking that, yet I can't help it. Coming here reminds me of the good times in growing up."

"In the gardens of the estate?"

"Yes, but unlike Mrs. Gallagher's, yours have heart and soul."

An hour or two. What could it hurt? She took his hand. "Yes, I will go with you to Garcia."

Victor's hand went up in front of him. "One favor, please. Don't dress fancy. I like you just the way you are."

A feeling of happiness bubbled up into a smile. She slid alongside Victor in the cart. As they clattered down the drive, her hip almost touching his, she had the strangest sensation that they were meant to be together.

* * * *

Now I've done it! I've become involved. He'd always been able to control his words, carefully thought them out to obtain the desired results. It wasn't fair to encourage Marisol any further. He had done enough damage by kissing her. If he were to exit this situation without causing either of them pain, he'd need to stay in control of his feelings. But here, with Marisol, words bypassed his active mind and spilled out of his mouth.

Victor touched his lips, still burning from the feel of her. He glanced at her, riding next to him, and his heart did one of those corny pittie-pats that only occur in romance novels. Okay, he had feelings for this woman, but it wasn't love. It was compassion. Yes, *compassion.* He...felt sorry for her. No, that wasn't quite right either. With her, his body cheered and tingled all over, as if he were a teenage boy again. No blue pills, no mind games, just pure desire.

Victor, you fool. You will get in tight with the emerald exchange and forget all about this woman.

No, not a mere woman. Marisol was life itself. While he'd only known her these few days, she had changed him, made him a better man—one more considerate of others. Through her eyes he saw hope. What did it matter if he had wealth? Without her he would revert to the empty shell of a man he had been.

As he and Marisol drove up to the main house, they passed Joseph, who was running circles in the driveway bouncing the soccer ball he brought back from Bogotá. The boy's hair was wet—from his much-needed shower, Victor guessed. Victor didn't think he'd ever gone two days without a wash. Yet being grimy and smelly hadn't stopped Marisol from kissing him, or from allowing him to kiss her back. He parked alongside the greenhouse, and then he and Marisol hopped out of the cart.

"Look what *Tio* Carlos gave me." Joseph balanced the ball in the palm of his hand. "An authentic soccer ball."

"Carlos didn't buy him that ball," Victor murmured to Marisol. He wasn't sure why he had to make that clear, but it didn't seem right to allow Carlos to take credit for the huge smile on Joseph's face.

Marisol leaned in to him. "I figured as much. That was very thoughtful of you, Victor." She took his hand in hers and squeezed it.

"Catch," Joseph shouted.

The ball came at him. Victor raised his good arm and snagged it, dribbled it, and kicked it to Joseph. He hadn't played soccer in years, but he'd been good at it. He could teach this kid a few defensive moves—if he were going to be around.

"I will tell Mama we will not be here for dinner before I get cleaned up, Victor." Marisol's dark eyes were dreamy, and so was the smile on her luscious lips. She reached back to take off her bandana, and her hair, that glorious chestnut mane, tumbled forward to frame her face.

His mouth went dry. "Don't...uh...take too long."

"*Oof.*" Joseph caught him in the stomach with the ball.

"Got to pay attention, *Tio* Victor."

He waved his hand in the air. "No more. I've got to shower. I'm buying your mom supper in town."

"Really?" Joseph beamed.

—and Victor was sorry he'd said anything.

"*Tio* Carlos is waving at you from his cottage," Joseph said.

Carlos. How could he have forgotten his brother was going to lay out his plan tonight—and show him those emeralds?

He watched Marisol disappear into the main house. He couldn't disappoint her. Women always took a long time to get ready. He'd make it quick, and then duck in the shower. Wiping the sweat from his brow with the hem of his shirt, Victor headed toward Carlos's cottage.

His brother held open the door, waiting. "Come inside before Rosario comes back to drag me off to dinner."

The swelling on his jaw had gone down, leaving a purple bruise. He smelled of soap and had put on clean clothes, but what was up with the muddy work boots? Victor would swear they were the same ones Carlos wore home from the mine.

"How're the ribs doing?"

"A hot shower and I am good as new. Well, almost." Carlos touched his lip.

"I've got to get cleaned up. I have a date."

Carlos raised one eyebrow. "Marisol?"

Victor smiled.

"You devil, you." Then he frowned. "You...ah...are not getting involved..."

"Oh no. Nothing like that."

Hands in his pocket, Victor scanned the room. A plasma TV took center stage on the far wall, blaring a baseball game in progress. From the uniforms, it appeared to be the Florida Marlins. He hadn't seen even a *portable* television at the main house. Obviously, Carlos kept his extra earnings close to the vest. "Nice place."

Carlos shrugged, as if being able to afford all the male toys in the world was *nada*. Picking up the remote, he programmed the rest of the game to record, and then clicked off the TV.

The room went quiet.

Turning, Carlos signaled Victor to follow him into a room with a plump king-size bed and a ceiling tiled with mirrors. The bed faced a second plasma TV.

Victor glanced at the tiny night table and noted a stack of DVD's. Porno, from the looks of the movie on top. Victor was no stranger to such flicks. He had acted in a few, but only with women. The pay was decent, and it wasn't his face the camera zoomed in on.

Locking the door behind them, Carlos sat on the edge of his bed, holding his sore ribs. Patting a hand on the fluffy red quilt, he indicated Victor should join him.

Surely, Carlos meant nothing by the motion, yet he didn't feel comfortable sitting beside a man on that love nest of a bed. "It's okay.

I'll stand."

Carlos raised his shoulder in a shrug. "Whatever." Crossing one leg over the other, he rotated the heel of his boot. Digging into it, he produced a fistful of huge emeralds. Their bluish-green color was intense, with carbon-colored vein networks.

Victor's mouth dropped open. The emeralds sparkling on the palm of Carlos's hand were many times larger than the half-carat stones he wore in his ears.

"Our first shipment." Carlos singled out the largest of the gems, one with a six-spoked star pattern. He held it to the light. "We are lucky, *mi hermano*. I was able to obtain only the finest quality. This five-carat Trapiche is very rare. You should be able to sell it for somewhere between thirty-two and ninety-five thousand American dollars."

"No shit? That one stone is worth all that? And all those beauties were in your boot the entire time Sanchez was beating on you? No wonder you were more worried about finding your boots and getting out of *La Esmeralda* than seeing a doctor."

"My ribs are broken, but they will heal. Doctors do not do anything except give pain pills. I take four already." Carlos took a few shallow breaths. "See much better."

Was Carlos trying to prove he was up to going on with their deal? Although Victor supposed the hard part, getting the gems out of the mine, was done. It was Victor's turn to finish the job.

He nodded, as if he planned to go along with the deal. He'd been thinking the whole time he helped the women in the field that the chance to get rich wasn't worth his life.

"You will have to change your flight. To meet the shuttle."

"Which shuttle? I thought they would go with me on my flight."

"Too risky. No, the shuttle will work the best. "Carlos's eyebrows went up. A sly smile stole over his face. "Customs spot-checks, but with so many flower crates they are sure to miss the one containing our emeralds."

Flowers? Of course. Garcia Jardines shipped once a day, sometimes more.

Marisol's lilies.

How could he do that to her?

The guilt of deceit pressed on Victor's shoulders until he swore he shrank to half his size. Soon, he would be face to face with Marisol and have to pretend he didn't know what would go down in her greenhouse sometime between today and tomorrow.

"Still with me on this, *mi hermano?*"

"I...uh..." His brother was counting on him; he couldn't let him down. Not now, when the emeralds were in hand and the deal was about to go down. He'd find a way to make it up to Marisol. Once he was rich, it wouldn't be hard to think of some means of pleasing her. Yet, even as he thought it, Victor knew Marisol was one commodity that couldn't be bought.

Carlos stared at him, eyes hard as black ice.

He wet his lips, and then smiled. "Of course."

"Good. I was afraid you were going soft on me." Carlos poured the gems into a small paper bag, the kind a hardware store uses to hold screws and other small items. Twisting it shut, he stuffed it into the top drawer of his night table.

He handed Victor a telephone book. "Call your airline. Get a flight out around five, so you can be sure to arrive in time to meet the nine o'clock plane. Use my phone." He pointed toward the hard-wired telephone in the living room.

Victor picked up the handset. Dial tone buzzed in his ear, a whisper of warning. *You will be rich, but at what cost?* How many women had he used for his own ends in the past? Now he was using Marisol—the one woman who didn't seem to care about his looks or prowess.

Carlos's breath was on his neck. His brother counted on him to keep his promise. Tracing one number at a time around the rotary circle of the desk-style telephone, Victor connected with the agent at the airline. This time, he didn't balk at the hundred-fifty-dollar change fee, or the higher cost for a direct flight. After reciting his credit card number, which he had memorized, he dropped the handset into its cradle.

It rang almost instantly. Carlos shot in front of him to grab the phone.

Victor stumbled, nearly falling backward over the sofa. "Hey. Watch it."

Carlos paid him no attention. He spoke in low angry tones with his hand cupped around the mouthpiece, and then slammed down the receiver. He turned, eyebrows raised, as if surprised to see Victor remained. "I have to go out now."

"What's going on?"

Carlos grabbed his shoulder. "Take care of your end of the deal, eh? See you later." Pushing past him, Carlos headed out the front door.

Victor followed his brother as far as the doorway and watched the Cherokee peel out of the drive. Why hadn't Carlos confided in him?

Weren't they brothers? Partners?

If he had a car, he'd follow to see where his brother went—protect him, even. Carlos could be walking into danger. He shoved his hand into his pocket and found the scrap of paper with Berto's number. He rubbed it between his fingers. He could use Carlos's phone to call him. Berto was a straight arrow though. For all Victor knew, Carlos could be picking up more emeralds from another hidey-hole.

Carlos trusted him enough to leave the emeralds behind in his presence, so he needed to trust Carlos. Right now, he was in limbo—he hadn't bathed in two days, and he had a date with a beautiful woman he shouldn't keep.

He plodded out of Carlos's over-the-top accommodations toward his own simple cottage, the guesthouse. He hadn't spent much time in it, yet he couldn't help feeling the place belonged to him. The bed was small but comfortable, and he really hadn't minded showering and dining at the main house. There, in the señora's kitchen, he had been treated as part of the Garcia family.

Gathering his toiletry kit, a towel, and a set of clean clothes, he set out to the main house. As he approached, his heart leapt at seeing Marisol disappear with a flash of yellow into her cottage. Was she thinking about him? Or how long she would be away from her lilies? Before he met her, he would've assumed she'd be hot for him. He hadn't been able to read her, like the others.

Señora Garcia's kitchen smelled of rice and beans. He would miss its warmth and the señora's home cooking.

"Excuse me, señora, may I?" He held up his toiletry kit and towel.

"Of course." The señora smiled at him, one hand on her hip. "I understand you and Marisol will not be joining us for dinner."

God, he hated this. From the smug look on the señora's face, Victor realized that, in the señora's way of thinking, inviting Marisol to dinner was as good as a marriage proposal."No...uh...we're doing a quick supper in town."

"No rush." Rosario distributed plates and utensils on the kitchen table. "She needs a break from those lilies. Keep her out late, or she will be right back in that greenhouse until dawn culling those stalks."

The greenhouse. Of course, the first place Marisol would go. Victor didn't know exactly when Carlos planned to sabotage Marisol's lilies, but he *did* know he'd have to keep her out of there once Carlos returned.

"I will tell Carlos dinner is ready," Rosario said, setting out the last plate.

"He's going to be late," Victor said. "He got a phone call and took off."

Rosario's forehead wrinkled. "Did he say how long he would be gone?"

"Sorry, no."

Rosario removed Carlos's plate from the table and carefully replaced it in the cabinet.

Victor felt for her—a husband who was never around and watched porno to get it up. At least that's the conclusion he had come to after seeing the setup in the bedroom. He didn't want to think poorly of his brother, but a guy was a guy.

The bathroom, white tiled and spotless, was barely large enough to accommodate a toilet and a curtained shower. Several soapings and rinses later, Victor slipped into his black silk shorts, glad not have to perform the task in front of a leering client. If Marisol learned how he made a living in Miami, she'd turn her back on him faster than a speedball.

As he buttoned his palm-tree-design shirt over his chest, Victor peered at his face in the bathroom mirror. Damn, he looked healthy, with a sunburned nose and reddish cheeks. The white crinkles around his eyes reminded him he had left his sunglasses in the Cherokee. Dark bristles of the start-up beard covering his upper lip and lower jaw gave him a roguish look he rather liked. Reddish highlights that would cost hundreds if done in a salon streaked his once nearly black hair. Without bothering with the gel, he finger-combed his hair, and leaned back, satisfied.

This is me.

He supposed he should shave before he left Colombia to appear more civilized when he flew home, but that could wait. Tonight, he had to deal with Marisol. Even if he *were* staying a few more days, and even if he *wasn't* in cahoots with Carlos, he had no business encouraging her. He was not worthy of her. He was scum. He should cancel.

And tell her what, big man? That you have a headache?

Marisol's smiling face flashed in front of him as if she were really there. He didn't want to tarnish that smile any sooner than he had to.

Gathering his things, he reached for the doorknob. *Deal with this like you always do. Put on that killer smile and let her think that you are good, and kind, and honest—and hope she doesn't see through your pretense.*

Victor's resolve disappeared the instant he emerged from the main house and went around back. Marisol, a vision in a trim yellow dress and ballerina flats, rested one hip against the white van. Her hair, dark satin and wet from her shower, streamed behind her shoulders and her naturally rosy lips curved in a smile. Even the Trapiche emerald could not compare with her natural beauty.

"Ready?" She handed him the keys.

"You bet." Victor's manhood did a dance under his slacks. Tugging down the front of his shirt to hide his reaction, he climbed into the driver seat and realized that, by tomorrow night, this very flower van would be implicated in criminal activity. When Soto found out Victor was involved, and he would, his life would be as worthless as the stones rutting the driveway.

Plugging the key into the ignition, he backed out of the space. If only he could turn back time to the night of the cockfight, he might have nixed Carlos's plan and salvaged an iota of Marisol's respect. His foot hit the brake to shift to first, and the van stalled out. *Damn. Forgot to clutch.*

"Victor, what is the matter? You seem upset about something."

He turned to her, putting on his most sorrowful mien. "I...have to leave tomorrow night. I can't stay until Saturday. I have issues to deal with back in Miami." *There, that was the truth, kind of.*

"Tomorrow? So soon?" She reached for his hand and looked into his face.

He did his best to keep his expression blank, but he saw the sadness in her eyes. "I'm sorry. I will handle things and find a way to come back to see you, and Joseph, too," he choked out.

"Marisol's lips tipped up in a half smile. "You do not have to make promises you cannot keep."

"But I *want* to keep them."

"Then get this truck moving. You promised me supper."

"So I did." A feeling of contentment welled up inside Victor. Marisol was okay with him leaving. She wasn't hounding him for a commitment.

Why wasn't she?

Chapter Fifteen

The village of Garcia didn't have much to offer by way of fancy dining, but fine food wasn't what Victor had in mind for tonight. He parked the van in front of Café Juanita, a tiny restaurant wedged between a two-story apartment building and Barra de Luis.

Marisol's hand moved to the door handle, ready to exit. Victor might be an underhanded bastard, but at least he could remember his manners and treat Marisol like the lady she was.

"Wait. I want to do this the right way."

"Very well." She rested her head against the seat and crossed her arms, a smile playing at her lips.

She was independent and strong; yet at that moment, she seemed as fragile as a child. He wanted to take care of her, be there for her. Be the man she looked up to. But that would never happen. His past would never go away. A pure-minded woman like Marisol would never forgive him all those years of deception. Then he had looked upon women as jobs. He saw now they were people, humans with hearts and souls. Now that he had found his own heart, he clearly saw the harm he had done to others.

Going around to the passenger side, Victor opened her door and extended his hand. After their work in the fields this afternoon, his hands were blistered and rough. Had she noticed how he had changed? He grasped her hand tighter than he should have.

With an open smile, Marisol hopped out. "My, such a gentleman."

If Marisol knew how many clients he had helped out of limos and fancy cars and then escorted to the bedroom, she wouldn't think him a gentleman.

Still holding hands, he and Marisol stopped to peruse the menu taped to the window. "Is the food any good here?"

"I only came once with Joseph. Not too bad."

Inside, the décor was simple with pale blue walls, chrome-edged circle tables and a counter backed by a cooking area with a microwave and a grill top. A coffee machine with a half-full carafe of dark brown liquid sat next to a countertop case holding pastries that might've survived the day's morning rush.

A stocky woman with short, dark hair, who must be Juanita, rose from her seat behind the counter and set down her newspaper. "Sit anywhere. I will be right with you." She disappeared through a door at the back of the kitchen.

Guiding Marisol by the elbow, he steered her toward a black vinyl booth by the window.

"The tail end of the sunset is my favorite time of day," Marisol said, settling into her seat. "The sky glows with color. See?" She pointed at the post office across the street.

The white adobe facade glowed pink, like Marisol's cheeks. He wanted to remember her like this—smiling, happy and content to be with him.

Reaching for her hand, he played with her fingers. Soothing the ridged calluses, he examined her blisters. "If you were my woman, I'd treat you like a princess. I would hire a maid to tend to your every wish, and I would..."

"Stop it, Victor. You and I know I am doing what I love. I would be miserable being waited on hand and foot."

"So you would consider it, being my..." The word caught in his throat. *What right did he have to bait her like this?*

A rueful smile played at the corner of Marisol's lush lips. She rested her chin on their clasped hands. "Would you really come back to see us, Victor?" Her doe eyes looked up at him, expecting truth.

Victor's mouth went dry. His heart wanted to burst and spill over. If he wasn't careful, he'd be a blubbering like a fool. He didn't want to leave her and go back to his life in Miami with a hole in his heart he could never fill. "I may not be able to."

Her lashes lowered, casting dark shadows against her cheek. She lifted her chin, let go of his hand, and drew back. "I understand." She grabbed the menu tucked between the salt and pepper shakers and a long necked bottle labeled, "Juanita's Pepper Sauce." As she scanned the offerings, he could see her marshal her dignity. She had put him on the spot, and he had turned her down.

"I am not very hungry, Victor. Here." She handed him the menu. "Find us something light."

"What will you have?" Juanita loomed over them, pad in hand.

He hadn't heard her approach, although from the sturdy orthopedic shoes she wore, her footsteps had to have been hard to miss.

"I will have coffee, black, Juanita," Marisol said. "Victor, I will be right back," she said without a glance in his direction. Grabbing her tote bag, she set off, assumedly to the unisex *bano* to the side of the kitchen area. Her pace was hurried. She held herself erect; lustrous hair, now dry and wavy, streamed down her back.

"A Club Colombo brew for me and..." He scanned the plastic sheet—all in Spanish—until he found a word he recognized. "Bring us an order of nachos."

Juanita looked at him cross-eyed. "Nachos?" She shoved a thumb over her shoulder. "I have my homemade chicken stew heating on the stove."

"The stew then, two bowls."

"Coming right up." With a bounce to her step that hit the tiled floor like hoof beats, she bustled toward the kitchen.

Alone at the table now, he took a moment to pull his thoughts together. He was in trouble. From her reaction, it was obvious Marisol cared about him. The old Victor would have zeroed in for the kill. The thought of running his hands over her firm breasts sent hot blood coursing through his veins. He would be gentle, let her call the shots.

But he had gone soft. It would be wrong to take advantage of Marisol. She was so much more than a one-night stand. Touching her hand had to be enough for now. He wasn't going to spoil their last night together by obsessing over what was to come. The emeralds awaited him. He would have everything he always wanted—except Marisol.

And tomorrow, he would leave her life for good.

In the meantime, their drinks arrived, Victor's in a bottle and Marisol's coffee in a Styrofoam cup. He took one look at the coffee's murky brown color and knew a woman used to fresh-perked, home-grown coffee wouldn't want to drink such swill. "Bring the lady a beer also," he said, catching Juanita before she left.

Once Marisol returned, she took a sip of the coffee and made a face.

"That's what I figured you'd do. I hope it was all right, but I ordered you a beer." He squeezed the lime down through the neck of his bottle. "Here." He passed over the beer to her. "Try it."

Marisol eyed the bottle for a second, and then took it from him. As she did so, her fingers lingered against his hand and sent a flash of heat to his crotch. Sniffing at the lip of the bottle, she took a sip and then wrinkled her nose.

"Not a beer drinker, eh?" He picked up the menu card. "Perhaps a glass of wine."

"Papa drank wine sometimes," she said, brightening. "Yes, I will try a small glass."

The urge to know more about her dug into him. Had there been any other men in her life? Obviously, she had sex with Joseph's father or the kid wouldn't be here now. Joseph. Maybe he could do something to help her with him—pay for college, even—once he made it big in the emerald business. "Tell me about your son." He dropped his elbow on the table and set his chin in his hand.

"Excuse me." Juanita set two bowls in front of them along with a basket of cornbread.

The stew was hot and spicy. As they ate, a silence fell between them, with Marisol's focus on their meal. She had avoided his question about Joseph, again. He knew he was being nosy, but he cared, especially if she had been raped. Carlos had been close-mouthed when he'd asked him about her, so perhaps her past was a deep family secret.

Marisol blotted her lips with her napkin. "Juanita makes great stew, but I have eaten enough." She pushed away her dish and flipped her hand under the back of her glorious hair. "Tell me more about this Mrs. Gallagher."

Whoa. Wasn't expecting that one. He took a swallow of beer to wet the dryness that cloyed at his throat. It had been foolish of him to mention his first paramour's name. Since he arrived in Colombia, he'd been off his game.

"Well, ah...she owned a huge estate in Coral Gables—that's the ritzy section of Miami," he added, figuring Marisol would have little knowledge of Miami neighborhoods. "My mother was a maid at the Gallagher estate and raised me as a single mother, as you are raising Joseph." He extended his hand in a communal gesture. "As a boy, I was allowed the run of the place, as long as I didn't get into trouble."

"This Mrs. Gallagher must have liked you, then." Marisol lifted the glass of wine Juanita had set in front of her and looked over the rim at him as she took a small sip.

Taking a square of still-warm cornbread, he bit off a hunk and took his time to chew and swallow it. "She liked me all right," he said, finally.

"Enough to pay for private schooling?" Marisol lifted one eyebrow.

Damn, the woman was astute. Had she sensed a relationship between him and the Gallagher woman? A wave of heat flushed his face. He was thirteen years old and back in that fancy bedroom mounting Mrs. Gallagher. Beneath him, she screamed, "Harder, Victor, harder."

"And more," he replied without thinking. "She made me..." He dropped his head in his hand. He couldn't go on. He didn't want to talk about this anymore.

Marisol gently pulled his hand from his face and covered it with hers. "It is all right, Victor. I understand. I, too, was taken advantage of. I was fourteen and a novice at Saint Andrew's."

"A novice? You were going to become a *nun?*"

Her shoulders shrank inward, as if she was waiting for him to berate her. "Yes," she whispered.

He lifted her chin with his fingers and saw that her amber eyes were watery. At that moment, they were not man and woman, but two kindred souls. What kind of man would go after a nun? Maybe some horny priest, which made stealing a child's virginity even more of a crime. "It was not your fault."

"I led him on."

"I doubt that. Did he rape you?" There, he said it. He had to know how far this bastard had gone with her.

Marisol looked down; her long lashes fluttered. "I thought he loved me."

Lying scum. "Well, where is this person now?" He straightened in his seat. "Why didn't he take responsibility for his son?"

A single tear glistened on Marisol's cheek.

Victor didn't know what to say or do. He only wished he could ease her pain. "Would you like another glass of wine?"

Marisol brushed the wetness from her cheeks and smiled. "Are you trying to get me drunk so you can have your way with me, Victor?"

"I thought about it, but now..." He returned her smile. "I wish..."

"Shush." She held a finger to his lips.

The nearness of her finger made him part his lips. Before he realized what he was doing, he had grabbed her hand. The tip of his tongue made tiny circles on her palm. He pursed his lips and began kissing the tender spot inside her wrist, which had gone limp. His breath came in short pants. God how he wanted her.

"You guys done with that stew? This is no boudoir, you know." Juanita stood over them, hands on hips.

Marisol withdrew her hand from his.

Crap. What had gotten into him? "Just a check, please."

He exchanged glances with Marisol, who suppressed a giggle.

With Victor in control of the wheel, they drove back to Garcia Jardines. As they pulled into the drive and passed the damaged fencing, a flare of rage shot through him. He might be leaving, but he would never forget the raw anger he felt for Gomez Soto. One day, someone would take that man down. If he had his way, he would be that person.

"Tomorrow, we will continue with clean up," Marisol said, arms crossed and jaw set firm.

Reality returned in one swoop. He would no longer hear Marisol's gentle breathing beside him. He would park the van in its usual spot and sometime between now and tomorrow afternoon, Marisol's lilies would be compromised. He glanced over at Marisol, so beautiful and pure. He wanted to remember her this way, relaxed and falling in love with a man who could never return her love.

"If Carlos has no plans for me, I'll help you in the greenhouse tonight."

"Thank you, Victor." She leaned in to kiss his cheek. Her hand brushed over his stubble of a beard. "I like it, Victor. Makes you look like a Hollywood actor."

He laughed. "I should keep it then."

"Have you been with many women, Victor? I mean since..."

What was it with her? Marisol had a way of springing questions he didn't want to answer. "He waved his a hand in the air. A few. How about you?"

Marisol turned her head and pretended to look out the side window.

I take that as a no, then.

As they passed the main house to park around back, Victor glanced over at Carlos's place. No Jeep. He would check with Rosario to find out if Carlos had called. He needed to talk with him now.

Tonight.

Before it was too late.

* * * *

Foolish woman. I am making a big mistake by falling for Victor. As she set off for her cottage, Marisol shook her head, trying to clear her thoughts. *He will ruin my life if I let him get any closer. I kissed him today, let him hold my hand, and then when he started to run kisses over my bare arm I melted like an iceberg. What is wrong with me? Where is my stamina? He is leaving. He said so.*

And he will not be back.

But Joseph. Victor's departure would affect him. He was finally showing interest in going to college and now the person who encouraged him, was going to be out of his life. Joseph would follow Carlos.

He would want to drop out of school and learn security—and then he would be up at those horrible mines, filthy as sin, a gun at his hip.

That was not the life she wanted for her son.

Inside, she found Joseph in his room, seated at the edge of his bed holding open a book. She tried not to smile and make a big deal over it. "Another test tomorrow?"

"I did not hear you come in, Mama." Closing the book, he stuffed it into his backpack. "No, I was just reading."

"I see." However, she did not see. "That did not look like a school book." She held out her hand. "Let me have it."

With a disgusted sigh, Joseph dug through his backpack and pulled out a glossy-covered paperback. He shoved it at her. "Here."

"Joseph, what has gotten into you? I am your mother. You will not speak to me in that tone of voice."

Joseph rolled his eyes at her.

"Enough! You are going right to bed."

She took it, half expecting it to be one of those dirty books Rosario told her Carlos read. She flipped through it. "You are reading about emeralds? Why?"

Joseph shrugged. "When we studied about the Emerald Revolution, I wanted to learn more about our mines. I will probably get extra credit if I write a paper on it."

"Ah." She had been wrong to accuse Joseph. "I am sorry. Come, give me a hug."

"Do I still have to go to bed early?"

"You may read your book."

She turned to leave, wondering if there were more to her son's interest in precious gems than getting extra credit at school.

With Joseph settled for the night, Marisol returned to the greenhouse. As her fingers moved, her mind flashed to that afternoon, when Victor helped them recoup what they could. If they could work together for the rest of their lives, she would be content. He was a good man. He cared about her and Joseph, and he understood what she had gone through with Father John. Like her, he had been taken advantage of. She could almost trust him. Even though he made no commitment, the possibility he would come back to visit made her hum as she worked.

The door from the kitchen opened.

Victor.

He said he would come help her. She fluffed her hair, bit at her lips to redden them, and turned to greet him. Her surge of joy fell away. "Oh, it is you."

"Of course it is us. Who did you expect?" Rosario nodded. "Ah, I see. You thought Victor was coming. Should Mama and I leave?"

"Of course not. But he *did* say..."

"He went after Carlos," Mama said. "I loaned him the van."

Rosario's hand covered her mouth. She appeared to be about to burst into tears. "My husband has not returned. He was beaten up today, and now he has missed dinner again. Victor told me he left after he got a phone call."

Marisol had been through this so many times with Rosario. "Did he at least call?"

Rosario shrugged. "No. *Nada.* And he left his cell phone in the bedroom, so I cannot call him."

"I am sorry." That was all Marisol could think to say. Maybe she was better off than Rosario was. At least she only had a son to worry about, not a wandering husband as well.

"You are back early," Mama said "Humph. The least Victor could have done is take you into Bogotá for a proper dinner."

"I would not have gone to Bogotá. Look what we have to do. Already the stalks are drying out. They are fragile, If we do not work quickly they will..."

Her hand flew to her forehead. "I...cannot do this anymore. I am tired of trying to keep one step ahead of Gomez Soto. If I were trained to shoot a gun, I would creep up on him at his fancy house and shoot him in his black heart."

"Calm down, Marisol." Rosario's hand was on her shoulder. "You have taken this burden to yourself. We are with you now. The work will get done three times as fast."

Leaving Mama and Rosario to cull the gathered stalks, she moved toward the solarium section, delighted to see new germination. "We will need to ready some beds for planting tomorrow." She bit at her lip. "With our fence down, Soto is liable to..."

Mama interrupted her. "Rosario, tomorrow you will go to the supply yard in town and order new fencing. Buy only the best quality and ask if we can have it installed on credit."

"Thank you," Marisol said, pleased Mama was finally taking ownership of Garcia Jardines. "That is what Papa might have done." She kissed her mother's cheek.

It was after ten when the three of them called it quits. Victor had not come to help, so she expected he met up with Carlos. Rosario left for her cottage, while Mama went inside the house to get ready for bed.

Marisol was sweeping up the work area, waiting for Mama's high sign that the shower was free, when a car came in the drive.

* * * *

A wasted trip. Victor circled in front of the main house and checked for the Cherokee for the umpteenth time. It hadn't been in its parking space five minutes ago, when he had driven past, and it wasn't there now. *Carlos, you should have talked to me. I am already in deep with you. Maybe I could have gone with you and, between the two of us, we could've handled whatever glitch you're dealing with now.*

He'd been everywhere Berto suggested, and still no sign of his brother. Carlos wasn't sitting at Barra de Luis tipping brews, nor was he at the Club Galilistico, where one of those awful cockfights was in progress. He didn't know where else to look.

Time to call it quits for the night. Victor parked the van in its usual spot behind the greenhouse. As he passed the front, he noticed the lights were on inside. He didn't expect much would happen in regard to the emeralds until Carlos returned, so the greenhouse should be off limits for now. Maybe his brother's absence meant the emerald deal was off. If the emerald scheme went bust, he could confess all to Marisol and have an iota of a chance she would forgive him.

You're dreaming again, buddy.

His heart stopped at the sight of Marisol. Her back was to him, slim hips swaying as she pushed a broom. He wanted her. Not just her body, all of her. He had said he would help her, and he meant it at the time. But now he didn't dare set fire to the flame that had kindled between them over dinner.

As he walked past the greenhouse, he couldn't shake the sensation of being watched. He twisted his neck toward the window and faced Marisol. She was behind the glass, like a bird in a gilded cage; one he could look at, tease even, but could never set free. Her eyes were expectant and her chin was up, those luscious lips ready for a kiss, or more.

You can't have her, asshole. Keep moving.

He turned away, pretending he didn't see her, waiting and ready for him. He could have taken her then, right there in the greenhouse, and she would have let him. He hunched his shoulders, trying to make himself as small as he felt. He was a nothing, scum. That one single incident where each of them lost virginity changed his and Marisol's lives. She sought chastity, while he became a male whore.

There. He said it.

Whore. Whore. Whore.

All the fancy trappings in the world didn't change the fact that, at the end of the day, he was paid for screwing women. But what did all that matter? Once Marisol learned the truth, she'd kick his ass out of the plantation so fast he wouldn't feel the pain until he landed.

* * * *

The roar of the van pulling up behind the greenhouse sent Marisol dashing to the window. Victor had returned. Her eyes slid over his manly frame as he rounded the bend and headed toward the door. The lights were low, but she was sure he could see her standing at the window ready to greet him. She rapped on the window to get his attention. He turned and looked right at her, yet he seemed not to see her.

She supposed he was too worried about his missing brother to re-member he offered to help her, not that she planned to work more this evening.

He moved ahead, casting a long dark shadow over the drive and leaving her behind. His shoulders were slumped, as if he were defeat-ed—which meant he had not found Carlos.

It was nearly midnight, bedtime. Yet she had hoped they could have a few minutes together before morning brought a new day, when he would leave. Standing at the window, her nose pressed to the glass, wetness trickled down her cheek. *I do not need him. If he really cared about me, he would cancel his reservation and stay on a few more days—or forever.*

But he would not stay. And he would not come back. Tonight would be all she had as a memory of the man she had come to care about. Meeting Victor was God's way of testing her again. She was be-ing punished. She was to live out her days as a nun, even though no convent would take her. Marisol turned from the window.

Once Marisol had cleaned up, her hair still wet, she slipped on her nightdress and headed out into the cool night to her cottage. Rosario's outdoor lights glowed in anticipation of Carlos's arrival. Maybe Marisol was better off not having to worry about a roving husband.

After checking on Joseph, she hung her wet towel on the door-knob and knelt at the altar to say her evening prayers. Following her usual bedtime rituals always relaxed her, but not tonight. She rose, knees satisfyingly sore from the penance of the ridged wood.

Her eyes strayed to her cot, wide enough for a single person. She envisioned Victor sharing it with her and suppressed a giggle. His feet would hang over the edge. The only way two would fit would be if they snuggled. A warm feeling gushed in her lower belly. She wanted to glow with the satisfaction she experienced so many years ago. It had been wrong then; but now she was a grown woman with needs, not a gullible child training to be a nun.

Rosario's words played in her mind. *You are too hard on yourself. You should take pleasure when it is offered. Victor is a man of the world. He is sure to have a condom in his wallet.*

Did it matter if she never saw Victor after tonight?

Tiptoeing past Joseph's room, she peered out the front door and up the walk. In the distance, the guesthouse gleamed like a jewel in the full moon. Rays of light streamed toward her. All she had to do was follow the golden road.

Her feet moved and she was outdoors. The night air was cool enough to raise goose bumps on her bare arms, but the adrenaline coursing through her veins kept her warm. One foot in front of the other, the soles of her calloused feet struck the dirt in the road. *Stop, go back. This is wrong.*

Marisol shook off the numbing words. For once, she was going to follow her heart. She broke into a light run, afraid she would change her mind.

As she neared, she saw the cottage was dark inside. Her breath caught at the realization that Victor would likely be sprawled across the bed, asleep. When she opened that door, he would know why she came. And there would be no going back.

She raised her face to a clear sky glittering with stars for an answer from God. A cool breeze whispered over her skin, sanctioning her mission. She raised her hand to knock and stopped, not wanting to break the magic of the moment.

With a twist, the door opened. She eased around it and closed it behind her. From the other side of the room, Victor's soft snores caught her attention. Moonlight streaming through the window outlined his figure on the bed. Alongside it, a suitcase lay open.

He does not know I am here. I still have time to leave.

But Marisol's body did not listen. Inching toward the bed, she stared at Victor's shadowy figure, head turned, one arm out to the side, sheet barely covering his man parts. His chest swelled and contracted with each breath, creating a hill of muscles that rippled to a narrow waist. His lips quivered with each heavy breath. His musky smell brought her nipples to stiff peaks and the area between her legs throbbed with need.

She eased down on the edge of the bed and pressed her hand into her crotch to stop the ache, but it did not help. Touching herself only made her want him more. Her fingers itched to pull away the sheet and touch the angles and curves of his smooth skin. She wanted to see him naked, to run her hands down the centerline of his chest and below. Her breath came in ragged gasps. She reached out and—

Victor eyes flashed open. "Wh..." He rubbed at his eyes. "Marisol?"

Marisol shrunk back. "I am sorry. I only wanted to..."

His dark eyes took her in, and the sensual look on his face sent her heartbeat careening out of control. Reaching up, she pulled the nightgown over her head. Her hair fell forward and she bent to him.

"Don't ever cut your hair," he said, his voice a hoarse rasp. He bunched it in his hand and drew it from her face. "Kiss me."

Her breath stopped abruptly. She ran her tongue over her suddenly dry lips, and then angled toward him.

His gaze, dark with lust, locked with hers. With one swoop, he wrapped his arm around her and drew her close. He took her lips with a groan, and pulled her on top of him. His hands were in her hair, his lips sent burning pulses to her aching extremities, and her breasts crushed into his chest. Through the sheet, his erection burned into her thigh.

He rolled them over, so he faced her, and smoothed her hair from her face. "Are you sure you want to do this?"

She ran her fingers along the hard line of his jaw. "I...uh..." He was giving her an out.

The scene with Mama when she arrived home in shame from the convent echoed in her mind. "You are nothing but a whore." She should leave now. Go back to her lonely cot and continue to pay the price of a single indiscretion.

Her lips slammed against his in rebellion.

She heard his breath catch, as he molded her to his body. The curling flame of his tongue parted her lips, sending fiery urges to her core. The sheet fell away and they were skin against skin. Arching her back, she moved her hips against him, wanting more. It did not matter that she might never see him again. Tonight, these few precious moments would be etched in her heart forever.

Her soft cries mingled with his, as he thrust into her, filling her. The world around her spun away and her lungs burned for air.

"Victor." She gasped as her last shred of control dropped away. Her body shook with a spasm of release.

Her body was moist with pleasure. The musky smell of raw sex caressed her senses. She would remember this feeling. Play it over and over in her mind.

Victor pulled out, ejected on her stomach, and then rolled over on his back.

Her body chilled in the night air, missing his warmth, and knowing it was time to leave. She sat up and kissed Victor's cheek. "*Gracias.*"

Twisting away from him, she grabbed her nightgown from the floor and dropped it over her head. The thin cloth clung to the wet spot on her belly. She covered the precious fluid with her hand.

Behind her, the bed creaked. Victor's hand was on her shoulder, warm and comforting.

"Why are you leaving?"

She could not let him see her crying. "Because you are."

Marisol patted his hand, and then stood, allowing his hand to drop away. Steeling herself, she walked to the door. The hurt that must be in his eyes seared holes in her back. She did not want to go, but he offered her no reason to stay.

She shut the door behind her, controlling the knob and swing of it so it made no sound. A solid wall separated them now. It was over. Marisol stood stock still for a moment as realization of what she had done seeped through her. She fell back against the door, her body cold. She was no better than that older woman who took advantage of him all those years ago. She had used him to please herself. Poor Victor. What must he be feeling now?

Bursting back inside, she ran to him and stopped short. He sat at the edge of the bed, head in his hands, and looked up at her. His hair was rumpled; his face hard shadowy planes; his eyes ice cold.

"I am sorry. I did not mean...it is just that you are leaving, and I do not think you will return. I needed you. Just this once. To remember."

"I understand." His lips formed a wobbly smile. Rising, he drew her into a tight hug, and then pushed her away. "Now go."

* * * *

With a flutter of her nightgown, Marisol disappeared through the door. Through the window, her moonlit figure appeared a shrinking shadow, moving out of his life. Victor pressed his forehead against the glass, letting its hard coolness calm the flush of shame that left his cheeks burning.

Had he been that bad a lover? He didn't know. He only knew what he had been told. But she hadn't come to him for love, she had come for sex. He was accustomed to being used, but not by someone as pure and innocent as Marisol. Okay, so she apologized. That didn't make him hurt any less.

It's for the best, he told himself. *Even if I had gotten a chance to speak with Carlos tonight, the fact remains I planned to deceive her. She had been quick to leave when he asked her to go. And he missed her like hell.*

To the far right, the night light Rosario must have left on for her husband was a tiny circle. Carlos had been right. Emeralds were trouble.

* * * *

Marisol's sobs echoed in the stillness of the night as she broke into a run. He had not stopped her from leaving. He had the chance, twice, but he let her go. If she stayed, she would have been nestled in his arms right this minute. When she thought of sex, she envisioned that one time with Father John. He had touched her all over, and she had let him. But with Victor, her heart sang a song she had never heard before. She had not wanted him as a man, but as a person. She wished she could absorb his essence into her. To be one with him, even for a short time, and tell the rest of the world to go to hell.

She had her wish. With her vow of chastity broken, she was free to move on with her life. Find a mate and settle down like Mama wanted her to. A tear trickled down her cheek and fell onto her chest. The only man she cared about enough to spend her life with would be gone by sunset tomorrow.

Chapter Sixteen

Victor's watch read three a.m. He sat at the edge of his bed, his mind running in circles over the mess he'd made of his life. It was a wonder he got any sleep at all. Rising, he pulled on his jeans and stuffed his feet into shoes. *Maybe a brisk walk will help.*

Outside, the floral scent made him want to linger. He would miss the open space and the gardens. Shoving his hands in his pockets, he strolled aimlessly toward the main house. The cottages were dark, except for Carlos's. No sign of the Cherokee. He should have stood watch at the greenhouse in case his brother returned to sabotage the lilies. The foreboding from the past afternoon returned. His gut clenched in apprehension. The longer Carlos was gone, the more likely something had happened to him.

And I gave up searching for him because I was pooped. As usual, I put myself first.

This was Carlos's world, he reminded himself. He knew how to deal with these people. The man was a member of the cartel, after all, and claimed his sources for setting up the emerald scheme were trusted. But who could Carlos trust more than his brother? Victor blew out a breath. He'd done what he could, given his limited knowledge of the area, to find his brother, and Berto hadn't seemed to think Carlos's sudden disappearance unusual. He knew Carlos much better than Victor ever would.

As he approached Marisol's darkened cottage, he paused. Was she inside in bed with her hair spread across the pillow, eyes closed in satisfied slumber; or was she tossing and sleepless with regret over what happened between them?

As he turned away, a glimmer of light refracted off the panes of the greenhouse windows.

Someone must be inside.

It had to be Marisol. Perhaps she couldn't sleep after coming to him and thought to work on her plantings. He would talk to her. She needed to know the truth. A few long strides deposited him at the greenhouse entry door. He wiggled the handle, found the door unlocked, and then eased it open to the now familiar odors of moist soil and greenery. It was late, and he didn't want to frighten her.

The scrap of moonlight that drifted through the glass lit the planting areas. Ahead, the door to the shipping area, which always stayed open, was shut. An incandescent glow of artificial light emanated from the crack under the door, sending bright streaks across the clay floor. The changing pattern of shadows verified movement inside.

Why would Marisol shut herself inside the shipping area at this early hour? Unless...

Oh crap, you fool. Carlos must be inside stuffing emeralds in the lilies. Maybe the missing car was a ruse to throw people off. He hadn't thought to search the woods behind Carlos's cottage on foot, but if he had, he might have come upon Carlos's Jeep, snuggled in the brush. Victor punched his fist into the palm of his hand. His brother pulled a fast one on him and he didn't like it one bit, especially after he'd spent half the night chasing after him.

He had to stop Carlos. Smuggling emeralds was bad enough, but involving the Garcia family in crime was off limits. Victor bit at his lower lip hard enough to draw blood. Surprising Carlos might not be a good thing. He carried a gun.

Slipping out of his shoes, Victor felt his way down the darkened center aisle until he stood in front of the shipping room door.

Careful now. He eased the knob to the right to undo the latch, opened it a crack, and peered inside at the slim figure fussing with the flowers.

A crate lay open on the table, alongside a vase of blooms. A pair of frightened, dark brown eyes turned to stare at him.

Victor held his arms out to the side. "Joseph, *wait.*"

The boy's breath came in short gasps; his eyes darted for escape. With a powerful thrust, Joseph's head ducked for the space under Victor's arm. His head mashed into Victor's pecs, pushing him out of the way and knocking him down. Victor's head bounced off the floor. Pain lanced through his skull.

He scrambled to his feet. "No. Stop." With a lunge, he snatched at the back of the boy's shirt. "Slow down, I'm an old man. Let's talk about this."

The cotton knit fabric slipped through Victor's fingers, and Joseph was out the door with a bang and a clatter. "Joseph. Stop. It's okay."

Damn. He went after the boy at a fast jog, each step jarring his head. Circumventing the plantings Joseph knocked over, he opened the greenhouse door and scanned the empty walkway.

The moon was down, but his eyes adjusted to the monotone blacks and grays, Victor caught his breath. Could Joseph have ducked inside his mother's cottage? Better check. *Marisol needs to know what Carlos has involved her son with—and I might as well tell her about my part in the plan.*

At the door, Victor scraped a hand through his hair, and then raised his hand to knock. A light went on inside. Like a white angel in her nightdress, Marisol appeared in the doorway, and he fell in love with her all over again.

"What is going on, Victor?" Her voice was clipped, annoyed even. "I heard you calling Joseph. What do you want with my son?"

This wasn't going to be easy. She hadn't been mooning over him, as he hoped, and now here he was barging in on her when the world should be sleeping.

"Joseph. Is he inside?"

She tilted her head to the side and spoke, as if explaining the obvious to a child. "Victor, Joseph is asleep."

Her gaze went over his shoulder, to the left. "What...what is the light doing on in greenhouse?"

"It's not what you think. Please, Marisol. I can explain."

"I just bet you can. Get out of my way." She pushed past him and stomped off for the greenhouse.

He grabbed at her arm, slim but hard with muscle. "No, you can't go in there. I mean. There's nothing to see."

"Get away from me, Victor. "

Crap, he couldn't let her see the mess in the shipping room. He followed her inside, helpless to stop her.

Whirling around, she glared at him like an angry cat. Her hand pushed at his chest with the strength of an arm wrestler. "You. Stay outside. This is *my* affair."

"No. it's not. It has nothing to do with you. Please. Let me check things for you. It could be dangerous."

"Pah. You are the one who is dangerous." She pushed again, harder.

His hands went in the air and he backed away. "Okay, be that way." He swiveled on his heel and left.

Damn hard-headed woman. I try to save her grief, and she gives me more. Nothing he could do. Marisol would think whatever she wanted to when she saw the emeralds.

He had to find Joseph and get him to confess his part to his mother, and then all would be square for the boy. She would forgive Joseph, but she might never forgive Victor.

Victor stopped at the door to Marisol's cottage, which she had left ajar. *Think.* Marisol said Joseph was inside the cottage. He might be, although Marisol would have heard him. He puzzled over the enigma, and decided to check out Marisol's claim.

An oil lamp lit the hallway, which allowed him to find his way through the tiny home. He peered inside a bedroom that had to be Marisol's—sparse with only a small cot, an altar, and some hooks bearing clothing. She was the opposite of everything he ever longed for, pure and simple. A woman like her required very little to be happy. All she wanted was truth, and love.

Across the way, the door was closed. He cracked it open, and then smiled at the lump in the bed. He fooled his mother in the same way, using a couple of pillows, when sneaking out for nighttime visits to Mrs. Gallagher's boudoir.

In Joseph, he saw himself twenty-five years ago—naïve, so willing to please, and about to become a man. If Victor could save the boy from a life of crime, perhaps he could regain some of the dignity he'd traded for the chance to be more than a maid's son.

Not here, which meant Joseph was still outdoors hiding. He hurried back outside and nearly rammed into Marisol.

"You bastard!" The palm of her hand stung his cheek. "You are no better than the others. You are a liar and a fake."

"Never mind about me. I'm worried about Joseph. He's not in his bed."

"You were inside my house?" Her voice rose two octaves. Chin jutted out, she spoke through gritted teeth. "You stay away from my son. Haven't you done enough?"

His shoulders dropped. Yes, he had done plenty, but not enough. "Marisol. Listen. I went to check on the light in your shipping room...at first I thought it was you inside. I found Joseph. Now he's run off."

"That is so low. You blaming my son to prove your innocence. I saw the emeralds. You played me."

"I will help you find Joseph. He can't have gone far."

"My son is asleep. Go back to your cottage and pack."

Slamming past him, she went inside.

* * * *

Victor rubbed at his eyes. He'd slept like shit and wasn't sure he had the energy to deal with everything. Carlos's plan had gone amok. His brother's greed was going to get him killed, and drag others involved down with him. Victor couldn't let that happen to people he cared about.

The señora would be frantic, but he needed to borrow her truck again. He rounded the main house to the back drive, and then ran to the old delivery van. Wedging his hand inside, he grabbed the keychain in his fist and slid into the driver seat. The engine started with its usual cough and stall routine. The roar cut through the night, silent except for the birds tweeting the approach of dawn.

Easing out of the parking space, he remained in first gear, driving just fast enough to keep the van from stalling out and relying on headlights to spot a flash of Joseph's red shirt. The boy had been gone less than half an hour. How far could he have traveled on foot, if he had traveled at all? He might've taken his bike, Victor couldn't remember if it had been in its usual spot. On wheels, the boy could travel much farther, but he would have had to follow some sort of path, which meant he could have gone as far as Garcia—Bogotá even. Maybe Joseph had ridden his bike to a friend's house? Victor realized how little he knew about Joseph's social life. Had he accompanied Marisol to the soccer game, he might've picked up clues that would steer him in the right direction.

As Victor inched the van past the plantings, he leaned out the window to scan the aisles on each side of the driveway. His insides squeezed at the sound of Marisol's plaintive wail as she searched for her son. The fact that she called after the boy repeatedly meant she hadn't found him. If the boy wouldn't respond to his mother's calls, he certainly wouldn't come out of hiding for the uncle who caught him in the act of smuggling. No, if he were to spot the boy, he'd have to circumvent the area and sneak up on him. He didn't want to chastise the boy. He just wanted to keep him safe.

He spotted the beam of a flashlight Marisol must be using to wend her way through the wooded area just beyond the plantings. She was on foot. *Not safe.* Maybe he should drive in and pick her up? *No, that will rile her even more. She hates me now. She'll spit in my face if I go anywhere near her.*

His mission was to find Joseph, and at the same time continue his search for Carlos. Leaving Marisol to search for her son on her own, Victor drove out of the plantation and onto the main road to Garcia, keeping his speed to a crawl and scanning the road for someone traveling on foot or by bike. He slowed as he passed Soto's plantation. He chewed on the inside of his mouth. If Joseph traveled on foot across to the backfield, he might have scaled the fence and crossed over to Soto Flores. He was only twelve, after all.

Soto's men might hurt the boy. He had read enough thrillers to know where crime was concerned young boys were a commodity. Though from what Carlos told him, Soto wouldn't post his best men at a plantation where he spent little time. No, Sanchez and Miguel would be near Soto—at his Bogotá estate, maybe.

Scanning the sides of the road, Victor drove on. Other than a pickup truck headed in the opposite direction, the road was clear into Garcia. The shops on Main Street appeared closed, except for the green neon sign of Barra de Luis, which flickered feebly as if it was about to go out. A light glowed inside the bar, it seemed odd that Luis's was open for service this late. But what did Victor know?

After parking the van behind the line of vehicles in front of the building, Victor headed for the bar, lips clamped. The bar was a cartel hangout. When he peered in through the Luis's window earlier, he had shied away when he saw Sanchez and Miguel tipping brews, but now he needed answers and he was going to get them.

A lopsided "CLOSED" sign hung on the locked door. The stools were unoccupied, and the counter was clear of glasses and bottles. The crown of Luis's head stuck up from the counter, as if he were seated behind it.

"Hey, open up." Victor's fists rattled the glass.

Luis stood up abruptly, his hand on the butt of the pistol he kept tucked at his waist. The man's chest swelled, as if taking in a deep breath.

Getting accustomed to having a gun pointed at me can't be a good thing, Victor thought. Hmmm. Luis's eye twitched, now. Likely, he's been robbed more than once. *If the bar is supposed to be closed, why is he here?*

Weapon drawn, Luis approached the door.

"Remember me? Carlos's brother, Victor," he yelled through the glass.

Luis's face went blank, and then he tucked his gun in his belt and cracked open the door far enough for them to talk. "You cut your hair."

Victor ran a hand through his cropped hair. Was it only a few nights ago he was here and had his wallet lifted? He'd bet Luis had been in on the theft.

"If you came for another Aguardiente, it is too late." He pointed to the sign. "I am closed for the night."

"I'm looking for Carlos. Have you seen him?"

"Not tonight." Beads of sweat popped out on Luis's forehead, even though it was cool outdoors.

Victor reached in through the opening and grabbed Luis by the front of his shirt. He looked down into frightened eyes. "You're lying. And don't bother going for your gun. I'm not going to hurt you. I want the truth."

Luis's body went rigid.

Figuring he'd made his point Victor released his grip.

Luis fell back and mopped his forehead with his shirttail. "I don't know anything. Leave me out of this. I am just a poor bartender."

No tattoo, and the man seemed sincere. "Okay, for now. But If I don't find him, I'll be back." Victor stepped from the door. The lock clicked behind him, and he headed for the van.

As he settled in the driver seat, Luis's inside lights went out. The neon faded. *Wonder if Luis was waiting for something or someone?*

Victor drove to the only other place he could think to go.

* * * *

The night brightened to the pale sky of early morning. Dewdrops glittered over the fields, but dark clouds roiled overhead. It would rain today. How fitting. Marisol shoved a chunk of damp hair behind her ear, smoothed a hand over her sore throat, and called again. "Joseph." The sound came out in a hoarse rasp. It was no use. He had taken his bike and might be anywhere. Why would he run from her?

Her flashlight flickered as the battery weakened and it was not light enough to see well without it. She had done her best on foot. Damn that Victor. Had he not stolen their van, she might have caught up with Joseph by now. How could she have been so gullible as to fall for Victor's nice-guy act? She should have known he would disappoint her, like every other man in her life. Lesson learned.

She dragged herself back to the complex, noticing her sister's outdoor lights remained on. If Joseph had gone to her, Rosario would be watching for Marisol from the window. With Carlos still missing, Rosario did not need to take on her problems as well.

Joseph could not have gone far. Maybe he circled back. In fact, right now he could be inside their cottage fast asleep. A surge of fresh adrenaline went through her as she pushed open their cottage door and shouted his name with what little voice she had left. The sound echoed through the emptiness.

Making her way down the hall, she stopped in front of his room. *Please let him be inside.*

Opening it, a bubble of relief exploded in her chest. She tiptoed inside, so as not to waken him. Her questions could wait until they both had a few hours of sleep, but she had to make sure he was all right.

"Joseph." She touched the lump in the bed, it felt wrong, not like a sleeping boy. "Joseph?"

She threw back the covers and burst into tears. Grabbing the pillow, she tossed it on the floor. "You are not my son, you fluffed up bunch of feathers. What have you done with him?"

Picking up the pillow, she hugged it to her chest and inhaled Joseph's musky scent. Throwing a childish tantrum was not going to bring back her son. Her little boy had slept on this pillow and he was missing. She fluffed the pillow and set it at the head of the bed, where it belonged, and straightened his covers.

A stray hair fluttered against her cheek. The breeze. *Where had it—* she went to the window and found it half open. *So that's how he got out without me seeing him.* How many times had Joseph pulled this disappearing act on her? And why? Was he sneaking out to see a girl, or getting into trouble with one of his friends? She thought she knew her son, but now she wondered.

Mama would know what to do. Perhaps they would call, Berto, although the man seemed not to have as much influence as he suggested. He had not helped much with fingering Soto for their break-in the past week, so what could he do for them now? Still...

Marisol ran from the cottage and rapped on Mama's door, which she now kept locked and chained. Nothing. Then she realized it was dawn and her mother would be sleeping. The bedroom was far enough away so she was not likely to hear the door. Turning away, she walked down the steps, plodding past the decorative hedging that hid the alarm system wires, around to the side of the house. On her toes, she peered into Mama's bedroom window. She was in bed curled to one side, as if leaving room for Papa.

The window had been left open at the top, which was typical of Mama. She never shared Papa's paranoia about attack. Even now, when Soto had shown his fangs, she did not believe she could be harmed.

Marisol tapped a musical beat against the glass. "Mama," she cried, but her voice came out in a hushed rasp.

Mama stirred in her bed, and then sat up. Her hand went to her mouth when she saw who it was. She came to the window, frowning.

"Let me in the front, Mama. We need to talk."

Mama pointed in the direction of the living room.

At the front door, Marisol waited, shivering in her soiled nightgown and gardening clogs, while Mama undid the bolts.

"Marisol, my child, what has happened to you?" Mama's arms were warm around her. "Why, you are chilled to the bone."

The night must have been cold, but until now, Marisol never realized it.

Grabbing the hand-knitted blanket from the sofa, Mama wrapped it around her shoulders.

"He is gone," she choked out. "My Joseph."

"That cannot be. He is just a boy. Where would he go?"

"You do not understand, Mama." She looked to the kitchen. "I could use a glass of water."

"Of course. I will make coffee."

"Yes, coffee. Good and hot."

Marisol pulled out a chair and sat at the table, her head in her hands, allowing the normal sounds of Mama rustling about the kitchen to soothe the ragged fear that something awful had happened to her son.

While the coffee perked, Mama set a small shot glass in front of her. "Drink this."

She obeyed, allowing the sharp bitterness of Papa's stash of malt liquor to send numbing heat down her throat and into the pit of her stomach.

Mama pulled up a chair. "Tell me."

"I have been everywhere. He took his bike. I walked as far as I could on foot..."

Mama's eyes went to Marisol's face. "Why, you are all scratched up." She rose, returning with a pan of warm water and soap. Kneeling in front of her, Mama cleaned the dirt from the scratches on her face, arms, and legs. "Why did you not take the van?"

"I was going to, but by the time I figured out Joseph was not in our cottage, it was missing."

Mama's eyes narrowed. "Victor borrowed the van earlier, but he returned. I saw it parked out back before I went to bed."

"All I know is it is gone, and so is Victor."

"Carlos?"

"No sign of the Cherokee. Rosario's porch light is lit."

Mama shook her head.

"I know. How can everything go wrong so fast? I cannot stand it anymore, Mama. Every step we take forward brings us back in place. Now the worst has happened."

Mama did not reply. She did not have to. Her face a stony mask, she dumped the dirty water into the sink, and then went into the bathroom. She moved in slow motion, as if trying hard to understand.

Mama returned with the bag of cotton balls and the bottle of iodine, which Marisol knew would burn. She did not care; she wanted to hurt; she wanted to feel something other than despair.

Once Mama was satisfied Marisol's wounds were in order, she set two mugs of steaming coffee on the table.

"About Joseph," Mama said, ready to listen.

Marisol closed her eyes to clear the horror of the futile hours spent tramping through woods and along the side roads. "I was in bed, but not asleep, and heard noise outside my cottage. A man's voice shouted Joseph's name. I ran to the door and found Victor, the man you thought was so nice. He was out of breath, as if he had been running, and was looking for Joseph. Then I noticed the light was on inside our greenhouse. I think Joseph noticed it from his bedroom window, went to check, and found Victor..."

Her hands flew to her lips. "I...almost forgot. Everything is out in the open."

Mama set down her cup. "What do you mean?"

Marisol bolted out of her chair, letting the blanket fall to the floor, and ran to unlock the connecting door. "Just come."

She and Mama rushed into the greenhouse and headed for the shipping room, finding the light remained on with at least a dozen stems wilting inside the open crate.

"Emeralds, Mama. Hidden in our lilies." She lifted a bloom from the crate, plucked out the cotton ball, and turned it upside down. An emerald as large as the tip of her thumb dropped into the palm of her hand.

"*Madre de Dios*." Mama picked up the gem and held it to the light; its intense green color reflected in her eyes. "Very rare, with wheel markings. Papa would say this emerald is worth millions."

The greed on Mama's face forced Marisol to take a step back. *Who is this woman?*

"All the blooms packed, so far, must contain emeralds of great worth." Mama picked up the small brown bag, lying open on the shipping table. "And look, there are more in here."

"Victor and Carlos know these gems are here. Do you not think they will try to retrieve them?" Marisol said.

She replayed the run-in with Victor. He had been hell-bent on finding Joseph. Her jaw tightened hard enough to make her teeth ache. Her son was in trouble and it was her fault for trusting Victor. Joseph must have surprised Victor, and then run off. What did Victor plan to do if he found Joseph? Carlos had to be part of this. He claimed to be Joseph's friend, but what would he do to a boy who stumbled onto his smuggling scheme?

"They must have Joseph," she said, sucking back a sob. "Leave the gems. Pretend we never saw them. We need to call the police."

"Police? Do not be foolish. Why should we put billions of dollars in their pockets, when all this can be ours? Why, we would never have to work another day. You can have your wish and keep Garcia Jardines going forever. We could even expand. Buy out Soto's lands, with plenty left over to send Joseph to the finest college in America. "She pressed her lips against the Trapiche emerald and added it to the bag, her fingers lingering on the stone as if she didn't want to let it go, even for a second.

"Those emeralds do not belong to us." Marisol snatched the bag from Mama's grip and rolled down the top to close it. She would not look inside. They were just stones, pieces of green rock that someone would be after. She held the bag as far away as her extended hand would allow.

"Dirty money, Mama. I do not want it, and neither should you.

When the time comes, I will find a way to pay Joseph's tuition...and we will run an honest business, one we can be proud of."

"Give me that bag, Marisol." Mama tore the bag from Marisol's grip with such strength that the bag fell open. The gems ping-ponged on the floor, like a cascade of marbles.

"Now, look what you have done." Mama knelt, scooping up the stones and shoving them into the pocket of her robe.

Marisol's insides crushed into a tight ball. *This is not happening.* "I will not be a party to this, Mama. You are on your own."

She stomped out of the shipping room, sniffing back a sob. Her own mother. No better than the rest.

Chapter Seventeen

Victor rode shotgun in the flower van with Berto at the wheel. Like police officers on a beat, they'd been everywhere, asking questions and knocking on doors. Still, no clue as to Carlos's and Joseph's whereabouts.

Berto stroked his jaw. "Soto's men must have Carlos. I am not sure why they would kidnap Joseph, though."

"The emeralds. Carlos must have told them about Joseph." Victor clenched his fist. If they found Carlos alive, he planned to show his brother a few karate kicks that would send him flying over the mountains.

"Of course, Soto's men can be very persuasive. Let us hope they are still alive."

The inside of Victor's mouth went dry. "What do you mean, *alive?*" He stared at Berto, wanting him to take back the ugly thought.

Berto shrugged. "Soto's band is tough. They will stop at nothing to get what they want."

Victor's mind spun in mucky circles. His brother could be dead. And Joseph—was Soto so heartless he would kill an innocent boy? "We have to find them. Tonight. I mean this morning."

He shook out his shirt and sniffed at it. In the few minutes he and

Berto had been in Club Galilistico, it had picked up the odor of blood and feathers from the cockfights. Angel had been flopped over the bar, gripping his glass of whiskey like a crutch. His bloodshot eyes laced with pain, and his jaw a swollen mess. With a boozy slur, he denied seeing Carlos.

"What now?" he asked Berto, as they chugged up the highway from Bogotá.

Berto scratched his head. "Soto's estate is up the road."

"You think he would…"

"We should have a look while we are here."

Berto veered off the highway, turned up a side road toward the gated entry, and then hooked a left and drove over manicured lawn until they reached a wooded area. He secreted the van behind a clump of foliage, wet with morning dew.

"Stay away from the fencing. He has it wired."

"Then how do we get in?"

Berto winked. "Follow me."

Berto lumbered forward, the pockets of his "lucky" brown jacket sagging with the basics for a search such as theirs. After fifteen minutes of tromping through untamed forest, they reached a clearing at the foot of the mountains.

Victor whistled. "Nice digs." A golf-course-smooth lawn rolled up to the backside of a three-story, adobe mansion with a tiled roof and terraces branching from every level.

Had Carlos's plan come to fruition, Victor might have owned such a house. He envisioned himself inside, sleeping on satin sheets in a king-sized bed. He would loll in bed as long as he wished and, when he decided to rise, would ring for his personal valet, who would bring him coffee and freshly baked croissants on a silver tray.

Victor wasn't sure he wanted that anymore. That lifestyle was as pretentious as his companionship business—all show, but hollow inside. He experienced a different existence the past few days. Even if he were to become the richest man in the world, it occurred to him he wouldn't be happy without being surrounded by people who cared about him.

"Not an easy house to secure," Berto said. "But then, Soto does not need to worry. He has installed the latest security system."

"How do you know all this?"

"I have friends."

Friends? Victor tried to think if he had ever had a real friend he could share secrets with, before Carlos. *Where are you, my brother?*

Staying deep in the brush, they skirted the clearing and sneaked onto the property through what Berto claimed was the gap in the wiring. One step in the wrong direction and they would be toast. They stopped, hidden, watching Soto's servants starting their day. A man in a white shirt and khaki pants scooped debris from a turquoise lap pool capped with a canopied Jacuzzi. Outside a six-car garage, a similarly uniformed figure hosed down a fancy white Jeep with a heavy chrome fender.

Berto scanned the property with a pair of folding binoculars.

"May I borrow those?" Victor held the binoculars to his eyes and focused on the man. *Bandaged shoulder.* "It's Miguel. I'll bet he knows something." He handed them back to Berto.

"Better to question him off the premises," Berto said. "I do not want to explain to Gomez Soto why we are sneaking around his property. I see a shed on the other side of the lawn. If we approach it from the rear, I doubt we would set off an alarm. We should check it out."

"Uh...yes, of course." A shed would make a great holding area for a small boy or an unconscious man.

Victor started after Berto, when, out of the corner of his eye, he noticed a flash of movement at the back of the mansion.

Two animals as large as horses bounded out and rolled over on the lawn, playing, and then stood, suddenly alert.

He pressed a hand onto Berto's arm and pointed. "Dogs. Great Danes. They've caught our scent."

"I know. Here they come. I am out of here." Tripping over his feet, Berto raced toward the van, leaving Victor standing within ten feet of the red wooden building.

Victor didn't know Berto well enough to judge him, but it surprised him a former cop would run rather than face a situation. Berto carried a gun, and all Victor had for defense were his bare hands. Well, Berto could be a coward, but he'd be damned if he was going to let two puppies keep him from making sure his brother or Joseph weren't being held inside the small building.

Like a couple of racetrack dogs, the Danes covered too much ground in too short a time. One, he might be able to handle, but two would wrestle him to the ground.

Victor lunged forward with the Danes barking at his heels, grasped hold of the door latch, a wrought iron, lift-up style, and pushed it open. As he ducked inside, he started at the clatter of tools of some sort. The shed was dark and smelled of rusty metal. Flies buzzed at his legs when his foot struck something small and squishy.

Outside, the barking turned ferocious. The building shook from the impact of heavy paws beating for entry. Victor threw his weight against the door to offer some resistance, but he didn't expect the thin wood to hold up forever.

He held his breath at the piercing squeal of a whistle. The barks became whimpers. The thudding on the door stopped. "Lauren, Bacall, you naughty dogs. Daddy does not want you near the tool shed." A female voice penetrated the walls.

Daddy?

"There is nothing in there for you." She spoke perfect English.

The dogs whimpered and pawed the door.

"Very well. I will check."

Crap. Releasing his pent up breath, Victor flattened his body against the backside of the wall nearest the door hinge.

The door banged open. Daylight flooded in. He couldn't see the woman, but from the strength and vitality of her voice, she was an adult—perhaps the daughter Berto mentioned. The dogs continued sniffing, still pressing against the door, squashing him flat against a handle of some tool. *Don't breathe.*

"Stop that," the woman said." It is only a bird. Poor thing must have flown in here and starved to death."

A scrape of metal against dry wood. "There, all gone."

At the snap of leashes being clipped to collars, Victor let out a breath.

"Come on, let us go."

While the door was closing, Victor glanced around—fertilizer, rakes, hoes, and a hand plow. No sign human life here.

He waited until he was certain the Danes and their mistress had gone back inside the house before he crept out, and sneaked through the brush to reach the flower van.

Berto sat waiting in the driver seat. "You were lucky. Soto's dogs are trained to kill on command."

"*Mucho gracias* for leaving me to investigate alone."

"*Da nada*," Berto said, visibly unfazed by Victor's sarcasm. "Find anything interesting inside?"

"Nope. Just tools and a dead bird."

Berto nodded, and turned the key in the ignition. "I did not think Soto would harbor anyone in his home. Knowing the way Soto operates, they would be held far from any of his properties."

Victor sucked in a breath, and then sputtered out, "Why didn't you say so before I risked my life to check out a red herring?"

* * * *

Marisol stumbled out of the shipping area, leaving Mama to gather up the emeralds. Her head pounded and the few sips she had taken of coffee curdled in her stomach. She pushed aside her mother's greed and focused on Joseph. It did not make sense that he had run off. Even if he was afraid of Victor, he should have returned home once Victor stole their van and drove off. Of course, her son was innocent. But if he noticed a light inside the greenhouse from his room, why would he not have roused her; or at least left through the cottage door, instead of creating a pretense of being asleep and sneaking out his bedroom window?

The greenhouse window vibrated with the impact of a large and weighty object.

Marisol threw herself on the floor and crawled under a table of plantings. Their plantation had not been bombarded since the attack; just before Soto had Papa killed. This had to be Soto's doing, and it had something to do with the emeralds.

"What was that?" Mama called, rushing out of the shipping room.

"Shush." She twisted toward her mother and motioned. "Down."

Mama hit the floor and crawled under the table nearest the shipping room. They waited for what seemed like hours, eyeing each other, until no further attack came.

Finally, Mama rose. "Gomez is at it again. First our gardens, now our greenhouse." Her arms crossed in front of her, hiking up the hem of her robe a few inches to reveal the flash of tan paper peeking from her pocket.

Drawing in a shaky breath, Marisol pushed herself upright and moved to the window. Her hand went to her throat and her heart pounded with fear. "Noooo." She shoved open the door and raced outside, with Mama's slippered feet padding behind her.

"Joseph's bike. It cannot be. How did they...? Oh, Mama, something awful has happened to my son." She fell into her mother's arms, soaking the shoulder of her robe with her tears.

Gently, Mama pushed her away. "Something is taped to the handlebar, Marisol."

Tears blurred her vision. When she stared at the two-wheeler, she envisioned her son mounted atop it, feet pumping as he cycled off to school. "It is going to cost us to repair that bike." She sucked back a sob.

Moving toward it, she smoothed her hand along the dented frame, dampened with morning dew. "It will rust." Bending down, she picked up the front wheel that must have fallen off with the impact and hugged its boney frame to her chest as if it were Joseph. Only then could she bear to look at the white paper wrapped around the handle-bar, glowing in the light of breaking dawn.

* * * *

Victor let out an exasperated breath. "Any other great ideas, Berto? So far, we've batted zero."

"You said Carlos left after a phone call?"

"Yes. He seemed agitated, but wouldn't tell me a thing."

"If he sensed danger, he would not have gone willingly. Let us talk to Rosario and find out if she has heard from Carlos. I called a trusted friend in the *policia*." Berto patted his belt, where he had clipped a two-way radio. "He is on alert for my call."

A trusted friend. Victor had heard the same expression from Carlos. He realized now, he could depend on no one to find his brother and Marisol's son. A pang of guilt forced him to look down. He'd taken Marisol's only means of transportation. She must be frantic. Maybe she found Joseph, though, and he only needed to worry about Carlos—although his gut said otherwise. "Do you have a working cell phone?"

Berto shrugged. "What would I need a cell phone for?"

"Like, now. Mine is back at the guesthouse. We could save ourselves a trip by phoning Rosario."

Berto clamped his lips. "Better we go there. We need to watch her face when she talks to us to make sure she is telling us the truth."

"You have a point." Even though he was ninety-nine percent sure

Rosario knew nothing, it would give him a chance to talk to Marisol and find out if Joseph was safe at home.

With Berto at the wheel, they chugged down the highway in silence. Cars and trucks whizzed past, blaring their horns. Victor wanted to press his left foot on top of Berto's to make the van go faster. The dashboard clock read sixish. A dusty dawn had arrived, leaving the sun behind a cement-colored sky thick with enough raw humidity to cause the peaks of the Andes to disappear into the clouds.

The engine droned on, lulling him to relax. Damn, he couldn't keep his eyes open.

By the time Victor awoke, the number of vehicles passing them had dwindled. He realized they had turned off the highway and were traveling on the two-lane road toward Garcia. Beside him, Berto's head nodded while his eyes kept fluttering closed.

"Can we pick up a cup of coffee somewhere?" Victor attempted to keep Berto awake.

"In Garcia, maybe."

"Good." Victor focused on the road. Drops of rain spattered at the windshield and all he could think of was Marisol's lilies. They would benefit from rain, but water would make taking care of the damaged area more difficult.

His eyes wandered as a white Jeep whizzed by in the passing lane. "Hey." He sat forward in his seat. "Did you see the plate on that car?"

Berto craned his neck, adjusting the glasses on his nose. "No, it is too far away now. You mean the Jeep?"

"I'm sure it's the same one we saw on Soto's property." His insides hummed with fresh adrenaline. "That's got to be Miguel, and he's headed toward Garcia."

* * * *

The slip of paper trembled in Marisol's hands. She reread the note and handed it to Mama. "They want the emeralds for Joseph."

Mama's face went hard. "Gomez is many things, but he would never harm an innocent boy. They are bluffing. I will call Berto. He will know how to handle this."

"But..." Marisol thought her heart would break as Mama left to go inside, her robe turning a blurry blue color through Marisol's watery gaze. The emeralds seemed more important to her than her grandson.

"What is going on?" Rosario called, hurrying toward her. "What... Oh my God, you look awful." Her gaze fell to the damaged bike. "What has happened?"

Marisol handed her sister the note. "It is Joseph."

Still wearing the red flowered dress she had on the past night, dark circles hung under Rosario's red eyes as they moved over the note. Her mouth opened in horror. "Joseph, in exchange for the emeralds? What emeralds?"

"I found Victor smuggling Trapiche emeralds in our shipping room. Joseph must have surprised him. He...was chasing after my son."

Rosario's mouth dropped open and her eyes widened.

Marisol could almost see her sister's mind working.

"Carlos left after a call and has not come back. I knew something was up, but I have learned not to ask questions." Her hand covered her mouth. "They must have my Carlos, too. I just saw Mama here. What did she say about this?"

Marisol let out a long breath. "She went to call Berto."

"Really? Berto?" Rosario's mouth twisted to the side.

"And..." the words stuck in Marisol's throat. Finally, she choked out, "She has the emeralds. Oh, Rosario, the look on her face when she saw them gave me goose bumps. I would not be surprised, if instead of phoning Berto, she is hiding the emeralds."

"Mama loves Joseph, she would never..."

"You did not see her face, Rosario."

* * * *

"Can't you drive any faster? We're losing the Jeep." Victor blew out an exasperated breath.

"I am doing the speed limit. Besides, it is raining and the streets are slick."

"Rain? You call this rain? Why, it's just a drizzle. Pull over. Let me drive."

With a screech, Berto swerved into the brush at the side of the road and jerked the car to a stop without bothering to downshift. The van stalled out. He shot open his door, hopped out, and walked around to the passenger side. "Go. You do."

"Sorry, pal." He laid a hand on Berto's shoulder. "It's just that we can't screw around."

Behind the wheel, Victor coaxed the van to restart and they were on their way. The white Jeep was no longer in sight, so pushing the old man out of the helm really wasn't going to make a difference now.

"Still want that coffee?" Berto asked.

"Might as well. Maybe we'll learn something at Juanita's."

Twenty minutes later, when they pulled into Garcia, Victor felt strangely at home. Even though a light mist of rain continued to fall, a silver-haired man swept the sidewalks outside his shop. Two dark-haired women sat, sheltered by an awning, on a cement step holding mugs and cradling fussy babies. The neon sign over Barra de Luis remained unlit. Victor scanned the vehicles parked alongside the road for signs of the white Jeep. *Nada.*

Hopping out of the van, they headed for the café and stood behind a line of locals getting to-go cups and sweet buns.

"Ah, you came back for more," Juanita's said, recognizing Victor from the previous night.

"No stew this morning. Just coffee. Two cups to go."

Berto nudged him and pointed at the tray of pastries.

"A couple of those, too," Victor said.

As Juanita tabulated the cost, Victor leaned in and spoke in a low voice. "You opened at five. Did you notice anything strange going on next door?" He tipped his head toward Luis's.

She handed him a white paper bag containing the pastries and napkins. "There was some shouting, but then it was quiet. I mind my own business."

"*Gracias, señora.*"

Grabbing their coffees from the counter, he and Berto walked outside. Berto started for the van.

"Wait. I want to check something out." Stepping onto the clay walk that fronted Luis's bar, Victor noted the closed sign remained in place. Posters glued to the glass on the upper door advertised Club Colombo beer. "I was here a few hours ago to ask after Carlos. It was after three, but Luis was inside. He denied knowing anything, but he seemed nervous."

"Perhaps he was worried about being robbed?"

"I doubt it. I think he was waiting for someone or something. The lights were on, but the closed sign was up and the door was locked. He wasn't open for business, so what was he doing in the bar at that time in the morning?" Victor jiggled the doorknob, and then banged on the upper part of the door, startled at his own grisly reflection. "Hand me your flashlight, Berto." He shot the light inside, scanning the shelved bottles and glasses. The counter was clear, no sign of life.

"You are wasting your time," one of the men who had just exited Juanita's said. "He will not open for business until eleven."

"Yes, I know, but I have to talk to Luis. Do you know where his house is?"

The man sized up Berto and Victor. "I do not know either of you." He narrowed his eyes. "Why do you want to see Luis?"

"We're looking for my brother, Carlos Rodriguez. I thought he might've stopped off here last night."

The man sipped his coffee. When he lifted his arm, Victor saw the green tattoo.

"I know this Carlos." The man's mouth turned down in a crooked sneer. "You should stop looking for him." Turning, he walked off.

"Does not sound good," Berto said.

"No. It doesn't." Victor envisioned Carlos lying somewhere, tied up, beaten to a pulp—or even dead. He'd almost lost him at the mine, and now— "I don't care. We can't give up until we get answers. Something fishy is going on at Luis's, closed or not, and we're going to find out what that is. Come on, Berto. Let's do this. There has to be a back door."

Taking the lead, Victor took loping steps to the corner, passing a tiny post office and a bank, and headed down a side street wide enough to accommodate a single car. Rain fell from the sky in a light patter, sticking his shirt to his body. Apartment buildings cast added gloom to the dismal morning. As Victor avoided a collection of trashcans, a scrawny black and white cat crept out and wove between his legs, purring.

"He likes you," Berto said.

"Yeah, must be my deodorant."

At the end of the street, they took a right and walked past a mail delivery truck and a dilapidated Buick. No white Jeep, which meant Soto's man might *not* be inside. The rear entrances to the buildings were unnamed, with plain wooden doors and corroded brass knobs. With the black and white cat at his heels, Victor counted down to the fourth door and turned.

"Go. Scat. Find a nice dry place to hang out."

The cat sat on its haunches, ears perked, and then laid down on the sidewalk with its face between his paws and looked up at him.

"Okay, be that way. Get rained on." Leaving the cat, he assessed the back entrance to Barra de Luis, which was covered with peeling decals advertising various liquors. The wood on the door around the knob was flaked, as if the place had survived a break-in. He tested the knob. Locked. Just in case, he banged on the door, and yelled, "Anybody in there?"

Above them, a man shouted, "Quiet. People are sleeping up here."

"*Policia*," Berto shouted back him.

Victor's sixth sense kicked in. "We have to get inside and check. Carlos could be in there, almost dead, unable to talk."

Berto shook his head. "I told that boy when he was growing up to stay out of trouble. He never listened. Does he join the National Police and make Nesto and me proud? No. He gets cozy with the cartel and the next thing I know he is working dirty security at the mines."

"Too late for regrets, Berto." Victor pressed his ear to the door. "I hear something. Not sure what it is."

"Kick in the door. It is hollow. It should cave easily," Berto said. "I used to be able to do that, but my leg bothers me now." He rubbed his right leg. "Gunshot wound to the knee."

Victor stepped back to get a running start and slammed the sole of his foot flat against the door. Pain vibrated up his leg. He was so out of shape. The door shook, but held firm. The cat was back, rubbing at his leg. With a light sidekick, he shoved it away. The animal hissed at him.

"Maybe we should let the police handle this," Berto said, pulling at his moustache.

"Why? For all we know the room could be empty. Any other ideas?"

Berto produced a pointed tool Victor didn't recognize. "Pick the lock."

"I don't believe you went ahead and let me jam my foot, when all along you had an easier way of getting inside." Victor took a few calming breaths.

Berto shrugged. "Sorry, *mi sabrino*. Forgot I brought this along."

A few clicks later, Berto turned the knob and inched open the door. They peered inside, the only light coming from their opened door. A musty odor tickled at Victor's nose. From the far corner, they heard a muffled bumping sound that was repeated at short intervals.

"You were right. Someone is in here."

Victor sucked in his breath, preparing for the worst.

Berto flicked on his flashlight. The beam scanned a room that was wider than it was deep. On their left, two five-tiered metal shelving units housed wine glasses, beer mugs, and boxed cocktail napkins. Cardboard cartons of liquor were stacked high on the right. The door that must lead into the bar was about a dozen feet ahead of them.

"The sound is coming from the left corner." Berto held his flashlight steady. "A door to another room."

"There's that noise again." Victor moved toward the door, his heart hammering.

Chapter Eighteen

Marisol's head swiveled around at the roar of wheels on wet dirt. Her blood ran cold. "Soto's car is coming down our drive. He has come to collect the emeralds."

Rosario's hand went to her mouth.

As the black sports car skidded to a stop in front of the main house, Marisol said a silent prayer that Mama would not open the front door. She had to have heard the car's low growl, and would realize Soto came in search of the emeralds. Marisol's throat tightened. With Rosario right behind her, she started toward the vehicle, loathing every step. Soto would be in the back seat, dressed for business in his expensive suit and tie. Was Joseph bound and gagged alongside him? With the car's blackened windows, it was impossible to see inside.

Prickles of moisture from the dampening grass wet her ankles, as if the plantation were crying right along with her. She sucked back the urge to burst into tears and straightened her back. She would deal with whatever was necessary to get back her son.

Sanchez's hulking body unfolded from the driver's seat. His classy black slacks and subdued sport shirt could not hide the fact that, underneath, he was as ruthless as his boss. As he moved, she caught the metallic gleam of the pistol shoved, nose-down, under his belt. Making no attempt to open the rear passenger door, Sanchez ambled toward them, a malicious smile on his smooth-shaven face.

"Nice of you women to greet me. I am here to check out Joseph's story."

They were in this together, she and Rosario, two women missing loved ones. And this man, this awful man who looked them over as if he were deciding on a meal, had to know where Joseph and Carlo were right now.

"My son. Where is he?" Marisol rushed toward Sanchez.

"And what about my Carlos?" Rosario came up beside her, her fists dug into her hips.

"If you want to see either of them again, you had better make sure I find the emeralds." Sanchez reached behind his back for the gun, black and ugly with a snub nose, a sleek flattened body and a rubberized handle. He pointed it at them.

Rosario gasped, as if she had never seen a weapon before, but Marisol knew different. Papa always carried a gun, for protection he said. Mama kept that gun hidden away. So far, they had not needed it.

"Those emeralds belong to the Green Fire Cartel. Your Carlos stole them from us," he said to Rosario. Sanchez stood a good foot taller than her; his words struck like a heavy rainfall.

Rosario drew up her petite frame. "I do not know what you are talking about. We have no emeralds. How dare you call my Carlos a thief? Why you...and to think I used to bring you coffee while you waited for your boss to make nice with our mama."

Marisol poked an elbow into her sister's ribs and hissed into her ear. "Do not aggravate him."

Sanchez grabbed Rosario with his free arm, twisted her to face the greenhouse, and then let go his hold.

"You." His fingers dug into the tender skin of Marisol's upper arm. He shoved her forward to stand beside her baby sister.

Marisol glanced toward Mama's. Right now, Mama could be behind that front curtain seeing Sanchez holding a gun on her daughters. Would she rush outside and hand over the emeralds, or try to ward off Sanchez by brandishing Papa's pistol? Mama never wanted to learn to shoot; none of them had.

They arrived at the door to the greenhouse with no sign of movement from the main house. The door opened easily, as Marisol had forgotten to lock it. Inside, raindrops banged at the glass like tiny gunshots. She scanned her plants as if seeing them for the last time, each seedling reaching for the light.

The door to the kitchen remained closed, confirming her suspicion. Mama must not be aware of what was going on. Perhaps she had gone back to bed after making sure the emeralds were hidden away, and was dreaming of the riches she would buy with the proceeds from them. Or maybe she had the police, or that do-nothing Berto, on the phone right this minute.

"The ship room. Where?" Sanchez growled.

Marisol nodded toward the far corner. She and Rosario exchanged glances.

"I know you do not believe us," Marisol told him," but Rosario and I do not know anything about these emeralds."

Sanchez stiffened and she could almost see his mind working.

"What about the señora? She must be inside the house. Why did she not come outside when I drove up?"

"She is a heavy sleeper," Rosario said. "It is only six."

"Well, let us wake her up. Maybe she knows something."

"You leave our mother out of this. If you want the real culprit, go find Victor Novak," Marisol spit out. "He took your precious emeralds. Give me back my son and leave us alone."

"Ah, so you lied to me. You do know about the emeralds. Victor Novak? That man would not have the guts to steal emeralds. But do not worry, pretty lady. Your son will be here soon. I sent Miguel to get him. When I hold a gun to his head, you will tell me what I need to know."

He poked the pistol into Marisol's back to propel her forward. She held her breath, not knowing if Mama had tidied the shipping room or left it as they found it, minus the emeralds. The door was ajar, allowing a beam of light to paint a path to the room a good twenty feet away.

As she and Rosario moved through the center aisle, Marisol's fingers brushed the tops of her seedlings, finding little comfort in assuring they remained healthy, alive.

At the shipping room door, Sanchez shoved them inside. "Bring me the emeralds."

The counter was clear of flowers; the shipping crate had been stored, the wastebasket emptied. Mama had done a thorough job of clearing any possible evidence that could have pointed to the emerald scheme.

Sanchez paced in front of the doorway, his gun at the ready, as she and her sister sifted through every drawer, every cabinet in a pretense of searching for the emeralds. Finally, he let out an exasperated breath. "You women are wasting my time. Joseph claimed the emeralds were in the ship room, hidden inside the lilies. I see no lilies here." He narrowed his eyes at them. "Maybe your son lied."

"No. We have lilies," Rosario said. She pointed at the refrigerated room. "In storage."

"Open it."

Rosario's hand shook as she pushed down the heavy chrome handle and opened the thickly insulated door to the refrigerated room. A blast of cold air wafted out.

"Now both of you. Inside, and start looking. Give a shout when you find them."

The door slammed behind her and Rosario like a death knell. The inside handle of the door had broken off, and they had not gotten around to repairing it. Marisol flipped on the light switch, tripping over the wedge used to keep the door ajar while they transported lilies. Despite the cold, the floral scent of dozens of ready-to-pack lilies filled Marisol's nose and sickened her stomach. The room was claustrophobic, not much bigger than a pantry—narrow, with shelves holding vases. She and her sister huddled between the shelving, chilled further by the rain-dampened clothing that clung to their skin.

"What are we going to tell him?" Rosario said in a quivery voice.

"We stall for time. Help could be on the way."

After a sufficient time had elapsed, Marisol banged on the door and shouted, "They are not in here. We have checked every lily."

The door swung open. They walked out, half-expecting Sanchez to kill them for not finding the gems.

But he did not. In fact, he had stashed his gun back in his belt, obviously deciding she and Rosario were not a threat. He let out an exasperated sigh and turned to Rosario. "Carlos must have hidden the emeralds in his house, then. We are going to search your place, Rosario. Too bad he cannot tell us where they are."

Rosario's face went white. "What do you mean?"

"He is gone, Rosario. You know, you are not too bad looking. Maybe you and I could..."

"You killed my husband. You...you..." Rosario's foot shot out and caught Sanchez hard between his legs.

Sanchez roared and doubled over. He slowly lifted his head. His face was a horrible mask of rage. Grabbing Rosario's arm, He twisted it behind her. "You bitch."

Marisol zeroed in on the handle of the gun sticking out from the back of Sanchez's waist.

"Do not even think about it." Sanchez's foot struck her.

She landed in a heap on the tiled floor.

Still gripping a sobbing Rosario, Sanchez pressed his foot into Marisol's ribcage. "I could crush you with one foot. Do not move." Throwing Rosario on the floor next to her, he pulled out his gun.

The thud of his work boots pacing in front of them sent vibrations through Marisol's body. He paused and towered over them, his weapon pointed down. Marisol stared into its snub nose.

"Now, where were we? Yes. We were going to search your house. But first, there is something I have been itching to do since I walked into this stinking place." Keeping his gun aimed at them, Sanchez stepped to the side and moved backward through the aisle between the plantings. Using his free hand, he made a wide arc, sending table after table of seedlings crashing to the floor.

Brushing the wetness from her face, Rosario buried her face in her sister's shoulder. Marisol gasped, but held her tongue. *What did it matter? What did anything matter anymore?*

"Stop," Rosario shouted, sitting up. "The emeralds are not in my house. I know where they are."

"Sure you do." Sanchez sauntered toward them. He held the nose of the weapon against Rosario's head. "Last chance, sweet thing. The truth, or I swear I will gun down your whole family. Your sister here." He nudged Marisol. "Then her son, and your mother."

Rosario licked her lips. Her throat moved as she swallowed hard enough to be audible. "My mother has them."

* * * *

Victor ripped the filthy bandana from Joseph's mouth and threw it on the floor. The boy's eyes were wide, his face pale and tear-stained, and his red soccer shirt muddy and torn. Joseph sat on the commode in the tiny bathroom in the storeroom of Barra de Luis. Thick rope held his spine against the water closet and was coiled around his wrists and feet.

"They were going to kill me. I had to tell them." His words came out in hiccupping sobs. "Mama was working so hard and *Abuela* needed money. Carlos told me if I put the emeralds in the lilies, he could sell them in America and we would all be rich."

A stab of guilt sliced through Victor's heart. Carlos hadn't told Joseph that Victor was in on the smuggling scheme—and it made no sense to reveal that fact now. Stooping to eye level, Victor took Joseph's face in his hands. "It's okay, son. It was good you wanted to help your family save Garcia Jardines, but you weren't going about it in the right way."

"Berto." He held out his hand. "Your pocketknife."

Joseph looked away as Victor sawed through braided rope as thick as an old-fashioned clothesline. Once his hands were free, he brushed the wetness from his cheeks and sniffled.

"Hurt?" Victor pointed to the red rings circling Joseph's wrists.

"A little." He pressed his hand on Victor's arm. "You have to stop Sanchez and Miguel. They went to Garcia Jardines to get the emeralds."

The emeralds. He caught Joseph hiding them, but Marisol had gone inside afterward. Were they still as Joseph left them, or did his mother clean up after him?

"How long ago?" Berto asked. He coiled the cut lines that had held Joseph and draped them over his arm.

Joseph shrugged. "I do not know. It seems like forever."

"Come on." Victor took Joseph's hand and the three of them started for the door, which they had left ajar.

With a slam, the door flew open with a flood of light. "Not so fast."

Miguel's dark figure cast a shadow on the aisle walkway. His gun gleamed silver.

Berto's hands went up, the coiled lines sliding onto his shoulder.

Victor pushed Joseph behind him and drew in a breath.

"You, too, *Vickie*," Miguel said in a taunting voice. "Arm's not doing so good. I will find a way to thank you for that later. Hand over the boy."

Behind him, Joseph sucked in a breath.

"Steady now," he whispered. "Stay right where you are."

"Keep those hands in the air, Vickie. I'd hate to shoot you and spoil the fun of beating you to a pulp." He motioned with his gun. "Come on, boy. I want your mama to hear you scream." Miguel smiled an evil smile that showed too many teeth.

Meanwhile Victor tested his foot against the lowest carton in the stack of three. The stack was weighty, but with the right angle, he could—

"Do you really want to do this, Miguel?" Berto said. "You have gotten away with petty theft, but now you are in deep with kidnapping. Do not add murder to the charges or you will be in the jail for life."

"What do you know old man?"

"Your wife will miss you," Berto continued, "and you will not get to watch your son and daughter grow up. You will be behind bars with other criminals, men. You are not a big man. You have heard the stories..."

The confident smile drained from Miguel's face.

Without moving the upper part of his body or taking his eyes from Miguel, Victor bent his right leg at the knee and rammed it into the stack of boxes. The top carton hit the floor on one corner, splitting the cardboard and spewing six packs of canned beer in the aisle. The cat, who must have followed them inside, leapt from the top of the adjacent stack of boxes and onto Miguel.

Miguel stumbled backward, tripping on the cans. "Get off me." He pushed at the cat, who clawed at Miguel's shoulders and seemed to have no intention of letting go. His gun hand flailed to the side. A bullet rammed into the ceiling. The burning stench of gunpowder filled the room.

Judging the distance, Victor leapt over the mess and landed on top of Miguel before he could take aim. Miguel expelled an involuntary breath as Victor's knees dug into his chest.

"Drop it." Victor slammed the thug's gun arm. The gun clattered to the floor and bounced out of reach. The cat followed the movement and went to investigate.

Berto stood over them, his gun drawn. "It is over Miguel. You are going to join the big boys in jail. Keep the gun on him while I tie his hands and feet." He passed his gun to Victor.

"Didn't know you carried, Berto." The pistol was cool in his hand. "We could have used this a few times tonight to get answers we needed."

"Everyone here carries a gun for protection."

Joseph crept forward, his face white and his eyes fearful.

"It's all right now, Joseph. We're going to go help your mama now," Victor told him.

"The cat." Joseph stooped to pet the animal. "He helped us. Can we take him with us?"

"He must belong to someone in the neighborhood, besides we have a job to do at Garcia Jardines and he would just get in the way."

"I see." Joseph dropped his head. "You are right, *Tio* Victor." He gave the cat a last pat. "Goodbye, Savior."

"I will have my friends in the *policia* ask around," Berto said. "If the animal is a stray, I will let your grandmother know."

"Gracias, Tío Berto." Joseph stood, ready to leave.

Using the ropes that once held Joseph, Berto set to work. "I will wrap this guy up and phone the police. You take the kid to the plantation in the van. I will be right behind you."

"But how will I..."

Berto smiled. "Simple." He dug into Miguel's back pocket for the keys to the Jeep and tossed them to Victor.

Raising his hands, Victor caught the keys and then drew Joseph alongside him. He stared down at Miguel. His face went hard. He knelt down and studied Miguel's wrist. *The designer knock-off with the scratch across its face.* "That watch. Where did you get it?"

Miguel just smiled.

* * * *

"Let us go find the señora." Sanchez poked the nub of the gun into the small of Rosario's back. "You. Get up," Sanchez ordered Marisol.

Holding her hand against the sharp pain in her side, Marisol rose to stand beside Rosario. "Now you've done it," she hissed.

"He said Carlos..."

"You know better than to believe the likes of Sanchez."

"Hey, quiet." Sanchez grabbed a roll of the sisal rope they used for supporting plants. "Hands behind your backs."

The thin fibers of the rope scratched at Marisol's wrists as he wound it around and between them. Without cutting the rope when he was satisfied, he ran a length to Rosario and bound her, as well.

"I should gag you two, but I would hate to hide your pretty lips. Besides, I need you to convince your mother to give me the emeralds."

Yoked like a couple of oxen, Sanchez used the butt of his pistol to nudge them forward.

"I cannot open the door, with my hands tied," Rosario said.

Sanchez reached around her and tried to turn the knob. "It is locked. Get your mother to open it."

"Mama, it is me, Rosario. Open up."

Marisol drew in a breath, her teeth rattling from the tension in her jaw. *Does Rosario not realize that once Sanchez has the emeralds, he will have no need to keep any of us alive?*

Behind the door, Marisol heard the shuffle of Mama's bedroom slippers, and then clicking noises.

"No, do not open it, Mama," she yelled.

Sanchez struck her across the mouth. She tasted blood, but it was worth it. The clicking noises stopped. Mama had heard her.

Sanchez nudged Rosario. "Tell her."

"Mama, Sanchez has us, he is going to..."

The door swung open. Mama stood a few feet away holding Papa's gun.

Sanchez laughed. "You going to shoot your daughters? Drop it, Señora."

"He has a gun at our backs, Mama," Rosario cried.

Mama's face was ashen. She set Papa's gun on the kitchen table and stepped aside to allow them into the kitchen.

Marisol inhaled the calming aroma of the fresh pot of coffee perking on the stove. Sanchez's large hand slammed into her back. She and Rosario stumbled toward the sink. Mama came hurtling after them, banging against the counter.

Sanchez motioned at Mama with his gun. "Step away from your daughters and keep your hands where I can see them. We need to talk about my emeralds."

Marisol scanned the area around her. If she could find a way to break the bond holding Rosario and her together, they might have a chance against Sanchez. She studied the countertop behind and around her. Nothing within reach that would help. Then she nudged Rosario and whispered in her ear. "We need to rub the line between us against the edge of the counter."

Rosario nodded, and they began work to fray the packing twine, while Sanchez was focused on Mama.

Mama's hands went to her throat. "What would I know about *your* emeralds?"

Mama was playing coy, and Marisol could kill her for it. "Give them to him, Mama."

Sanchez checked his watch. "Miguel must be running late. I wanted you all to watch me kill the boy. Too bad, he is smart boy, one day he might have joined our cartel. What about it, señora? Are those emeralds worth more to you than your grandson is?"

Mama's lower lip trembled, and then Marisol saw her eyes harden like two brown bullets. "You killed my husband. Now you want to kill my grandson? God will send you to hell."

"Hell? I am already in hell. Now give, old woman. Or I will start with your daughter." He grabbed hold of Marisol's hair and yanked back her head, exposing her throat.

She stared at the ceiling. She could die right here in Mama's kitchen. His face was close to hers. His dark eyes glittered with greed and she could smell his foul breath. She tried to twist away. His hand tightened in her hair and she grimaced.

Sanchez's lips curled in smug satisfaction. The snout of his pistol jammed into the soft spot under her chin. When she swallowed, the cold metal dug in further.

Chapter Nineteen

Wipers scraped vertical arcs across the windshield of Miguel's white Jeep as Victor turned into the drive of Garcia Jardines and spotted a black dot, which had to be Soto's Jaguar, parked in front of the main house. *Too late. They are already here.* He scraped his lower lip with his teeth. Getting inside without being seen would take some finesse. Swerving onto the scruffy lawn, he parked behind the guesthouse, where the Jeep would be hidden from view, and killed the engine.

"Wait here," he said to Joseph, indicating the guesthouse. He stepped onto the slippery, wet grass and pocketed the keys.

"I am coming with you." Joseph pushed open the door on the passenger side and ran to his side.

"Oh no, you're not. I'm not going to rescue you twice. Didn't you see Señor Soto's car in the driveway?"

"But Mama is in trouble and it is all my fault." Joseph's breathing was hard and his face filled with pent emotion. He brushed a hand through his short dark hair. "I wanted to help *Abuela* save the plantation. I never meant..."

"Shush. It's not your fault." Victor tucked Miguel's gun into his waistband as he had seen others do. He hoped to hell the damn thing wouldn't go off.

He pushed open the door of the guesthouse, shaking off the feeling of homecoming. Marisol's floral scent wafted into his nostrils. He sucked in a ragged breath. *I let her go. And now, I've really blown it with her.* Joseph looked up at him as if he were a God, but Victor knew different. He was no God—far from it. But the boy didn't deserve to be disappointed in him.

"Go on inside and barricade the door behind you. You can watch from the window...just don't get caught."

Joseph nodded, though rebellion flashed in the boy's eyes. Rather than abandon Joseph, he might be better off taking him along. At least he could keep track of his whereabouts and try to protect him. He sighed in resignation. "All right. You can come. Stay right behind me."

Joseph's face sagged with relief. "I know how to get into *Abuela's* house."

"Good, because we can't go through the front door."

"They might be inside the greenhouse."

"I know." A vision of the glittering green emeralds strewn across the packing counter flashed before Victor's eyes. He could've snatched them up and run off instead of chasing after Joseph. The old Victor would've never given the boy a thought. But Joseph touched a part of him that hadn't worked in years. His heart.

As they crept down the drive, Victor kept an eye out for incoming traffic. Berto should have been right behind him in the van. As they neared the main house, Victor's gaze strayed to Carlos's cottage. Was his brother really dead, or had Miguel stolen Carlos's watch after beating his brother unconscious?

Dropping into a crawl, Victor and Joseph snuck along the hedge bordering the driveway. Soto's black Jaguar lay in wait like a sleek cat. There was no sign of Sanchez's telltale stream of cigar smoke emanating from the driver's seat. The man must be inside with Gomez Soto. Where was Marisol? And what would those men do to her, the señora, and Rosario? The memory of Joseph, captured and restrained, sent involuntary shivers down his spine. He scanned the upper drive. *Come on, Berto. All you had to do was call the police, then hop into the van.*

Realization sunk like a boulder to the pit of his stomach. *No time to wait for help.* He fisted his hands at his side. He had taken Miguel twice already. Certainly he could handle a frail old man and his bodyguard. Besides, he smoothed his fingers over the handle of Miguel's gun, he had help.

Joseph nudged him. "*Tio* Victor. Around back." He pointed to the far side of the main house. "*Abuela* usually keeps her bedroom window open for air."

"Glad I brought you along, sport." Victor put his arm around Joseph's slim shoulders and felt hard muscle. Trying to avoid trampling the flowerbeds that framed the main house, they stooped below window level and crept to the rear.

Joseph stopped and pointed to a single window about six feet above the ground. The window was cracked open at the top, which meant it was not locked.

With a leap, Victor managed to grab hold of the lower sill with the tips of his fingers and pull himself up. He peered in at a rumpled bed. Empty, as he expected. The door to the hall was ajar.

"You'll have to get on my shoulders."

Victor stooped to allow Joseph to straddle his shoulders.

With the extra height, the boy managed to open the lower half of the window. "I hear voices. Think they are in the kitchen." Joseph heaved himself inside with Victor's help.

"Come on." Joseph leaned over the sill and held out his arms to Victor.

With a leap, Victor grabbed hold of the sill.

Latching his hands around Victor's wrists, Joseph tugged, stepping backward as Victor's belly scraped across the sill. When he was far enough in, Joseph let go of his hands so he could drop the remainder of the way to the floor and "walk" himself the rest of the way. His feet dropped onto the tiled floor with a thump.

Victor froze, waiting. No footsteps headed in their direction. "Good."

Joseph started for the door.

"Oh no, you don't," he said in a hushed voice. Grabbing the back of the boy's shirt, he motioned for him to hide under the bed. Joseph complied with a sulky expression.

"Now stay there. I have to focus and don't need you distracting me."

Victor peered around the doorway and down the short hall, which led to the living room. From the kitchen beyond, a male voice shouted orders. Pressing his body flat against the wall, he edged toward the open doorway, holding Miguel's pistol in his right hand for bogus support. The chamber of the gun was empty, he had discovered. He would need to bluff his way through this.

Sanchez's voice rang out. "Hell? I am already in hell. Now give, old woman. Or I'll start with your daughter."

Daughter? Marisol. Oh, shit. Victor's heart pounded. In his mind's eye, he envisioned the layout of the kitchen, a square shaped room overwhelmed by a huge table. The bathroom was opposite the end of the table and adjacent to the door to the greenhouse.

"No, please," the señora cried. "I have the emeralds. Let her go."

"Where are they?" Sanchez demanded.

"Here. In the kitchen."

Victor caught a glimpse of Sanchez's back. The thug's arm was bent and... *Oh, fuck. He's going to kill Marisol.* Victor's heart stopped beating. If he jumped Sanchez, the gun could go off. *A distraction.* That's what he needed. He felt in his pocket for the keys to the Jeep. Taking careful aim, he hurled them toward the table. They landed with a metallic thump.

Sanchez's gun came away from Marisol's throat. He swiveled around, poised to shoot. "Who is there? Show yourself."

Victor ducked back out of sight. All three women were in the room, but it was Marisol who Sanchez tortured, her face white with fear, eyes like a deer in the headlights. Raw rage tore at his gut. His trigger finger itched against the cold metal of the gun. Then he remembered. *No Goddamn bullets.*

He shoved the gun into his waist and ripped the sneaker off his right foot. He hurled it toward the kitchen where it landed in the doorway.

Sanchez's gun went off. The sneaker flew up, hit the ceiling, and then tumbled back onto the floor. Victor flattened himself against the wall outside the kitchen, his nostrils twitching at the smell of gunpowder. *Close one.* He checked the bedroom door, hoping Joseph didn't have any brave ideas about coming out of the bedroom.

Another shot. Sanchez must be just on the other side of the door. Victor's heart pounded with a mix of fear and rage. No time to play chicken. In seconds, they would be face to face.

Time stopped. His senses sharpened: the smell of coffee—the *bloop, bloop* of the pot perking on the stove; the odor of Sanchez's cigar-smoke on his clothing wafting through the doorway and, oh, God, the heart-wrenching sounds of sobbing women. He honed in on Marisol. Pain seared his heart. Sanchez seemed to have no qualms about firing his gun. No telling when he would turn on the women. He must not let that happen.

A red haze blurred Victor's vision. He flashed back to his wrestling days in school. He was on the mat at Lawrence, preparing to finish off his opponent. With a lunge, he dove low and fast. One arm scooped at Sanchez's ankles. The man was sturdy as a tree, but caught off guard, he slammed back against the table.

With a hot flash, a bullet burst from Sanchez's gun, ricocheted off the stove, and pinged into the floor. In the haze of the moment, Victor thought he heard screams.

No time.

He plowed into Sanchez before the man could right himself, and used his weight to force Sanchez backward over the table. The gun clattered the floor.

Sanchez's powerful arms and legs wrapped around him in a squeeze hug. Victor's arms were pinned to his sides and his lungs begged for breath. Sanchez's sweaty face was close enough to bite off

Victor's nose.

Have to break the hold. He managed to loosen the leg grip enough so he could move his foot on the floor until it struck Sanchez's weapon. With a sideswipe, he kicked it out of reach. Sanchez's attention focused on the weapon, which allowed Victor to struggle away. When Sanchez stood, Victor jacked his knee into the man's crotch.

With a howl, Sanchez's meaty hand clutched at Victor's throat. "You need to die, now." His words spewed out in a beastly growl and his face was dark with feral anger. The pressure from Sanchez's hand increased. Victor couldn't swallow. He couldn't breathe. Now his eyesight blurred. If he didn't make a move to break Sanchez's iron grip, he would be no help to the women. *Think. Hands free. Use them!*

Remembering Jake's training, Victor drew on his last bit of strength. He stiffened his arm like a weapon and karate chopped at Sanchez's sinewy forearm, breaking the hold on his throat.

With his vision clear and his breathing easy, he twisted away, and then rammed his shoulder into Sanchez's armpit, pushing the man away. Dancing back, he sent a karate kick to Sanchez's side.

With a loud grunt, Sanchez dropped to the floor like a sack of manure, rolled over, and tried to sit up.

Victor readied to deliver another blow when—

The base of the coffeepot came down on Sanchez's head. The lid flew off and landed on the man's stomach, along with the basket of grounds. Sanchez yowled in pain as boiling coffee spurted up and over his face and upper body. His eyes crossed and took on a dazed look. Then he fell back, his large head thumping on the floor.

"Nice work, Señora." Victor relaxed his stance and rubbed at his sore Adam's apple. "Knocked him out cold."

"Mama." Joseph burst into the room and threw his arms around his mother's waist.

Berto sauntered in behind him, and pointed his pistol at the downed and dazed Sanchez.

"Maybe you want to join the *polica*, Victor. They can always use good men," Berto said.

"Where the hell have you been?"

"What do you mean? I had to wait for the police to show up to haul Miguel to jail."

"You *waited* for them?" Victor took an exasperated breath.

"You think I was foolish enough to tangle with this brute alone?" Berto took out a pair of handcuffs and clipped them on Sanchez.

Victor cocked an ear at the scream of a siren.

"The *polica*," Berto said.

"What about Gomez Soto? He sent these men to kill us," Marisol said.

The sweet sound of her voice struck a sad chord in Victor's heart. He tried not to be hopeful. He saved her life, and rescued Joseph, but he had lost her trust.

Berto shrugged. "Word is he flew to Miami for his sister's funeral."

"You all set here, Berto?" Victor nodded toward Sanchez, who lay on the floor.

"*Sí*. Your father would be proud of you, Victor." Berto patted his shoulder.

I doubt that. "I could use a lift to the airport."

"Take the white Jeep. I will run by and pick it up after this is settled."

Victor glanced toward Marisol. She held Joseph to her as if protecting him from evil. She looked away from him, as did the señora. Rosario sobbed at the kitchen table. Sanchez must have told her about Carlos. Victor wasn't convinced Carlos was dead, but maybe he didn't want to believe it. He had let them down. All of them. Without another word, he retrieved his shattered sneaker from the floor and started for the front door.

"Where are you going, *Tío* Victor?" The boy grabbed at his arm.

He turned and laid a hand on Joseph's shoulder. "I have to go home now."

"Are you coming back?"

"I don't think so, son." His voice cracked at the word.

Joseph shook his head to the side. Then he pivoted toward his mother. "Mama, you have to stop him."

Marisol shot Victor a look of disgust that turned her beautiful face into an ugly mask. "No, I do not."

With a ragged breath, Victor strode to the front door.

"Whoa. Back." A uniformed police officer shoved at his chest. "No one leaves."

The rifle in the officer's hand was pointed business end down.

"It is okay, Huardo," Berto called from the kitchen. "Victor is Nesto's son. He is with me."

"Ah." Huardo nodded his head, sizing up Victor. "I see the resemblance." He touched his finger to his cheek, just under his eye.

The mole again. It would haunt him every time he looked in the mirror—the life he might have lived if his mother had only told him about his true father.

"I need to leave. I have a flight to catch," Victor said, taking a second to shove his foot into what remained of his sneaker.

"Sure, no problem." Huardo stepped aside to let Victor pass.

The door slammed, making Victor officially an outsider at Garcia Jardines. He stepped onto the wet cement porch and took slow steps down to the drive. The tinny sound of rain on metal forced his gaze to the black Jaguar. He swiped off the water drops beading on the highly polished hood. He'd never own that red Jag now. It was just a car, anyway.

An officer read a newspaper behind the wheel of the idling police sedan parked behind Soto's ride. Victor searched for a last look at the flower van, and then realized Berto must have tucked it out of sight.

He started down the drive, stepping over the rain-filled ruts. His hair was damp, his clothes stuck to his skin, but what did it matter? He didn't belong here. Less than a week ago, he had found a family and now, his brother was likely dead. He was alone again. Fighting to survive. Burnt by the green fire. Because of his greed, he had lost the only woman he cared about. And the boy—what would happen to Joseph now?

Too many questions, and none of the answers involved him anymore. He hoped the Garcias would have a reprieve while Soto ramped up his A-team.

For the last time, Victor opened the red wooden door to the guesthouse that had become his home. He was almost packed. Leaving his muddy sneakers at the door, he threw on a dry shirt, grabbed his windbreaker out of the roller bag, and put it on. From the lining of the pillowcase, he retrieved his passport and extra money, and stopped as the scent of lilies assailed his senses. The bed linens were rumpled from his restless hours after Marisol left his bed the past night. He gathered the sheets in his arms and buried his face in them, inhaling them, inhaling *her.*

Enough feeling sorry for yourself. You have a life to live, and it isn't here. Jamming the linens into a pillowcase, along with his used towel, he carried the bundle to the door and left it there. As he did so, he caught a glimpse of himself in the crackled mirror.

"Loser," he said to his image. Grabbing his air ticket, he shoved it into the inside pocket of his jacket. All his life he had allowed his lust for money to determine his fate. No more.

"It's up to you to save yourself," he told his reflection. Raising his chin, he squared his shoulders and pressed his lips together. He would go back to Miami and begin anew. From now on, he would sleep in his own bed, wear only the clothes he could afford. No more cruise ships. No more snaking after wealthy matrons. He'd find a job at a restaurant, in South Beach, maybe, and put what money he could save toward completing his degree in finance. Only then would he be worthy of a woman like Marisol.

After a last look around the sparse room, he pushed open the door and rounded the backside of the house, where he had hidden Soto's white Jeep. When he turned on the ignition, he half expected the Jeep to choke and stall like the flower van always did. Pulling away, he navigated over the rutty footpath onto the driveway and drove past the damaged lily field, sodden and untended today. Marisol would worry.

He brushed a hand through his cropped hair. *Not your problem anymore, buddy.*

* * * *

"Come on, asshole. Wake up," Berto said to Sanchez. "You're too big to cart to the police van. Huardo, I need a hand here."

When Sanchez sat up, the lid of the coffeepot clattered to the floor. Mumbling to himself, he rubbed at the red, blistering spot at the top of his head. "What hit me?"

"I did," Mama said with a satisfied smile. "That will teach you to come around here terrorizing my family." She pointed her finger at him. "You tell that boss of yours he is on my black list. If he ever shows his nose on my property again, I am going to run him off in our brand new flower van."

"What do you mean *new* van?" Marisol said. Her lip, where Sanchez had slapped her, burned hot and the crusted blood pinched when she spoke.

Rosario lifted her head from the table, where she had been sobbing, and blinked away her tears.

"The emeralds belong to Carlos, is that not right, Berto?" Mama said.

Berto scratched his head. "I suppose. No one else seems to have a claim on them. From what Victor told me, Carlos risked his life to get them...and he may have died for them. Oh, good. *Gracias*, Huardo."

Berto and Huardo grabbed Sanchez under his armpits and got him standing.

"I hope you rot in jail." Marisol touched her sore lip.

Sanchez's lips curled in a sneer. "Maybe you will come visit me, *chica."*

She slapped his face hard enough to leave a palm print.

"I have wanted to do that for a long time. Berto get him out of our sight."

"Right, señorita. Come on. Move those legs, asshole. Walk."

Once they had left, Mama bustled to the kitchen drawer and pulled out the paper bag.

Marisol's heart stuttered in its rhythm. *The emeralds.* Because of them, she almost lost her son. She reached for Joseph. He shrugged her off, moved to a kitchen chair, and sat glaring at her. She must make him understand that even though Victor had rescued them, he had schemed with Carlos to deceive them. She drew in a breath. And to think that, hours beforehand, she had gone to Victor's bed.

"Look, Rosario." Mama dug into the bag and pulled out a fistful of emeralds. Trapiche. Your husband left you well-to-do."

Rosario pushed away Mama's hand. "I do not want them. I only want my Carlos back."

"But look." Mama pushed a gem into Rosario's hand. "See the deep green color, the wheel markings. This one alone is worth *millions.*"

Rosario rolled the emerald between her fingers. Its green glitter reflected a circle against the pale skin of her cheek. "I would not know what to do with this, or any of the other emeralds. They almost cost us our lives."

"Bah, they brought Victor and Berto here to save us. Now they will bring us prosperity...or at least you, Rosario. They are yours, after all. What will you do with them?"

Rosario pressed the gem back into Mama's palm. "We have a

plantation to run, Mama. Now we have the money to make it work."

Marisol rose to hug her sister, cheeks dampened with tears. "Oh, Rosario, you would do that for us?"

"You, Mama, and Joseph are all I have now." She sucked back a sob. "We have always lived at Garcia Jardines. Now we have the money to hire more workers and even buy more property." Rosario's hand curled into a fist. "We will fill that Elite order, Marisol, and bring in new buyers for your lilies."

Marisol's heart swelled with joy. Then she sobered. "What about Gomez Soto? He knows of these emeralds. Even though Miguel and Sanchez are in jail, he will have others come after us for them." She glanced at Joseph, who now leaned forward in his chair, eyes alert with interest.

"I doubt Gomez even knows about them," Mama said, shaking her head.

"The Jaguar," Marisol said. "Why would Sanchez have been driving Soto's personal car alone? Soto has a fleet of cars his men can use."

"And I do remember Gomez being worried about a sick sister in Florida."

"So, Mama, you think Sanchez and Miguel went behind Soto's back?"

"It is possible."

"Then we are rich!" Joseph shouted, leaping from his chair.

Marisol's chest heaved with relief. It was going to be all right.

Mama sighed. "Yes, but I do not know how we are going to turn these emeralds into pesos? We have to sell them, and then managing all that money..." Her hand brushed against her forehead. "Just the thought makes me dizzy."

"What about *Tío* Victor?" Joseph said. "He is a money man. He would know what to do."

Marisol sighed. "Your *Tío* Victor is a thief, Joseph. Do you not know that?"

"No, he is not, Mama." Joseph looked at the floor.

* * * *

Victor was a new man, fresh and clean. It was not too late for him to start over and live a life he could be proud of. Maybe someday he would meet someone like Marisol and have a family. A son, like Joseph, who would look up to him. He pressed his lips together. His wife wouldn't have fancy clothes, but then he doubted that kind of woman would ever appeal to him after Marisol.

He would be an ordinary, hardworking man, not a phony hot shot preying on women or trying to pull off a smuggling gig. His mother had been a housekeeper, but he had never thought less of her for it. In fact, he had respected her even more than all those pretentious rich folks who wallowed in money. She had worked hard and earned every honest cent—and he would, too. First he would find a job and figure out how to complete his degree in finance. Then he would set up a business as an accountant, or maybe a financial advisor. One day he would be able to look at his image in the mirror and be proud of himself.

As he drove through the village of Garcia, Victor realized he would miss it. While he certainly didn't need another Aguardiente from Barra de Luis, he could go for another bowl of Juanita's chicken stew. In fact, he checked his watch, his flight wasn't for a few hours and he was damn hungry. Swerving into an open space, he was righting the car when a blaring horn caught his attention. He checked the rear view mirror. A white van was barreling down the road.

He drew in a breath. All the plantations used white vans to transport flowers. Perhaps the dealer needed to make the Miami shuttle. Or it could be Berto. Perhaps he forgot to tell Victor something—like, *"Goodbye, nice meeting you. Come back to see us."* But that didn't make sense; Berto would have hopped a ride back to Bogotá with his officer friends.

An arm shot out of the window on the driver side, an arm too slim to belong to a man. Victor's heart thudded so hard beneath his rib cage he could hear it echo.

He turned off the ignition and got out. The van pulled up in the space behind him and stopped with a jerk. The door shot open.

"Victor." Marisol ran toward him, her hair flying around her face like dark wings.

He forced himself to stand in place with his arms at his side.

Marisol put a hand on his arm. "Victor. Thank God I caught you in time. I am so sorry." She threw her arms around him and kissed him.

His hands hovered at his sides, wanting to wrap her closer but not sure if he dared. He was dreaming this. How else could she be here? If he tried to touch her and his hands met air, he would wake up, and she would be gone.

But her were lips too soft and moist and needy to be a figment of his mind. No, she was here, hugging him, kissing him, as if everything were all right. His arms went around her and he was in heaven. For this minute, she belonged to him.

Marisol pulled back. Her face was tear-streaked and one side of her lip was swollen and bruised. Her high cheekbones lifted and plumped in a wide smile.

"I forgot to thank you."

"I don't understand."

"Joseph told me. Oh, Victor, I blamed you for corrupting my son, and all the time it was that...that" —her mouth twisted in distaste— "Carlos."

Victor exhaled. He had to tell her. Watch the joy drop from her lips. Then she would leave him. This time, it would be for good.

"Victor, you are crying." She brushed the wetness from his face.

He wasn't crying. He never cried. He drew away, knowing she wouldn't touch him once he told her the truth. "No, it's just rainwater. Look, Carlos didn't tell me he'd involved Joseph or I would've never...."

She drew in a breath and stepped away from him. Her face lost its soft, hopeful glow and her eyebrows knit. "*You* were in on it, too?"

"Carlos was to get the emeralds to Miami, and I was supposed to be there to meet the plane and sell them."

"You led me on. We had dinner. I bared my soul to you." Her voice rose.

"I'm sorry. I'm no good for you. You were right. I'm a lying bastard."

Her face softened. "You could have stolen the emeralds and run off with them, but you gave them up to protect my son. Once he had the emeralds, Sanchez was going to kill Rosario, Mama, and me. But you risked your life to save us." She grabbed his hand. "I could forgive you." She dropped her head, and then looked up at him hopefully. "Maybe we could start anew. Here. Now. Joseph begged me to bring you back to the plantation."

"And you?"

"I am begging you to come with me. Will you?"

Victor wanted to grab her in his arms, tell her *yes*, and leave it at that. She would never know about his past in Miami. Who would tell her? Then he remembered his vow in front of the mirror. He was not that man anymore.

"I can't lie to you." He brushed the back of his hand against her cheek, half expecting her to flinch away. "I've only known you for a few days, but in that time, I've learned to care. I'm not the man who arrived from Miami any longer. That man was a selfish, pompous, bastard who screwed women for a living."

He heard her breath catch in her throat. "You did *what?*" She froze, staring at him as if she didn't want to believe the words that had come from his mouth.

"I was nothing but a lying gigolo." Turning from her, he pressed down the handle to the white Jeep.

Her head rested on his shoulder, and her hot tears seared through his shirt, cutting through to his skin like a knife.

He shifted around and took her face in his hands. "I never meant to hurt you."

"No, Victor. You did not hurt me. I hurt for *you*. Who you were and what you did does not really matter. What matters is who you are now. I see a man who cares."

"I have no money, Marisol. Nothing to offer any woman."

"You do not need money to love someone."

Victor's chest tightened, his throat closed, and tears welled in his eyes. He kissed her forehead, the tip of her nose, and then touched his lips to hers. "I could fall in love with you."

She lifted her head, stood on her toes, and drew him into a kiss.

"Hey," Berto yelled from the back window of the police sedan. "You two could get arrested for that. You are both parked illegally."

Sanchez sat alongside him, trussed like a roasting pig. He stared straight ahead. He and Miguel had failed Soto, and they would pay in more ways than one.

Laughing, Marisol grabbed Victor's hand. "Come, Victor, we have to get back to the plantation. Mama is having a celebration over our riches."

"Riches?"

"The emeralds. Carlos brought them from the mine. He died for them. They belong to Rosario, now. We need you to negotiate a good price for us."

"So, I would be a money man, then?"

Marisol kissed his cheek. "*Our* money man."

Victor's life spread before him like the good part of a novel. He could stay here and work, where he had family and love. He would live in the guesthouse, help with the plantings, and defend the Garcia's against future harassment by Gomez Soto. Hell, he could take online courses and complete his degree right here in Colombia, so he would be better qualified to do right by the Garcia's finances. And maybe one day, when he proved worthy of her love, Marisol would consent to be his wife.

"Victor, what is the matter? Do you not want to come back to Garcia Jardines with me?"

A lump formed in his throat. He smoothed his hand over Marisol's silken hair, and then cupped her chin. "More than anything in the world. But..." He shoved his thumb toward Café de Juanita's. "Do you think we could have a bite to eat, first?"

About the Author

Joy Smith merged a successful career in non-fiction with fiction-writing. An avid sailor, she spent the past thirty years cruising the Atlantic Ocean and the Caribbean Sea with "Captain My Way." In addition to GREEN FIRE, her published works include three boating books, a wedding planning book for moms, and a children's book. Joy and her handsome captain live in Connecticut and sail out of Mystic. During her spare time she continues to develop recipes, crochets prayer shawls and blankets for those in need, and is on a never-ending diet that would really work if she could stay away from ice cream and chocolate. She would love to hear from you. Contact Joy via her website at www.joysmith.net.

My Dear Reader,

If you enjoyed GREEN FIRE, I would love it if you would spread the word by recommending my book to your pals, posting a review on Amazon, Goodreads, or Barnes and Noble websites, or sharing on your social networks.

I really appreciate your support and wish you the best of everything life has to offer.

Thank you,

www.ingramcontent.com/pod-product-compliance
Lightning Source LLC
Chambersburg PA
CBHW060533180626
46817CB00002B/544